the girls

BRUNO BOUCHET

HODDER

A Hodder Book

Published in Australia and New Zealand in 2001
by Hodder Headline Australia Pty Limited
(A member of the Hodder Headline Group)
Level 22, 201 Kent Street, Sydney NSW 2000
Website: www.hha.com.au

National Library of Australia
Cataloguing-in-Publication data

Bouchet, Bruno.
  The girls.

  ISBN 0 7336 1378 0 (pbk).

  1. Breast - Cancer - Fiction. 2. Interpersonal relations -
Fiction. I. Title.

A823.3

Text design and typesetting by Bookhouse, Sydney
Printed in Australia by Griffin Press, Adelaide

To Maureen Bouchet

Ship Building

8.00 am

The girls were familiar to James after twelve years of marriage, but today something about them was different. Perhaps it was because Maureen was standing near the bed in her knickers, with her arms outstretched, absent-mindedly moving her chest from side to side, like a belly dancer in slow motion. It was not her normal Saturday morning activity. Her eyes were closed as she swayed, listening to a silent incantation.

'Having a good time there?' His croaky morning voice woke Maureen from her dream dance. She moved closer, rested her knees on the edge of the bed and leant over, so her breasts hung above his head. He looked up at his favourite nipples. He could have described them with his eyes closed. He adored the way they could change colour: a purplish blush sometimes, and different light would render them brown, a gentle breeze of cold breath and they would contract and rear up before his eyes with the tips going hard. Up close the seemingly regular ring of the aureole was a random scattering of bumps, like a magical toadstool ring. If his fingers danced within one, he could make a wish. Today his fingers did not dance, he just stared right at the nipples until his eyes crossed, refusing to glance at any other part of her breasts.

'Good morning, girls. How are you today?'

'You tell me.'

'As gorgeous as the day we all first met.' Maureen stared at him. His eyes left her nipples to meet her eyes—a difficult journey, even after so many years of marriage.

James smiled. He knew she was looking for a sign that he had remembered the anniversary of the first time he and the girls had met, their first date. It did not have the prestige of their wedding anniversary, but it had been their own personal one, their 'little anniversary'. Something they shared that few other people knew about, a private celebration of the fun that had begun these fourteen years together.

They used to mark it each year with a different event: dinner, a night away, a candlelit champagne bath. Seven years ago, suddenly neither of them had felt like celebrating and so they quietly let it slide. The following year Maureen reminded him of the date and they did dinner. After that James was in Perth on business, and then Maureen was in Melbourne with work. The yearly link in the chain of celebrating had been lost and it did not seem worth trying to reconnect.

Maureen gave up reminding James and it slipped from his memory. They still celebrated their wedding anniversary with enthusiasm, each taking alternate years to plan a surprise event for the other, but the little anniversary had fallen into disuse.

James knew Maureen would still remember it. She did not forget these things. No birthday was ever missed, no card ever late. It was what Maureen did best: thinking of others. She chose presents that were personal, appropriate and clearly from her, even though James' name was on the card too. She always made him sign his name, hating generic couple signatures ('Jim 'n' Reen,' she would grimace).

James would have let it go. Nobody really cared about signatures, he thought. It was more convenient if one person, preferably not himself, did it all. He was a delegator. That was what he did best, getting other people to do things. Three years ago he thought he was doing them both a favour by having their signatures printed on Christmas cards. Maureen's was scanned from a letter and transferred to the card selected by James' secretary. Maureen had been furious and personally shredded all 200 cards.

Now, as Maureen scrutinised his eyes, he was determined that for once she would not read his mind. Failing to find what she wanted, she pulled away from him and turned to the drawers to select a bra. He watched her hesitate over which one. Perhaps he should drop a hint, let her know discreetly. No, this time he wanted to be the one to organise everything perfectly. He wanted to be the capable, thoughtful one who took the burden on himself, and to do that he had to hold it all back for the surprise. This year, of all years, had to be special. She had to understand without him saying it that he was there for her.

'You know we're having a Reenies' coffee morning, don't you?' She finally selected a bra and slipped her hands through the straps. He did know she was meeting Irene for coffee. (He also knew she was annoyed, because she fastened the bra herself and did not stand with her back turned for him to do it.) The Reenies was what Maureen and her closest friend, Irene, called themselves. A Reenies' coffee morning could go on all day and usually ended with several bags of shopping and a round of cocktails. James was counting on it. He had phoned Irene repeatedly to ensure she kept Maureen away from the house all day.

'I need the time to decorate the house, get the caterers in and set it all up.'

'Sounds bigger than Ben Hur,' Irene had replied.

'Bigger than the *Titanic*. I'm doing a nautical theme.'

'You, or the party organiser you've hired?' Irene did not believe he would do it himself. She had even been surprised to hear his voice and not his secretary saying she had James 'on the line for you'.

'I'm doing everything,' James had declared proudly, 'and you mustn't breathe a word.'

'I won't, but don't trust that vile friend of yours not to cock it up.'

'You agreed to lay down swords.'

'He doesn't have a sword. It's more of a penknife.' James groaned.

'Sorry, but if I've got till Saturday to purge the bile I feel towards him, it'll have to flow thick and fast now.'

'That vile friend of yours' was Irene's ex-husband, Stephen. James' best friend, he and Irene had actually met during James and Maureen's first date. They were responsible for the ill-fated coupling.

James had first met Maureen while managing a principal sponsorship agreement with *Danse Contemporaine* for one of his corporate clients. A management consultant, he specialised in sponsorships, matching products to art, events to firms. Maureen was in her first week as administrative assistant with *Danse Contemporaine* and immediately proved her mettle. She had been the only person in the dance company to realise the implications of the contract stipulating James' clients would have the right to impose corporate colours on costume and stage design for at least two productions in the season, plus product placement in another. This clause had been a gambit on James' part, inserted so it could be negotiated away rather than something more important. No-one had objected until Maureen joined the company a few days after the contract signing. Their first encounter was when a frosty Maureen turned up at James' office.

'Exactly how do you think we might work office computers into the set of *Invasion*, a dance interpretation of James Cook's landing in Australia?' she inquired.

James laughed and rattled off a spiel about contemporary reverberations. Maureen simply snorted and raised her eyebrows. The ice maiden attitude irked and fascinated him. He refused to budge and Maureen had refused to let it go. In rehearsal Maureen had made James watch as Captain Cook danced around a dot-matrix printer while a flu-ridden Aborigine died over a 15-inch monitor and large grey hard-drive. At the rehearsal James had bet Maureen a dinner that the critics would love it. She had faith in their critical appraisals and took the bet. James won. They had uniformly praised the presence of the computers as 'inspired' and 'a bold reminder that we have not advanced far in 200 years'. Maureen, delighted that the company had garnered rave reviews, was still disappointed to learn a shameless piece of product placement had gone down so well. She had to pay for dinner at the restaurant of James' choice.

Both James and Maureen had brought back-up with them to the pre-dinner drinks in case of disaster. As they sipped their Mai Tais, politely trying not to talk about work, the two back-ups, Stephen and Irene, had sat at the bar. Both were waiting for signals. If Maureen knocked her drink over, she needed rescuing. If James took his jacket off, he was in trouble. The 'everything's fine, you can go home' signal was a loud laugh and waving arms around—for both of them. After half an hour no signals had been given. James, sweltering in his jacket, was determined not to remove it. Maureen, normally a woman of grace, handled her glass nervously.

James was overawed by Maureen. She was the most perfect woman he had ever met. Intelligent, elegant, beautiful and possessing an extraordinary capacity for generosity. Beyond that there seemed even more, as if all her charms and accomplishments were a veneer masking something even greater. Then there were her breasts. They were so perfect, so cuppable, so distracting. She had been the type of woman that would have terrified him normally. 'Top Shelf Bird,' as Stephen would say. James had never reached above the second or third shelf before. This was his first shot at a major prize.

The first woman for whom it was worth risking failure and humiliation.

James was not the corporate philistine Maureen had initially thought. A confident and tough negotiator, he had a clear sense of what was appropriate, a genuine appreciation of the arts, even if it was a little too focussed on promotional opportunities. His hands were solid. Powerful fingers, she thought, with wide strong wrists. It was the hands that did it for her. Even in meetings when her eyebrows remained aloofly arched, her mind wandered to the feel of those hands on her body. Once he had caught her looking at them. His reaction—quickly hiding them under the desk and becoming flustered—surprised her.

As they sat in the latest renovated bar—smoked glass tables and purple carpet—they talked, they smiled, they giggled a little, but no signals were sent out. At the bar, an impressive slab of fake pink marble with brass edging, Stephen was on his fourth beer, Irene finishing her third white-wine spritzer. There was nothing to do but wait and watch.

As Irene turned to order a fresh drink, she heard Maureen's voice suddenly audible above the muted tones.

'I'm so sorry.' She turned and saw a drink had been spilled. It was time for her entrance. James was saying not to worry and removing his jacket to sponge it off.

The man who had been sitting at the bar close to Irene and tossing her the occasional glance got off his stool. Suddenly both Maureen and James froze, turned to the bar and started laughing hysterically, waving their arms as nonchalantly as they could. They both stopped, each realising that not just *their* friend was watching them. Stephen and Irene laughed, waved in unison and turned back to the bar.

'I'm Stephen, your counterpart for the evening.'

'Irene...I suspect we can leave them now...Well, that was a productive fifty minutes.'

'D'you fancy going for our own drink? If you want to bail out at any time, you can spill your drink and laugh hysterically.'

Irene hesitated. This guy was an obvious charmer, and irritatingly confident with it. On the other hand, he was attractive and she was several drinks down the track.

'OK, but if you remove anything other than your jacket, I'll leave.'

As they left, carefully not glancing back at their friends, the music volume cranked up to indicate the end of happy hour. 'Walk Like an Egyptian' was playing. Irene dreaded the idea that this meeting might lead to something. It would be a bit tacky, she thought, meeting your true love propped up at a bar during happy hour with the Bangles playing what might become 'their song'.

'Walk Like an Egyptian' did become *their* song, much as they both loathed it. One thing had led to another, to marriage, a daughter, infidelity and divorce. The break-up had meant the usual best friends complications as the dinner party and holiday team was broken up. Maureen and James had tried to keep seeing them both, but separately. However Stephen and Irene always managed to both turn up, both swearing blind that they would not be the one to 'start' and both tearing into each other on the slightest pretext.

Stephen and Irene established an unwritten rule: James could see Stephen alone and Maureen could see Irene, but the two together was a different matter. It was more than a fear of leaving the other one alone with their friends. There was a dedication to fighting that bordered on addiction. They were more aggressively territorial over James and Maureen than over their daughter. Sophie was off limits for arguing. However much they hated each other, she always came first. James and Maureen were a safe arena for combat and were the site of their fiercest battles.

The clashes intensified when Stephen started bringing dates to their gatherings. At their first 'new partners' occasion, Stephen was sitting next to a grinning redhead who, if an actor, would have been typecast as 'the other woman'.

'Couldn't find anyone fluent enough in medieval French to bring, eh Irene?' Stephen seized on the fact Irene had turned up alone. Irene, in turn, pressed her linguistic skills to the fore and addressed her comments to Stephen's date, first in Spanish (calling her a fourth generation Andalucian whore) and then translating it as, 'your dress flows over your legs like an Andalucian mountain stream'.

Stephen knew enough to suspect her translation was inaccurate but he was too afraid of hearing the truth to challenge her. The snarling continued for half an hour: Stephen baiting Irene, Irene attacking his date. Irene won. 'Tactics,' she crowed silently to herself, 'brains win in the end.' She could never have driven Stephen away from the table with a direct attack, but if his girlfriend ran off in tears, he would have to follow.

Maureen loathed these moments. Failing to control the situation or resolve their conflict for them, she felt responsible for the resulting unhappiness they all felt. Much as she liked him, she admitted Stephen should probably never have married. He was the nearest any man had come to proving it was physically impossible for a man to remain faithful to one woman. If only

Maureen had been strong enough to go on that first date without a back-up. It was her fault.

'You're going to be early. Can't see Irene being up and ready at this hour.' James sensed Maureen was in a hurry to leave.

'I want to do a bit of shopping beforehand.'

'I'd better warn Amex.'

She did not respond to the deliberate provocation. Normally he would get a lecture on which of them actually did the most spending. He was almost goading her to force his secret out of him, bursting for her to find out how wonderful he was being.

He could not wait to see her face as she learned that he had not only remembered their little anniversary, he had organised an entire dinner party himself, from concept to completion. It would be no ordinary dinner party, but an all-singing, all-dancing cruise-liner experience in their very own dining room. The place would be transformed beyond recognition and he, James Ting, was going to do it with his own hands.

'Don't know when I'll be back.' Maureen waved airily over her shoulder as she walked out the front door. Down the drive she stopped to pick a dead head off the rose bush, and waved again without looking. She dismissed him with a double flick of her hand in the knowledge he would be watching her. He smiled. Even when irritated she was incredible.

•

It was her favourite stop on any of her trips. The Milk Bar at Black Hill meant Nicole would reach home that day. She adored the dusty chandeliers. Each had a single piece of crystal missing, but it was not the same piece in each one. In the years she had stopped off at the Milk Bar, they had never changed: no further damage, no repairs and certainly no cleaning. Once she had asked Marie, one of the staff who seemed to have been there as long as the chandeliers, what had happened, but she had no idea. 'Nothing ever changes here,' she had sighed. Nicole liked to think that somewhere there was a trucker with some rather special earrings courtesy of the Black Hill Milk Bar, which he only wore in his cab.

The chandeliers hung over the posh carpeted dining area, tastefully cordoned off with a horizontal rose trellis nailed to pillars. She decided not to be posh. She had been on the road since midnight, driving down from Brisbane. She was feeling grubby. It was a burger-in-the-formica-area kind of moment.

'Nicole, burger with the works, no beetroot, no egg?' The girls at the Milk Bar knew her well.

'Perfect, Marie. How you doing?'

'Oh, the same,' Marie sighed, dropping another tray of moussaka into the bain marie. 'Nothing ever changes here.'

'That's what I love about it—a constant in this ever-changing world.'

'You would say that, you're only visiting. It's like living in a theme park, where the theme's boredom... On your way home? Where you been?' She brightened up at the idea of others getting out.

'Townsville, Rocky, Brisbane, and then the best Milk Bar in Australia.'

Marie rolled her eyes. 'God help us.' Nicole was one of the few people she liked in the place. A highlight in the daily parade of grumpy truckies, she got special treatment.

'Sit down, I'll bring it over. Going posh?'

'No, here's fine.' Nicole took her chips with her and sat down to read her paper until the burger arrived. Not the kind of food she would be eating at Maureen's that night, she figured. She laughed to herself, thinking of how once she had forced Irene and Maureen to meet her here after a long trip away. Nicole had bounced in after sixteen hours of not washing or sleeping to see them perched on the vinyl benches, nibbling on the corners of burgers. She knew they had arrived before she entered: theirs was the only VW Golf in the carpark. Irene sipped her coffee and winced.

Nicole had slapped her on the back in best truckie fashion. The coffee spilled on the table.

'I'm surprised it doesn't burn a hole, I can feel one developing in my stomach.' Irene was under attack from germs at every angle, not to mention the truckers watching her. A few nodded warily at Nicole.

'This is great,' Maureen announced gamely. Nicole laughed, shouted her order and sat down, shoving Irene across with her hips. Irene made no attempt to hide her disgust. Maureen looked like she was enjoying it. Nicole was not sure, it was hard to tell. Maureen was no snob, but she did have hygiene standards. This place could not possibly have met them, however flexible they might be. Irene shuddered as a fly landed on her burger and refused to be wafted off. A loud burp echoed from the table behind.

'You know, for someone that chose to be a woman, Nicole, this toxic testosterone dump defies logic. I can understand the truck driving. Feminist statement, marvellous. But why embrace the worst excesses of what you rejected?'

'Ignore her,' Maureen interceded, 'It's good for her to be challenged, and I'll have a banana milkshake.' The last part was shouted to Marie, who had dumped a bowl of fries and turned before eye contact could be made. Maureen tore into her burger, chewed, swallowed and let rip with a burp. She and Nicole laughed as Irene tensed even more, afraid that the squalor might be contagious.

'So it is true?' Nicole was brought out of her memory by one of the truckers, who sat down opposite her. He was not a 'mate', but she had seen him before. He delivered to the same depot in Sydney. The others who had been sitting with him watched with smirks on their faces.

'It?'

'You're really a man?'

'No...'

'Shit, you guys.' He looked round at the other truckers, thinking he had been the subject of a joke.

'...but I used to be.'

His face fell. It was always a shock to them. Nicole did not conform to the instant stereotype the words 'sex change' conjured up in their minds. They expected either a big bloke lumbering along in a floral print or a gravel-voiced anorexic drag queen. Instead she looked like a woman: black hair, short but stylish, what was generally considered a good figure and short neat nails, although driving all day sometimes made them a little dirty.

'You, you... had it chopped off. Jesus!'

Nicole had been through this conversation. She knew what would be asked next and when it would turn nasty. The boys would have their joke. The look of horrified bewilderment spread across his face. This guy had chopped his dick off, become a woman, and then started driving trucks. As usual, curiosity got the better of repulsion.

'So can you, like...still come?'

Nicole glanced at the dried egg on his stubbled chin.

'Not with you, mate, no.'

When the answer finally registered, he lunged across the table to grab Nicole and land a punch. As his head moved forward it connected with her pre-emptive fist. It smashed into his nose. He reeled back, took a plastic knife from the table and stabbed blindly at Nicole. She knocked the blade out of his hand with the back of hers. He stood up, reached across the table, grabbed her shirt collar with both hands and clenched his neck ready for a head butt. Nicole saw his move, raised her arms between his, knocking them open to release herself. He grunted as she jumped up on the seat and let fly a kick into his padded stomach resting on the table. He doubled over, allowing her to slam his face down in a bowl of hot chips drenched in sauce. With one chip sticking to his nose and ketchup flowing like blood down his cheeks, he moved off the bench, trying to get away from the table, which was trapping him. He miscalculated the edge of the table and fell to his knees. Nicole delivered a jump kick to the side of his head, just strong enough to remove the chip from his nose and to make him wobble over with another grunt. Cheers went up from the other table and Nicole marched over to collect the upheld $10 notes that they owed her.

'Did it again, Nicole. You're the champ.'

'Guys, you're gonna have to find someone better if you don't want to keep making donations to the Nicole's new breasts fund.'

'You can afford some right jugs now!'

'Yeah, but *you'll* never drink from them.' More roars of laughter went up. Nicole walked out on a high before her victim came to. She was a real trucker alright, she thought: driving hard, fighting tough. The guys respected that much at least, she reckoned. As she climbed into her cab, a voice shouted, 'Wait. You forgot your burger.' It was Marie, running out with Nicole's meal.

'You should be careful,' she added as she passed the burger through the cab window, 'Louie's a right bastard. The others can all be a bit rough, but him... I don't like him.'

9.00 am

James set to work as soon as he was sure Maureen was out of sight. There was no danger of her returning having forgotten her keys or phone. He clapped his hands and rubbed them together in readiness. Holding them out in front of him, he tried to look at his fat fingers with pride. Today he was going to be happy with his hands. They were going to do exactly what he told them to.

'Right.' He clapped them again. What first? Irene was teed up to keep Maureen busy. That would be no problem. He pulled out the schedule which had been hidden in his briefcase. The day was meticulously organised, unlike himself.

For a highly successful management consultant—employed at Ting & Co (specialising in sponsorship co-ordination)—he was surprisingly disorganised. It was his management philosophy that he did not need to be organised. His job was to motivate, grasp the big picture and give good advice. His assistant did his organising, saw to timetables, and ensured he was in the right place at the right time with the right notes. She did it brilliantly, but his brilliance had been in choosing the right person for the job. It was about delegation. Ship captains should be too focussed on the destination to bother with the petty details of how to get there.

He was successful at what he did, as their very pleasant Woollahra house indicated. In his sponsorship work he had brought about some brilliant combinations of companies and events. It was he who saw that the state's leading waste-services provider should hook up with free public events, disposing of all the waste after the event in an environmentally responsible manner. He created free concerts in a city centre park, performed on a stage made up entirely of dump trucks. Under his guidance waste management reached dizzy heights of public awareness and appreciation. His clients' trucks got happy cheers and waves as they trundled their toxic waste through residential suburbs.

Today was not about telling other people what to do. Today he was doing everything himself. He had decided on the nautical theme, drawn out his vision for the decorator by hand and sat through endless auditions for the evening's entertainment.

This had been his biggest ordeal so far. His company's leading sponsorship position meant excellent contacts in the world of arts and entertainment.

There was a ready supply of performers keen to get a foot in the door of Ting & Co and one step closer to a sponsorship deal.

Through his office had paraded a virtual Royal Variety Show of performers: a unicycling ventriloquist who crashed into his desk while drinking a glass of water and reciting 'The Man from Snowy River', a mustachioed drag queen with a patter so obscene James thought there had to be sex organs he'd never heard of, and three opera singers who claimed to sing the whole of Verdi's *Otello* in twenty minutes. He had finally settled on a group of three actors who would burst into the house, stage a hijack and force everyone to play party games. They would dress as pirates and do a bit of swashbuckling. A perfect surprise for everyone, it would be heaps of fun and in keeping with the nautical theme. Captain Bloodbath and his Cut-throat Crazies would be a sensation.

James' greatest pride was that he was going to make the dessert himself. His assistant had persuaded him that attempting the entire meal himself was not the best option and had located the woman reputed to be Sydney's hottest in-home caterer. Dessert was the compromise. No shop-bought, no chef, just James Ting, raw ingredients, and the *Paramount Desserts* cookbook. He had to go for the hardest recipe from the most uncompromising cookbook. Maureen deserved the best, and he was going to make it with his bare hands. Besides, how difficult could 'Soft Meringue with Muscat-poached Fruit and Vanilla Mascarpone' be?

Very. As he opened the book, kitchen apron and sheer determination at the ready, he checked the list of ingredients.

'5 tablespoons Vanilla Mascarpone (see page 16).'

It sounded a bit tricky, but James had self-confidence enough to manage it. Until he turned to page 16 and spotted a vital ingredient he was missing: time. Not only did the boiled cream, vanilla bean, lime zests and citric acid have to be chilled for five hours until it started to set, he was then to line a conical sieve with wet muslin, hang the sieve over a two-litre bowl, pour in the chilled cream and leave it for twenty-four hours. A whole day just to make a page-16 aside! Rubbish, he thought as he boiled the cream, added the zest, put in a teaspoon of vinegar instead of citric acid and then whacked it all in the freezer to facilitate the setting.

Turning back to the main recipe, eggs were to be beaten for the meringue. This he could manage, thanks to ten minutes of airport lounge television with Delia Smith. Sadly his flight had been called before Delia had defined how stiff a 'stiff peak' was. Stiff as a shirt collar, cardboard, concrete? He guessed at shirt collars and stopped beating.

'Line a 4 cm deep, 32 cm x 24 cm cake tin with baking paper: then lightly grease the paper with hazelnut oil.'

Did it have to be so specific? What if it was only 30 cm, would the cake blow up? He went through their high-tech teflon-coated cake tins, all wrapped in a protective layer of dust and found one that matched closest. Logic triumphed.

Baking paper, he figured, was an old-fashioned term for kitchen paper. He took the roll, pulled off several sheets and covered the tin. Olive oil would be healthier than hazelnut. He spread as much as possible before the paper absorbed it all.

Stiff egg whites were poured in, and it went into the oven. He turned the oven setting to 160°C and smiled with satisfaction. Soon he realised there was one knob for the temperature and a separate one for turning the oven on. It had a bewildering variety of options: floor heating, ceiling heating, fan, grill spit, fan with grill, floor and ceiling heating with or without fan. He opted for fan with grill in order to get a nice brown top on the meringue. Back to the marscapone. It had begun to crystallise in the freezer. His colander was neither conical nor sieve-like, but it served the same function. Rather than rip up Maureen's old blouses for muslin, a kitchen superwipe would do. He used a fresh one for anti-bacterial hygiene.

'Yes!' he shouted. It was such a long time since he had done real, on-the-job problem solving, James had forgotten how resourceful and inventive he could be. He peeped at the dripping marscapone. It was dripping too slowly so he squeezed it through the superwipe with his hand until he had nothing but a milky stained cloth and a bowl of liquid with a fine decoration of blue fibres through it. It went back to the freezer for rapid chilling.

James' all-conquering self-confidence collapsed faster than a souffle as a high-pitched whine indicated that in minutes his meringue had gone from anaemic to black to setting off the fire detector. The ear-splitting noise grew more resonant as two phones erupted in a torrent of calls. With the house phone in one hand and mobile in the other and call waiting on both, he juggled four calls at the same time, and even five calls when Tara from the Hunter Valley Wine Society called to see if he was interested in membership. Switchboard operators were far more skilled than he had given them credit for, he thought, as he attempted to turn off the oven with his foot.

Fifteen minutes after smugly setting the oven for his perfect dessert James had a black meringue, frozen marscapone lumps impregnated with cloth fibres and a sooty oven. In a dizzying cascade, setbacks had tumbled over each other out of the phones and into his ears: a shipment of chrysanthemums was infected with some unpronounceable bug that sounded like Latin for 'forgot to order them', and so were unusable for recreating an underwater bank of sea anemones; his chef was under threat of an Apprehended Violence Order for hurling a sub-standard snapper at her former fishmonger; and his secretary had called with the news that a performance artist for whom he had secured a career-launching sponsorship was determined to perform some tribute art at the house that evening. All bombshells were delivered to the continued scream from the smoke detector. He felt like Fate had swept down and flicked away everything from him—divine retribution for being too smug.

Finally, as he wafted smoke away from the detector with his free hand, James was down to just one call. It was Stephen.

'I really need you not to start on this one. This is Maureen's day and everything else has to be put aside.' James said this before Stephen could even draw breath.

'Tanya just wants to be sure she's in no physical danger.' The concern for his current girlfriend sounded almost serious. James could hear her tut audibly.

'We're in bed,' Stephen added as if by explanation. He always did this, thought James. He really was not interested in where Stephen and Tanya were or what they were wearing.

'She's a black belt in forms of martial arts Jackie Chan hasn't heard of,' James said. 'Irene won't touch her.'

'Nadia still has puncture marks on the back of her hand from the last time Irene said she wouldn't start on my girlfriend.'

James recalled Nadia, the last girlfriend to witness one of Stephen and Irene's scraps. She was the one before Tanya and had only lasted three months. She had got beyond the 'introduce you to my friends' point, but fell at the 'compulsive relationship with the ex-wife' hurdle. Nadia had kicked off hostilities by saying 'And this must be your mother' when Irene was introduced. It was doubly hostile as Stephen was Chinese, and Irene was not. Nadia proceeded to talk her way through dinner as if reciting from the latest issue of *Cosmetic Surgeon*. She pointed out who had had what done at the other tables. Given the provocation of Nadia's detailed account of how *her* mother's vein-removal operation had resulted in the thighs of a sixteen-year-old, James thought a fork in the back of the hand was getting off lightly.

'Nadia was different,' he said. 'I'd have done it myself to shut her up. Irene will not be spoiling tonight, Maureen's too important to her…and to you, I hope.'

'Just make sure she doesn't start…and what about what's his name?'

'Nicole.'

'Yeah, Tom.'

'She hasn't been Tom for several years now. Don't.'

'I'm not.'

'*You are* and you're not even here. Stop it... Gotta go, another call. Hello, James Ting speaking.'

'It's Justin from Entertainment Express.'

James responded with an 'err', unable to place the name in the frenzy of recent phone activity.

'Captain Bloodbath,' Justin clarified.

'Sounds more like Captain Sorethroat.'

'That's why I'm calling,' the alleged terror of the high seas whispered down the phone. 'We're not going to be able to take over your ship tonight. I can barely speak. I can't afford risking my voice... I've got an audition for the Abba musical next week, it could be my big...'

'Listen mate,' James erupted, 'that's enough. You're sick, fair enough, but get someone else. It's your respon-sibility... hold that thought... Yes, James Ting...'

'This is Sounds Good. Your background sea effects and music CD is ready. Can you collect by 11.30? I've got this gig to bump in and the tech crew are com-plete wankers...'

'I'll be there.' James switched back to Captain Bloodbath.

'Tonight's going to be perfect and you are not going to ruin it.'

'But it's short notice…'

'Yes it is, isn't it.' Justin had trapped himself with his own logic. 'I don't care what you have to do, but tonight at 11 pm precisely a band of high-sea desperadoes will burst through my front door, make us walk the plank and then play charades. I don't care if it's you or if you have to dig up Errol Flynn, but it will happen and you will see to it.' Years of making subordinates jump had perfected James' voice of irrefutable authority.

'Yes, of course,' the scourge of the Caribbean acquiesced.

James ended the call and waited for the next ring. It did not come. He sighed with relief and wiped half-heartedly at the black soot on the oven. He needed flowers to replace the chrysanthemums, something that could represent a sea theme. He would have to go to the florist before Sounds Good, but decided to brief them immediately.

It was time for technology to lend a hand. He abandoned the cleaning effort, thinking there was no point when a culinary army was coming in later to mess up the kitchen anyway. He drafted a short email on his mobile, asking his florist for suggestions, and dispatched it. They should have options ready by the time he got there. Another email to his solicitor at his home, giving him Captain Bloodbath's details, and instructions to get a fax off to him that morning threatening legal action if a home invasion did not take place. Next, a phone text message to Irene, assuring her of Stephen's good behaviour. She would be with Maureen, so he did not want to alert his wife that something was happening by phoning.

After the flurry of disasters, James realised that the only person involved in organising the evening who had not called with a problem was his designer. His silence was more worrying than all the other calls. James made a pre-emptive call. Marcus answered the phone while in mid-conversation with someone else.

'It's got to be shagpile, anything else would be just really really boring...Yes?'

'It's James Ting,' James announced slowly.

'Hi...No, tell him no...Sorry, what can I do for you?' He spoke as if it was an inquiry from a member of the public.

'Construct a ship in my house. I want a status report.'

'Fine.' There was a pause as James waited for something else to be said.

'Well?'

'Fine...that's the status. Florist told me about the flowers. Over them! So I'm opting for a wall of cornflowers.'

'You're opting?' James was getting riled.

'Oh, yes. Sorry, I'm suggesting. Your decision and all that. Go see the florist, they'll explain. Look, pretty busy here. Everything's fine, don't worry, pat pat on the hand. I'll be there at 12.30 to install it myself. Happy? Good. Bye.'

•

Stephen would never have believed he could find such a muscled body so attractive, had he not been presented with the proof so many times since he met Tanya. Tanya was defined, with strong shoulders and firm biceps. He was relieved she had big breasts. If she had been flat-chested too, he might have started having doubts about his sexuality. Here she was sitting on top of him, her arms clenched in a victory bicep pose. He was no six-stone weakling himself. He kept in shape, went to the gym and still played touch footy. His father had pushed him into football at school, it was the Australian thing to do. At school he had hated it because he had had to do it. After he left school and had a choice, he discovered how much he loved sports. The muscle obsession of his early twenties had paid off: a few years hard work building up and the rest had been easy to maintain, even easier now he was dating such an athlete. It was just as well he was fit. Tanya was not even thirty yet and he was hovering close to forty. She was a physically demanding companion.

He tried to flick Tanya over with his hips, but her thighs tightened around him. There was no escape. Tanya was the sexual predator and he was her victim, pinned down by firm kick-boxing legs. Like all white skin, hers had a slightly rough feel. He loved it— arousal by exfoliation.

It was these legs pinning him down that really did it for him, even more than the defined shoulders. These legs were dangerous. He resorted to tickling in an attempt to liberate himself, but she was one move ahead. Closing her eyes, she breathed deeply and switched the nerve endings in her skin off. In a flash, her eyes opened, her hands swooped down, grabbed his and forced them above his head. With one hand she pinned them to the bed frame. It was a question of positioning: her one hand able to keep his two in place. He was powerless. With her free hand she grabbed his chin, titled his head so he looked directly into her eyes. It felt like she had begun to grind her hips, but as he opened his eyes, her outside body did not appear to be moving. The pleasure radiating through his body was the result of pure internal muscle control. This sex was not penetration, it was enclosure. He made another feeble attempt to move: resistance triggered an even firmer grip on his body and a smile of satisfaction on his face. He relaxed and took it like a man.

Sex with a martial arts expert was like nothing he had experienced before. As an ex-dancer Irene had been able to do the splits when they first met. That had seemed wild, until now. Tanya's total muscle control produced effects he did not think were humanly possible. He did not know if vaginal dexterity was a real term (he should ask Irene, he thought) but Tanya had it in abundance. She was not always this dominating, but before competition it helped focus Tanya's mind. Stephen loved competition days. This morning's exertions helped prepare her body for the far greater challenge of the national Taekwondo championships.

'I pity your opponents, you're in top form,' he said, once she finally released him.

'I feel it. It's the Trinity, mind, body, soul—they're in harmony.' She tapped the side of her head. 'Mind's the hard part. Today I'm focussed, I feel I could move objects.'

'You moved my object easily enough.'

'I'm serious. The mind, it's awesome but most people waste it on thoughts. It's so much more than ideas. It's power.'

Stephen was relieved Irene was not present for that comment. She would have torn it to pieces, in several languages. He groaned silently: three Irene thoughts in one love-making session. If only he could have sex and not think of her.

'Take Irene,' Tanya continued, weaving Stephen's own thoughts into her mind-power analysis. 'She thinks too much. If she didn't keep thinking about you, she'd have let go and we'd all be happier.' Stephen blessed the irrefutable logic of a mind honed for action.

'I love you.' He grabbed a kiss and went off to the shower. She did not respond.

Things were going well between them, apart from the Irene issue. They had passed the six-month mark, enjoying each other's company. They had agreed they were going along for the ride, but they both knew that a 'where are we going' conversation was inevitable. She followed him to the bathroom as he showered. Tanya was not showering: the lingering smell of sex on her body would be off-putting for her opponents.

'We're fine with things, mate, aren't we?' Tanya asked. They always called each other 'mate'. Stephen had used it first. They had been off-road mountain biking. Stephen's bike had got a puncture and he was repairing it on the spot. Holding one plastic stick in place he needed the second to remove the tyre from the wheel. 'Pass the spoon, mate,' he'd said. Tanya laughed and he explained he had always used spoon handles to do this job as a boy, he did not know what else to call the sticks.

'It's not the spoon, it's the mate,' Tanya replied. 'Here you go…mate'. She handed the 'spoon' over.

'Thanks…mate.'

After that it stuck. It worked, they were mates who had great sex together.

In the bathroom, Tanya needed some reassurance that Stephen's expression of love was not leading to other things. In her experience, when a man started saying 'I love you' after and not during sex, he was thinking about settling down and taking care of her. She removed the thought from her mind. It was sucking power and disturbing the Trinity's equilibrium. Stephen hesitated with his answer from the shower.

'Great, mate. Never better! Especially if she's moving on now.' Tanya was satisfied. 'She' was always Irene and as long as 'she' hovered in the back of his mind, Stephen would not get any settling down notions. Tanya went to prepare her clothes.

Stephen was less satisfied. His 'I love you' was an exuberant expression of the moment. In his experience, 'are we OK?' was a woman signalling she intended to pose the 'where are we going' question to which co-habitation was the only acceptable answer. He felt a quiver, the one he always felt at that thought. It came from where he imagined his pancreas was, sending panic juices around his body which triggered the chemicals in his brain that caused evasive action.

The café where the Reenies were supposed to meet had undergone a makeover. Pretensions to Italian authenticity had been abandoned and it was now called Buzz.com. Customers were expected to use their internet-enabled phones on approach to place an order. On arrival they took a seat and received an email when their order was ready for collection at the counter. The coffee could then be charged straight to their phone bill. For those still suffering without WAP phones, orders could be placed via a conventional phone call, through a maze of message-bank options. They would receive a text message when the order was ready.

Irene had been sitting at her outdoor table for some time, wondering where all the cute young dark-haired waiters in stiff white jackets who used to hover so attentively were. Someone returning from the counter with their WAP-phone-placed order explained there was no table service any more and gave her the number to ring. Irene did not have an internet-compatible phone. A mobile phone itself had been compromise enough for Irene. She had succumbed to the black-mail of her child's safety being at risk if she was not constantly contactable—an internet-capable phone did nothing to enhance Sophie's safety and so could be resisted. Determined to have at least some human inter-action with her coffee, she marched up to the counter but found nobody there. Coffees appeared from behind pure white panels which raised automatically and fell again as the drinks were removed. She returned to her table ready to fire scathing words down the phone. She did not get the opportunity. The order was received, her credit card details were registered, she was thanked and informed there would be a five-minute wait, all without any interpersonal communication.

She boiled with frustration and waited, silently imploring Maureen to arrive so she would have someone to express her outrage to. They could vent spleen together and leave vitriolic messages on the cus-tomer feedback by dialling 9 on the list of service options. Eventually her beep came up and she resent-fully collected her coffee from the moving panel, deliberately spilling some on the pure white surface. Taking her first sip, she was ready to tut with distaste. She couldn't. It was frustratingly good coffee.

By the time the remaining foam of her café latte was drying out in the bottom of her cup, Maureen still had not arrived. She was never normally late. Irene was used to being the one pressing through the café, apologising breathlessly. She always ending up running the last few yards, knowing she was late and Maureen would be waiting. The only time Irene could remember Maureen being late was in their final year at ballet school and, of course, it was no run-of-the-mill tardiness.

Their end-of-year production had been *Giselle*. The Reenies were in the corps. Act II required them to be Willies, virgins who died before their wedding night, rising from their graves to haunt men who spurned their lovers. Maureen had vanished after the first act. Even as the ethereal virgins assembled for their second-act entrance, she had been nowhere to be seen. Only when they were on stage, as their queen, Myrtha, literally danced up a storm, did Maureen appear, sneaking into her position and whispering nonchalantly, 'Cracked a rib celebrating the harvest.' Everyone within earshot started. A hissed reference to a herd of cows from the dance master in the wings quickly made them regain their composure.

During the inevitable Act I 'villagers return from the fields to celebrate the grape harvest' dance, Maureen's thug of a partner had got carried away, squeezed her too tight during a lift and cracked one of her ribs. She had calmly completed the scene and reported to their dance master, who delighted in seeing her suffer so stoically. He gave her the option of dropping out, but gleefully bandaged her up and squeezed her back into a costume, fumbling with the lace and causing her tardy entrance. For the rest of his teaching career, he told the story as an example of what a 'real' dancer did.

It took a cracked rib to make Maureen late. She had the unnerving skill of arriving precisely on time, striding up as imaginary bells tolled the hour.

As Irene waited, the first happy flush of caffeine dissipated her anger at Buzz.com. It was a beautiful sunny morning, a special day for Maureen, and for once Irene had arrived first. All was right with the world. She wanted to make a huge gesture of kindness to humanity and decided that sending a text message to Stephen was as magnanimous as anyone could get. For Maureen, who always made everything perfect for her, she would make something perfectly nice. She toyed with what to say. There were so many beautiful phrases from so many lovely languages. There was one appropriate line from an obscure early French poem. Part of her wanted to send it in the original form, but that would irritate Stephen. She could send the original, then translate it into English in a second message but Stephen would think she was being patronising, and he would be right. She tapped it into her phone in modern French.

'*Paix: c'est l'amour des copains*—see you both tonight, Irene.'

This could be the start of the end of hostilities. They had been divorced for over three years but in her head she still played out revenge conversations where she finally expressed herself with all the eloquence that three language degrees and a life of translating documents could confer. She would say what had always eluded her: exactly how she felt. She thought if she could just once sit him down and make him really understand the pain he had caused, it would be over, and she could let go. That conversation never took place outside her head. Stephen always got in first with some provocative swipe that knocked her down to his slanging-match level. He denied her the verbal precision that was her greatest power, blinding her with her own anger. He was brilliant in his own blunt, cheating, childish way. She could feel 'that conversation' starting again and quickly pressed the send button on her text message before the rising bitterness changed her mind. It was the first conciliatory gesture and she was glad to be the one to make it.

She phoned for another coffee and contemplated ordering one for Maureen but decided to call her instead. Diverted immediately to her message bank, Irene grew worried. Holding the phone in her hand, she didn't care how desperate she looked. She had not realised that even a hint of a world without Maureen could be so unsettling.

The phone did ring. It was not Maureen, but Sophie.

'Mum, I can't stand it any more.' Sophie was spending the day and night with Stephen's father and grandmother. Annoyed at being shunted off to make the day run easier, she had been with them all of an hour when she phoned through the first complaint.

'You've barely got there. What's the matter?'

'Great Gran's trying to marry me off. I'm only twelve. I don't want to be married.'

'Now, don't exaggerate.'

'She's showing pictures of men in Hong Kong, asking which I like. She says she's being modern by even asking me.'

'She's just a bit confused, thinks you're Aunty Joyce. Go along with it. Revel in your heritage.'

'But she wants me to try on her wedding dress.'

'How sweet. It'll be just your size, darling.'

'But Mum, it stinks. If the next time you hear from me is in Hong Kong, it's your fault.'

'Yes, darling. Say hello to Pops and Great Gran.'

As she ended the call, Irene had visions of Sophie on a therapist's couch in years to come. 'I was terrified of this dress and my mother just didn't care.' She smiled ruefully, resigned to the fact that being a parent meant everything she said would be used against her as evidence. A text message announced her second latte was ready for collection. She had been wise not to order one for Maureen.

11.00 am

The flower shop demonstrated Marcus' alternative to the chrysanthemums for James. He really wanted to not like it, but failed. Everyone in the shop cheered as the staff did a live performance of how the corn-flowers would look. Although all eyes were on the performance, James experienced a sensation of being watched. He glanced over his shoulder, sure someone had suddenly ducked behind a display. He put it down to stress from the morning.

He moved on to Sounds Good to collect his CD. Sounds Good had been recommended by a soundscape artist who had prepared an aural artpiece for the lobby of a major client. The large ground-floor space with carefully positioned speakers made visitors feel like they were in a park. A stream could be heard to the left of the door, birds twittered in the lift area and if you wandered by the bank of potted plants twenty-six minutes into the cycle you could hear some young lovers getting carried away. James was no expert, but different sounds coming from different directions was impressive to him and so he went with the recommendation.

The door was locked when James reached it. It was 11.35; he was virtually on time. He pressed the door-bell—no response. There was no shop window and in fact it was no shop at all, just a grubby apartment door. Through the bubbled glass he could make out a corridor lined with boxes. Stacked high on either side, they formed a narrow tunnel. He phoned his contact number for the place to see where 'the guy' was. James had never quite caught the guy's name. He seldom used it and when James had asked, he mumbled something that could have been anything from Aaron to Constanza. James had opted to combine them and called him Ronstanza.

'Where are you? I gotta go.' Ronstanza answered, obviously somewhere at the far end of the tunnel.

'Can you hear a buzzing noise?' James pressed the bell again.

'Yeah.'

'That's me at your door.'

'Cool.'

A figure appeared from between the boxes down the corridor and opened the door. He looked hastily to either side, checking they were not being watched, pulled James into the corridor and shut the door. There was not much room in the tunnel of boxes.

Ronstanza had to squeeze past James just to shut the door. His shirt had that damp feel of months of unwashed dirt. He walked back down the corridor towards his studio, but suddenly stopped half way. There was a gap in the boxes creating a little lobby that was the full width of the corridor. By way of explanation, he turned and said:

'I don't like answering the door just because someone rings.'

'Right.' James attempted a smile.

'It's a rough business,' Ronstanza nodded sagely, as though warning James off breaking into the industry.

He pulled the CD from between two boxes that formed part of his mini-lobby. 'Used all the music you wanted and worked in the sound effects. The MIDI system's a beta program I'm testing. There's a couple of bugs skewing some of the levels, but you'd have to be a professional to notice.'

James nodded, pretending he knew what that meant, and handed over the payment. It was cash only, no receipt—probably linked to the door paranoia. He tried to peer ahead to see what the studio that was supposed to produce such marvellous sounds was like. He could see nothing.

Ronstanza started manoeuvring him back towards the door when the buzzer went again. Shocked into sudden action, he grabbed James, pulled him back to the mini-lobby between the boxes and pressed him against the wall. This must have been where he was hiding when James called. James started to speak but the guy clapped a hand over his mouth. He could smell dope on the fingers under his nose. The buzzer went again. Ronstanza cocked his ear, waiting for the tiniest sound to indicate what would happen next. His mobile blasted into the silence and they both jumped, knocking boxes down onto the floor. It was the caller at the door. He had come to collect him for the major gig he had lined up.

'You were expecting him?' James could not believe this happened every time someone called at a business listed in the Yellow Pages.

'Yes, but there are others…everywhere.'

'I think they're called customers.'

James left with the CD and the faint smell of Ronstanza's fingers still under his nose. Perhaps he should have been hired for the evening—paranoid fantasy as dinner entertainment. It could have worked.

Back in the car, James chuckled at how much he was enjoying himself, learning new things, meeting different (and in this particular case, very strange) people. He had forgotten how much he enjoyed learning. At school he had been teased as a suck but he loved learning. Starting new subjects had been his favourite time. It was like unlocking whole rooms in his mind. He got a rush of excitement as a difficult concept suddenly made sense and all the implications and connections pulsed round his head. This project was the first time he had felt that pulse in years.

Maureen and he had attempted a seamanship course when they had considered buying a boat. It resulted in them spending an afternoon on a floating gin palace on the harbour with Chance and Lorraine, a bleach-blond couple with heavy tans whom they'd met on the course. Everywhere they turned on the boat, there was a place to store a drink safely. It could have spent an hour tossing on the high seas without spilling a drop of Gilbeys but they hadn't got to test it. A much trickier test was in store as the anchor was dropped in a quiet cove, surrounded by tree-covered hills. No houses within view, and, as James looked at the shore, no clothes on the people. The obelisk standing unashamedly erect at the headland should have given it away, he thought. Dread steered towards reality as their hosts disappeared below decks 'to get more comfortable'. The brief disappearance had given them time to act. Maureen used her mobile to call James. He let his phone ring a couple of times and answered testily as Maureen put hers away. Pretending it was work, he started swearing as their hosts re-emerged to prove their heads were not the only place where peroxide had been applied.

'Shit. Why the hell didn't you call me sooner? Do you realise how serious this is?' James tried to focus on his play-acting and not on the roots in need of re-bleaching which were presenting themselves at eye-level. The 'crisis' sadly meant the blonds had to put their clothes on and motor to the nearest jetty to drop them off.

Much as they loved the sea, James and Maureen rapidly lost their enthusiasm for a boat. They decided a holiday cruise might be more suitable. Luxury, comfort and a strict dress code. The cruise never happened. It had become a joke between them, the holiday that always got put off in preference for some land based vacation. They had a secret fear that whenever they did book on a ship, they would discover Chance and Lorraine in the cabin next to them.

James loved the way he and Maureen worked as a team. A couple of years ago he had done a men's magazine quiz on how strong their relationship was and they had scored well. As a man, such quizzes were new and so he took it seriously, and proudly showed Maureen the result. Lately he'd been wondering if they would score so well.

There was something Maureen had not been telling him, and, if he was honest, he was not asking. Maureen never had to ask what was wrong with him. She was so intuitive she sometimes seemed psychic. Intuition was a lot harder for him. He wanted to see and understand all the things in her that she did in him, but he couldn't. Over the years he had managed to memorise the signs that there was something wrong, but he could seldom guess what it was and had to resort to asking her. She would sigh and eventually explain, but only after a volley of 'nothing, I'm just worn out'.

Recently he had not pushed her beyond the initial denials. Instead he opted to pour her a wine or give her a neck rub. In bed he would sit up with her head in his lap as he ran his fingers as gently as he could over her face. Terrified that his hands would suddenly jerk and poke her in the eye, he focussed on controlling them. As his thumbs touched lightly on her closed eyes, he felt moisture on them and quickly switched to using his other fingers so she would not know he had noticed her tiny tears.

Their sex life had changed recently too. Even after fourteen years, they had enjoyed regular sex, but now for the first time ever they had gone over a week without sex. Perhaps she was worried he was losing interest. Perhaps *she* was losing interest.

The phone rang. It was Irene. 'Maureen didn't turn up. I waited over an hour. I've called her.'

'She wouldn't just not turn up.'

'I know. I'm worried.'

'I'm heading home. Meet me at our house.'

The only other time he could remember Maureen disappearing was when her mother died. Even then she had left a note. She had walked out of the house, leaving 'gone for a walk' on a Post-It note stuck to James' phone. She had driven to the vast Royal National Park south of the city to pound cliff-top tracks for several hours. Returning with a tanned and invigorated face, she smiled, announced she was 'better now', and spoke no more of it.

The next day she set about organising the simple, moving funeral. James never learned what had gone through her mind as she stormed through the park. He had felt cut out of her grief right up to the funeral. As the curtains closed on her mother's coffin, she squeezed his arm with both her hands and tears seeped through her tightly closed eyes. It was a relief for him to be leaned on, but he suspected it had been as much for his benefit as for hers. Outside she reverted to her normal capable self. As everyone stood waiting to leave the crematorium a cloud of dense smoke burst from the furnace chimney, contrasting starkly with the pure blue sky. As if heavier than normal smoke, the cloud immediately fell upon the mourners. Everyone tried not to cough or think about who the smoke might be. Maureen smiled, tapped her chest and said, 'Part of her will always be with us.'

12.00 pm

Stephen was attempting a nifty shortcut through Darlinghurst in his jeep. Tanya had wanted to be at the Taekwondo venue early to have maximum time to focus on her objective. They were running late because she had spent too long pulsing the five tenets of Taekwondo through her body. Courtesy, Integrity, Perseverance, Self-Control and Indomitable Spirit. She needed to know each tenet, not intellectually but physically.

As the parts of her body took on a true under-standing of the tenets, Stephen had received his text message from Irene. Its generosity caused a wave of pity for her, an uncomfortable sensation which he did not mention to Tanya. It was not pity that Irene was single, virtually forty and in the shadow of her best friend, it was pity about the book sitting in a bag under his car passenger seat: the first English translation of the classic French medieval text, *Le Chevalier d'Étoile*.

His first thought when he had seen the book in a shop window was disbelief that Irene had actually done it. This text was her passion. In the early days of their relationship, hours had been spent in bed with her translating passages to him aloud. It was not his sort of reading, but with her bewitching French voice, it was fascinating. It meant nothing to him, but her voice took on a sensual richness with the words. As ardour settled into love and regular routine, exhausted nights and early starts, the reading sessions faded out. The rich arousing tones became more of a gentle lullaby wafting him to sleep, and so Irene stopped reading aloud.

Irene's life goal was to bring this work to modern English audiences for the first time. Its humour and its passion would make it a huge success. There would be a new trend in contemporary fiction as everyone suddenly unearthed lost texts. The French chivalric tradition would reign supreme, for a couple of years at least. Once a year Irene would have a flurry of activity on the book: researching and mapping critical points. She wanted to breathe life and relevance into the text. It was not a question of a simple word for word translation, it was a regeneration of the text and that took time, too much time. Marriage, motherhood and life with Stephen distracted her. Life without him distracted her more. One of his most successful taunts in their battles was to ask how *Le Chevalier* was going.

Stephen had been alarmed on seeing the book. Perhaps she was right: he *had* curtailed her potential. Alarm dissolved to triumph inside the shop when he saw who had actually written the book: Jonathan Townsend. From the promotional blurb on the cover, it was a hit, over 100,000 copies sold in the UK alone. This, his vengeful mind thought, would make a marvellous present.

'I can't wait to see her face when she opens it,' he said to the assistant as he bought the copy. Now, after her message, he was ashamed of what lay in the bag, grinning with yesterday's glee.

'D'you want me to stay and cheer from the side-lines or whatever you have?' He distracted himself from the bomb Tanya was sitting on.

'If you want to be there, that's fine. I won't be able to pay you any attention,' she replied with a matter-of-fact directness Stephen adored.

'OK, I'll leave you to kick butt.'

'Fine,' Tanya smiled and betrayed as much nervousness as she was capable of.

'You're great, you know that?' Stephen smiled back. There were no complications with Tanya, no second guessing. She had a man's characteristics and a woman's body. The perfect combination, he thought. Another compliment may have been a mistake if he was trying to stave off the inevitable 'talk', but his mind/mouth filter seldom worked in time. He was pleased that he had managed to pay the compliment and stop short of adding 'not like Irene'. Tanya was too busy exploring the tenets of self-control and indomitable spirit within her physical being to weigh the importance of what he had said.

'Christ, there's Maureen. What the hell's she doing here?' Stephen suddenly made the trinity wobble. Tanya sighed, adding perseverance to the tenets currently required. Stephen pulled over.

'Maureen,' he shouted out of the open window. She did not turn or respond but dashed down the next alleyway. Moving the car forward Stephen looked down the narrow lane. She had vanished.

'That's strange. She's supposed to be with Irene. Something must be up.'

'Why?' Tanya replied as chirpily as her martial arts focus allowed.

'Weird.' Stephen was puzzled.

'It'll be nothing. No point botching up the whole day wondering.'

Stephen continued to stare out of the window and down the empty lane.

'Mate, I'm trying to maintain a trinity here.' Tanya pressed on his thigh to draw his attention to the present and her increasingly precarious mind, body and spirit equilibrium.

'Sorry, mate. I'll call James after I drop you off.'

•

As James turned the car into his street, he could see there were two vans in his drive, piles of cooking equipment and several people making straight for his car. He parked across his own drive and climbed through the materials in the path to the front door where his chef and designer were getting impatient.

'I do not wait.' Ulrika, the frosty chef, was standing at the door, ladle in hand and clearly unafraid of a second Apprehended Violence Order.

'I gave up hanging around in '96, James. It's not something I have to do at my level.' Marcus had been there ten minutes already.

'And you won't have to. I'm here.' James answered them both at once. The phone rang.

'Mr Ting, it's Captain Bloodbath. About this...'

'Not now. Fix your mess and then call me.'

The thought of another volley of calls like this morning's was too much. Drastic action was required, so he switched his phone off. Alone and unconnected to the world, he listened to the babble of voices around him. No-one really seemed to be communicating. He headed for the front door. The minute his key turned in the lock, he was trapped in a race between Ulrika and Marcus to get through first.

They jammed themselves and James in the doorway.

'You don't have any idea of the scale of what I'm trying to achieve in these few hours, do you?' Marcus resumed what was obviously an ongoing dispute with Ulrika.

'You mean the table decoration? I'll get one of my assistants to do it in a spare moment.'

'Pizza Hut can supply the food, but only I can transform that lounge-dining area into a luxury ocean liner dining ambience.'

'Monster.'

Ulrika wriggled to unleash her ladle on her rival. Seizing the opportunity of a slight movement, James pushed himself through, shoved both creative geniuses backwards, and closed the door.

'I'm not opening until you both shut up,' he shouted through the glass.

'But...' in unison.

'*Shut up*!...You're both important, but I'll tell you now, if either of you starts, you're *both* out and I'll call Pizza Hut and arrange the flowers myself. Hear me, both of you or none. Agreed?'

An arched eyebrow apiece indicated they hated being reminded who was paying their bills. They nodded. James opened the door, let them in and walked out to check his car was not blocking the traffic. He switched his phone back on, afraid he had missed something important.

'Any news?' Irene arrived as he finished retrieving his voicemail.

'Yes. Stephen saying you'd sent him a text message. Thank you.'

'I did it for Reen. Heard from her?'

'No, she'll have a stack of messages on the phone. What's she doing?'

'How was she this morning?'

'Strange... sort of.'

'Oh yes?' The assumption rang out of Irene's response. Much as she liked James, it was impossible not to be suspicious of a man who could be friends with Stephen for so long.

'What does that mean?' James understood well enough.

'Have you been having an affair?'

'Great. Yes. I've been matching Stephen woman for woman all these years and every Monday morning we call each other and laugh at how stupid women are.'

'Have you?'

'It may be hard for you to believe, but Maureen's the only woman I've made love to for exactly fourteen years and today I'd really like to celebrate the fact, but I can't because...' He did not want to finish. It was too premature to make assumptions. There was no big deal in anyone disappearing for a couple of hours.

Irene understood his hesitation. She hugged him and whispered sorry in his ear, hating that Stephen made her mistrust all men.

'It's only been a few hours,' Irene reasoned.

'But her phone!' Vanishing was one thing, but it was inconceivable that anyone would disconnect themselves from the world for so long.

Stephen rang to report that he had seen Maureen. It added to their bewilderment. The back streets of Darlinghurst were not one of Maureen's regular haunts.

'Perhaps there's been some crisis with one of the dancers from the company. She could have gone along to be supportive in whatever it is they're having... doing.' Irene's voice quivered as she spotted her own desperate attempt to force an explanation.

'Or...' James' eyes lit up with inspiration, 'she could be organising a surprise of her own...Are you in on it? Tell me if you are. Don't give it away, just set my mind at rest.'

'No...but she would do it entirely on her own, wouldn't she? She's probably worked all this out and is planning a counter surprise.'

'That'd be Maureen,' James cried. They smiled, comforted by the logical explanation.

'We should have known,' Irene shook her head. 'No-one can outdo her.'

'So proceed as normal and wait to be surprised.'

'Fine, I'll have the Reenies' Day on my own. Her loss!'

James returned to the house. It was not that Maureen always had to outdo everyone. Her surprise would not be an attempt to beat him, but would probably make the evening even more enjoyable, and give him something special too. Still, within the relief, there was a tinge of disappointment. Just once he had wanted to do all the giving.

Inside the house, preparations were under way. The furniture had been cleared out of the dining area and into the study across the hallway. The carpet had been rolled back and removed.

'I can have my people cart that stuff if you want.' Marcus referred to the furniture that had just been removed. 'It's so twentieth century.' James hoped this was a weak attempt at self-parody, but suspected it was not. He moved on to the kitchen, determined not to stop the activity that Marcus' people had begun.

As James entered the culinary arena he noticed the ladle still had not been put down. With her assistant behind her, Ulrika posed on the far side of the island bench, waiting for him.

'What's this?' She slammed the ladle hard down on

the single-sheet granite island bench top. The force caused the abandoned ingredients and implements for 'Soft Meringue with Muscat-poached Fruit and Vanilla Mascarpone' to shudder. She then pushed the ladle to the left, sweeping the *Paramount Desserts* cookbook onto the floor.

'I might have guessed this mess would come from that book.'

'It's one of the top...'

'I am the top,' Ulrika glowered.

James confessed his pathetic attempt at dessert that morning. He asked if there was any chance Ulrika could see her way to completing the evening by preparing a dessert herself.

'Knees,' she announced. James' mouth dropped open.

'On your knees... No knees, no dessert.'

He rationalised that submission was the fastest resolution to this kitchen crisis. He sank to his knees, with every human-resource-management bone in his body creaking.

'Conditions.' She had not finished and banged the ladle on the single-sheet granite with each condition. 'I choose how I complete the menu...For the duration this is MY kitchen...You remove that book immediately...and you beg.'

Each bang brought back the memories of the cost

and difficulty of finding the sheet of granite when they had refitted their kitchen. Maureen had been forced to travel to the quarry personally to approve the selected slab. The slamming ladle shuddered through him.

'Fine. You choose. Your kitchen, book's out and I'm begging...please.'

'No, I don't know any dessert that takes less than twenty-four hours. If you had listened to me in the first place...'

'Surely...'

'Don't interrupt. I have a pimento wattle-seed ice-cream in my freezer. I might create something to go with it.'

'Great. Let's do it.'

'I require $100 for a taxi.'

'$100. Where d'you live, Melbourne?'

Ulrika shrugged her shoulders. The man was on his knees in his own kitchen, the upper hand was hers.

'Fine.'

'Good...David,' she addressed her assistant, too used to these scenes to have moved before being addressed, 'you may prepare the surfaces.'

1.00 pm

Nicole reckoned she was making good time. Another three hours would see her in Sydney. She could deliver her load, go home to get changed and then get round to Maureen's. If the worst came to the worst, she could go straight there after the drop-off. She always carried a presentable dress in her travelling bag. Occasionally she glammed up while driving. There was nothing quite like pulling over a few miles before the delivery, smartening her hair, doing her make-up and slipping into a slinky dress and heels. It did not pay to drive too far in heels, but the discomfort was worth the reaction as she pulled up at a depot, opened the door and descended a glamour girl instead of a stinking trucker. It was possible to be feminine and tough.

She used to love driving the truck. Sitting there, high above everyone else on the road, was a real feeling of power. She liked the physical aspect of the work. It was hard, but ballet training had stood her in good stead.

In the last few years it had been difficult to make

a living. Diesel prices, repayments on her truck and competition between independent drivers meant many trips barely earned her any money. She was luckier than most. Her repayments were less than those faced by most drivers, thanks to her parents' will and a loan from James and Maureen, but it was getting harder and harder to meet them. All her contracts 'assumed' she would abide by all trucking regulations, in terms of hours spent driving per day, but then demanded delivery times that made driving by the rules impossible. Often she had less than forty-eight hours to get from one end of the country to the other and yet was supposed to stop, revive and survive every two hours. High voltage caffeine and guarana drinks were not enough and, along with most drivers she knew, she had a regular prescription for 'diet pills'.

As awful as it was to see wired faces at truck stops, she remembered what one driver of thirty years' experience had said to her. She had walked into the women's toilet at one truck stop to see a driver pulling a syringe out of his arm. She ran out immediately. The older driver sympathised but told her to get used to it, and added, 'I'd rather a driver coming down the road towards me at 100 k in the middle of the night was wired on speed, than clean and falling asleep at the wheel.'

It had taken just one scare, a slight swerve across

the white line, a blaring horn and a split-second shift back into her lane for Nicole to ensure she always had something to keep her awake.

She shuddered to think how anyone with a family coped with the lifestyle. She just had herself to support and there was nobody at home to miss her or worry about her long hours. It made life on the road easier. Maureen would have been horrified if she had known the grim reality lurking under the dusty light of The Milk Bar's chandeliers.

Maureen, Irene and Nicole had all been friends since ballet school, dancing and graduating together, although not in the same roles. Nicole had still been Tom. There was a time when Nicole could only talk about her days as Tom in the third person. In her mind she pretended he had been some younger brother that had died. 'Tom was such a queen, I couldn't stand him,' she would laugh. It had been true. She had spent years hating Tom, despising any masculine aspects of herself. Puberty and adolescence had been a nightmare, the 'girly' taunts and abuse were nothing to the loathing she felt looking in a mirror. The lines of her body grew angular, hair appeared and her voice ran riot over octaves. The taunts sustained Tom. As long as he still looked like a girl, and acted like one, he was winning the war with his hormones.

Ballet had been a mixed blessing. It was the perfect

'girlie' option. An arts environment was kinder than others but the intense training and figure-hugging tights only emphasised a masculine body.

The operations came several years after ballet school. The decision arrived by itself, a visitor in the night that stayed permanently. The hurdles meant pain and difficulty but it was an easier war, one waged with the outside world, not a civil war raging inside her.

She thought of herself as the Little Mermaid, sacrificing everything to be what she wanted, transforming herself into a woman. After the operations, the only part of the fairy tale that rang true was the agony. In the story, every step the Little Mermaid took as a woman was like walking on broken glass. For weeks Nicole felt that broken glass right inside her body with every step. She had been ripped apart and re-assembled.

Maureen and Irene were the only friends of Tom that made the transition to being friends of Nicole. The only ones that had overcome her change and not treated her as if a hard shake would make everything fall apart. Maureen had led the way. As soon as Nicole was fit enough after the final operation, she had taken her down to Melbourne to go shopping. They shared changing rooms, tried on underwear, and went to the toilet together in bars. In one changing room they had looked at their breasts together in the mirror, admiring their own bodies, saying what they liked. They touched each other's breasts. Maureen closed her eyes, did a blind feel test and declared they felt exactly the same. Nothing could have welcomed Nicole more to her new gender. Maureen's breasts were perfect. If Nicole could have a taken a photo of them to her surgeon and asked to have the same, she would have. The trip to Melbourne had been silly and superficial but it was one of her most treasured memories. She never really wore the gorgeous underwear bought on the trip. Occasionally, when she needed cheering up, she would put it on and look at herself in the mirror.

It was Maureen who, indirectly, had got her into trucking. Nicole had tried office jobs and shop work, and had made it into beauty consulting. Her boyish figure which she loathed as a man now gave her a glamorous model-like quality. Designer clothes fitted her perfectly. Make-up demonstrations in department stores were her big earner. She became a shopping mall attraction. She gave tips on making yourself more feminine and discovering your inner model, all couched in terms of self-actualisation.

'It's about discovering your uniqueness, finding out who you really are and letting that shine through your styling and the colours you choose. Don't be sucked in by the latest look or style. Ask yourself, is this me, is this true to my inner self?'

The answer was invariably yes, and resulted in a sale. Nicole could not decide if she was a complete fraud or the most appropriate person to say what she said. The thrill of attention did not last long. Each housewife who approached her with a photo of Elle Macpherson saying 'According to this magazine we're the same body type, I want to look more like her,' seemed more like the last one than she could possibly stand. Nicole would run out her stock answer: 'They're right, you should go for the natural tones and minimal make-up look that she does. With Elle, less is more.' More than advice, they sought the compliments their husbands never paid them.

Maureen suggested that now she had been a woman for a few years, perhaps it was time to embrace her masculine side.

'I don't mean go back to Tom,' she explained, 'but we all have masculine sides, just like the feminine sides we're always telling men to get in touch with. Perhaps there's enough distance between Nicole and Tom to discover that part of yourself.'

This opened up a whole new area of her life, a giant stride towards being a whole person. She had cherished the grace of movement the years of ballet had given her, and she now learned to love the strength as well. The perfect woman did not have to be 'everything a woman should be' all the time. She would be comfortable enough with who she was to allow herself to be both. Her career inspiration came when she moved apartment and hired a truck to shift her furniture. Sitting high above the road crunching the gears was fantastic. The next week she enrolled in driving school.

A deafening horn and a shuddering jolt to the left blasted Nicole out of her reverie. She swerved, and a sweaty shiver ran over her skin. Before she could work out what happened, the horn blasted again. There was another truck driving alongside her on the opposite side of the road. The passenger window was down and she could hear the driver shouting.

'You fucking bitch, you're disgusting.'

He turned his steering wheel again to ram his truck into her. She moved her truck to the left, but not in time to avoid the sound and feel of their containers colliding. She glanced over. It was Louie, the guy she had beaten up at The Milk Bar. He was angry, angry enough to endanger both their lives.

They were on a straight stretch of road, one lane in either direction. A bend was fast approaching but Louie ignored it as he continued racing close by Nicole, oblivious to the damage he might be doing to himself or his truck. Nicole could feel her lorry rock to the left. A slight lift in her wheels felt like a death-defying circus act. One degree too much and the entire truck could fall over.

Another nudge produced a metal crunch. Something smashed. He had come up close, caught her side-view mirror in his, and pulled away. It bounced off the sides of both trucks and dropped onto the road behind them, coming to rest on the white lines.

Nicole knew he wanted her to brake. It was a game of brinkmanship. She felt a surge of determination to beat him. She had the upper hand. There was no way he would dare turn a blind corner in the oncoming lane. She could show him who was the toughest. The corner glided towards them. Louie looked over and smiled. He was not shifting. Nicole smiled back, refusing to lose face. She had beaten him before and would do so again.

The corner was a few seconds away. Nicole swallowed, realising she could not do it. The horror of Louie rounding the corner into a car was too much. It was not worth the risk. She cursed that split-second quiver in her stomach that said she had lost, and performed a textbook emergency brake. Louie surged ahead, crossed into the left-hand lane and rounded the corner. Nicole's truck came to a stop before the corner. There was no other traffic on the road, only the throb of her engine.

Her shoulders slumped and her hands pressed to

her face, feeling the wet of tears. Driving trucks every day, the fact they were huge killing machines escaped her attention. It was like working in a dynamite factory and tossing the sticks around because you were so used to them. Days like today reminded her of the lethal aspect of her job. She let the tears flow.

'Tears are good.' Every therapist she had ever visited had used that line like a mantra whenever the water-works started.

'Tears are good. You're alive. You're driving to Sydney and celebrating Maureen and James' anniversary. Life is good.'

She held her hands out in front of her. She could see the road, beyond that trees and then blue sky. Her hands looked as if they were being held in front of a video screen, she could almost see a line around them like some special effect photography. The slight tremble did not help. When they appeared as still as she felt capable of, she dropped them and breathed out slowly through her mouth.

Her quiet moment of recovery was soon shattered. From around the corner ahead of her, she heard a truck horn blaring, again and again, screeching brakes and then a crash. Back into emergency mode, she moved into gear and drove around the corner. Four hundred metres ahead on the left-hand verge a car had turned over in the slight ditch and slid to rest against a tree. Louie's truck had pulled over a little further on. He was running back to the crashed car.

Nicole stopped, jumped out of her truck and joined him at the crashed car. Louie could not keep still. Pacing around, putting his hands to his head, he looked at the car and groaned.

'Shit, shit. He was asleep at the wheel. He swerved over. Idiot, fucking idiot.'

Nicole crouched down to the car to see who was inside. There were no passengers, just the driver. He appeared to be unconscious.

'We should get him out. He's hanging upside down,' Nicole said.

'Don't move him, don't move him. It's evidence.'

'It could be ages before an ambulance gets here. It can't be good to be upside down.'

She opened the car door. 'He's not trapped. We could lay him out by the road and wait. Come on.' Louie helped manoeuvre the body out of the car and lay it on the grass verge.

'Have you phoned for an ambulance?' Nicole asked.

'No, I can't. You do it.'

'Fine.' Nicole stormed to her truck, got her mobile and made the call.

'I've gotta get out of here,' Louie announced, 'They'll crucify me.'

'It's an accident. You can't run off.'

72

'For God's sake, look at me. I'm wired as hell. The cops'll blame me. I'm finished, I don't fucking believe it. All because that idiot fell asleep.'

'That idiot could die.'

'Good, he's killing me off. Oh shit.' Louie's face broke. He looked at Nicole and sank to the ground. He sat, shaking his head. Nicole sat down beside him.

'It's not fair.' Tears literally burst out of his eyes as he broke into sobs.

'I haven't slept in five days. I can't afford sleep. If I miss another drop-off, I'm out of it. I can't afford to miss one. The truck repayment's due. And now this. They'll test me, I'll lose my licence.'

'I know, it's hard.' Nicole was relieved it was her who had backed down as she approached the corner. Otherwise she would have been facing this situation.

'Do you? I bet this is a hobby for you. What did you do before driving?'

Nicole smiled weakly, unsure whether to attempt a lie. She decided against it. 'Make-up demonstrations'.

'Very nice. Want to know what I did before I drove? I sat in my dad's truck with him when he drove. He died in his truck, an accident. Some idiot just like him fell asleep behind the wheel of an oncoming truck. Wiped out.'

'I'm sorry.'

'Sure, and the insurance company. The bastards wouldn't pay out because they tested his body for drugs. Said it was his fault for being on speed. The bastard that fell asleep though, his family got a full payout.'

'Believe me, I know how hard it is. If I knew when I was starting out...' Nicole felt a strange connection with the twitching maniac who had tried to run her off the road. They were both drivers after all.

'Trucking's my way of being free,' she continued. 'I'm on my own, don't have to put up with sneering all day, just the odd fight at a milk bar.'

Louie continued, oblivious to what Nicole had said.

'My wife couldn't stand it any more. She took off with my son, married some guy that works in an office. They're probably better off. I can't look after them. I used to be so proud. I was a truckie, you know. A real man's job, but it's all gone. A man's supposed to look after his wife and kid, I couldn't do that. You can't do that doing a bloke's work any more, you've gotta use a computer. They've made it so hard. Then, today I get beaten up by a woman.' Louie shrugged in disbelief, 'Not even a real woman.'

'I'm sorry, I...' For all his anger and aggression, Nicole could feel his pain.

'At least you chose,' he said, staring at her. 'You

chose not to be a man. I had it taken away. I'm done when the cops get here. That's it.' He looked at her with a boyish pleading in his eyes.

'You'd better go. No point two of us copping late penalties. I'm ... er, sorry about before. Mates?'

Nicole was touched. She felt they had connected, despite their fight and differences—a rare moment of empathy that made her glad to be human. In such a moment she wanted to do something to prove their fragile friendship and thought of what she might do if this had been Maureen or Irene sitting in desperation.

'Look, why don't you go?' she said. 'Get going before anyone gets here. I can say I just found this car like this and stopped to help. The driver won't recognise your truck. There's no-one else here. After all, it wasn't your fault, was it?'

'You're right, but I can't do that.'

'You must.' Nicole was sure now. There was no reason for him to stay. She could get him out of this.

'Really, you won't say anything? You didn't see a thing. Just the car. You're the best.'

He jumped up quickly and ran towards his truck. Relief had focussed his mind and body as he leapt in and drove off without a hesitation. Nicole remained with the unconscious car driver. She dispelled any nervous doubts she had—there was a bond between truck drivers, no matter how much they fought.

•

Weighing-in for the competition had been a shock for Tanya. She had always been 64 kilos, the perfect weight to put her right at the top of the women's middleweight category. She weighed in at 66 kilos, enough to take her up to welterweight and face women up to 9 kilos heavier than her. Her entire size and weight advantage strategy had to be replaced with one of speed and agility, and within an hour. As she stepped down from the scales, Vernon, the most experienced fighter in her club and her dedicated trainer for the day, registered the shock on her face. He took her to one side, held both her hands, looked in her eyes, said, 'Baekjul Boolgoo,' and walked away.

Tanya valued the focussed communication. 'Baekjul Boolgoo,' she repeated to herself, 'Baekjul Boolgoo'. It was the last and, right now, the most important of the Taekwondo tenets: Indomitable Spirit. The changing room was charged with competitors focussing. A deadening silence as the air was thick with waves of minds, bodies and spirits melding. Rumours of a number of American competitors taking advantage of the 'open' status of the national championships had proved correct.

Putting on her protective competition vest, Tanya pressed her hand on the large red dot in the middle of it. This dot was one of her opponent's targets. The very vest that was supposed to protect her was the item that attracted the blows. Kicks to the chest and head were the best way to score points. Punches could score in theory, but someone had to knock their opponent virtually to the floor with a punch to gain the point.

She sat down, blocking out the heavy atmosphere of the changing room, and took a moment to explore and understand Baekjul Boolgoo. What did 'indomitable spirit' really mean? It meant relishing the challenge. It meant the spirit was ready for her to move up to this new weight. It was an opportunity for learning and growth which she must seize. It was a difference of two kilos, a weight that was within the control of her body. Therefore it must be her destiny, another path had been chosen for her. She would walk down it with Yom Chi (perseverance, the second of the tenets).

It was the sense of control she was now achieving that had drawn Tanya to Taekwondo. She had always been good at sports. At primary school she was a legend. Running, swimming, team sports—she did them all and won everything. It made her popular and she was elected class captain. Her gang ruled the roost in the playground and everyone wanted to be part of it. Boys and girls alike looked up to her and no-one, it seemed, dared cross her. The fact that she was not the best academically only added to her stature. 'Who wants to be good at maths?' she would sneer if anyone dared to question her academic skills. Not that the other kids did very often. No-one challenged Tanya.

High school was different. From a mixed public primary school, she got sent to an all-girls Catholic high school, St Angela's. Within the first two weeks she realised she had the misfortune of going to the only school in Australia where sports were a low priority. Nobody cared if you could run faster, jump higher and dive better than everyone else. Conjugating verbs was more important than scoring goals. Tanya was confused and angry. From being the most popular girl in the school she had become the butt of jokes, jokes which she could not respond to. She tried to find clever insults, but all the lines which worked at primary school just brought derision. All she could do was seethe and get more angry. The worst blow came from a girl who had been at her primary school. As a group were laughing at a wrong answer she had given in French, she leaned forward and whispered to Tanya, 'Nobody likes you, nobody ever did. It's just we're not scared of you here.'

Her misery was brought to a head when her parents were summoned by the principal, Sister Judith, for a meeting. There had been reports of bullying in the school. At first, they were appalled to think that anyone could be so awful to their girl, but then Sister Judith made it clear Tanya was doing the bullying. If she could not make the girls like her, she could make them scared.

It was agreed she should channel her 'aggression', as the nuns defined it, into sports where she could control it. In a school where loving games was a cause of ridicule, it was not much of an outlet. Team sports proved useless to her. Apart from Sister Judith's doubts about arming Tanya with a hockey stick and unleashing her onto a pitch with twenty-one other girls, she realised Tanya could only throw herself into team sports if other girls did too. Matches against other schools were disasters with ten girls having to be dragged off the half-time bench and Tanya sprinting the field trying to be the whole team. It just made her more frustrated and the other girls even more scared. She was pushed into solo pursuits and found some happiness. Running and swimming exhausted her blissfully, but it was not until she discovered martial arts that Tanya found her calling.

It had been Year 10, when she was fifteen, that she first learned about Taekwondo. Initially the nuns did not like the idea of Tanya training her body into a lethal weapon during school hours, but after Sister

Judith took the trouble of researching what the sport entailed and read the magic words 'control' and 'respect', she could not get her to the classes quickly enough. It was the solution to all their problems. Tanya found a sport and people she could enjoy. Controlling her power, keeping everything in check, became important to her. She vowed to abide forever by the tenets of Taekwondo. Self-control was the ultimate virtue in her new religion. Gradually, she learned to get on better with the other girls. They would never be her friends, but they no longer tensed up if she sat next to them in class.

For her first match at the national championships, it turned out Tanya need not have worried about the weight disadvantage. Her opponent was of middle-weight height but heavyweight width. If it had been wrestling, Tanya would have been doomed. As it was, a minimum level of agility would counter each lunge. At the start of the match they sized each other up. Tanya's opponent shrieked out words of intimidation and bounced around. Tanya knew calm could be much more threatening, and remained as still as a coiled snake while the other girl jumped about shouting. In the midst of a scream, Tanya struck: a foot right on the girl's blue circle and a point on the board. The three rounds, each of three minutes, passed without any real challenge. She took it easy, being eight points ahead by the final round. In fact she took it too easy and earned a caution for not being aggressive enough. Whenever that happened, she always thought of Sister Judith and how pleased she would have been that Tanya was being penalised for non-aggression. At the end of the match, her opponent, a girl of sixteen, observed all the courtesies and then ran off in tears to her mother, standing by the other trainers in a Parramatta Eels tracksuit. Tanya heard the words 'not fair' and received a glower from the mother. Allowances, they felt, should have been made.

•

'I will not be Captain Bloodbath.' The words thundered down the phone.

Justin, the original Captain Bloodbath, sighed and whispered, 'Michael, you can have any name you want, just do the gig. I thought you might actually want some work for a change.' Desperation had set in for Justin. James Ting had meant business. Justin had even received a solicitor's fax, threatening legal action, on a Saturday morning. That meant real power. He was scared and running out of options. With Saturday being the busy night in the city's restaurants, all the actors Justin knew were working.

Michael was a desperate last resort. He had resigned from the final year at the National Institute of Dramatic

Arts because they did not take acting seriously enough. Michael was there to be real. When he performed there was no audience: there were emotional participants. If they did not cry and hurt as much as the characters on stage, the production was a failure.

'I won't be some pathetic Hollywood fabrication.'

'Michael, it's an easy $250. Think of it as a subsidy for your real work.'

'It's a compromise, Justin. One you're happy with, but not me. My work's too important.'

'It's a dinner party entertainment. They want a bunch of pirates.'

'All the more reason to hurl them out of their rich sham of a happy life.'

Justin groaned, 'It's for James Ting. If you're serious about your art, he can set up some amazing sponsorships. He's an important person to know.'

Michael recognised the name. 'He should be in prison for selling art down the river. You know in the '80s he made his name by insisting sponsors had their products on stage during performances.'

'That's just a myth. There's no way...'

'He wouldn't know real art if it held him at gunpoint.' Michael worked himself into indignation.

'But it's so you. No audience, just participants, and best of all, most of them don't know they are an audience.'

Michael's voice changed tone. Suddenly the event had possibilities.

'Mmm...He wants an invasion. I *could* give him one. Allow his guests to experience real terror for the first time in their lives.'

'Whatever,' Justin croaked with relief. Michael would be ham enough to create a fun night.

'Terrorist theatre invades the home. It could be a whole new movement. The government should be funding this type of experience across the country, shocking people out of their TV comas into the real world. Communicating directly with people in their own environments, not some artificial arena spectacular. This is really exciting, Justin. I have to do it.'

'Great. I'll give you the details, and you'll have to use Sasha and Colin. They're booked and relying on the money. No budget for anyone else, really.'

Justin was beyond caring how real Michael was planning to make it. He had a voice to preserve and Abba lyrics to memorise. He gave Michael all the details and hung up to gargle.

Michael was firing with the redefinition of theatre. He immediately called the few people he could trust with his vision. Bugger those soapstar wannabees Sasha and Colin, Michael was going for real actors. This was a big opportunity to strike a blow at the commercialisation of art. James Ting stood for everything Michael despised. Art as a corporate promotional tool. Tonight art would strike back: bite the hand that fed it and say 'no thanks'.

His initial enquiries did not prove fruitful. Calls to the few he respected as creators revealed that a couple had sold out and had found gainful employ on a Saturday evening. One of them was touring Korea with *Pokémon the Arena Spectacular*. He was disgusted. He did manage to get the one person he really trusted. He knew Janine would never sell out and get paid work. She made a point of going to auditions unrehearsed and performing whatever was flowing through her mind at the time. Seizing control, she would finish her performance when she was ready, not when some power-crazed producer yawned 'thanks'. Her last presentation had become a mourning for the murder of the inner child of a stockbroker. Screaming out share prices, she stabbed imaginary teddy bears and beat the floor with her forehead for fifteen minutes. It was not what the producers were looking for to advertise their orthopaedic mattress.

Janine was as excited about the project as Michael was. Janine was excited about any of Michael's projects. He was a visionary leader whose genius would be celebrated in years to come. She adored his lack of compromise and his integrity. He pursued the perfect dramatic experience like a surfer waiting for the perfect wave. He would rather be lost at sea forever than ride in on anything less than 'the one'. From what he said, Janine believed this small innocent entertainment could be the one—the perfect performance that would change theatre forever.

•

The base platform on which James' ship was to be built was complete. He was standing on it with Marcus, both of them swaying gently.

'It's kitsch, but I love it. If it wasn't so naff, I'd sing "In the Navy". God, I'm brilliant.'

They swayed in unison as if rolling on the ocean waves.

James stood there with his legs apart, feeling satisfied for the first time that day. The board they were standing on had been mounted on tough coiled steel springs, all of a slightly differing height. As a result, when anyone moved around, the floor swayed beneath them in an irregular sea-swell kind of way. It was his idea and he had made it work, creating exactly the effect he wanted.

The platform was the outline of a ship. The sides of the cruise liner would be built up around it to thigh height. Everyone would have to walk up a gangplank to board the ship to sit at the dinner table. The guests would feel the gentle sea motion as they sat eating dinner on James' ship, but they would have no idea where it came from.

He looked from the platform at the array of timber, pre-prepared ship parts, drills and sawdust. It looked like an impossible task to complete that afternoon.

'Don't worry. That was the hardest part. This bit's boring now.'

Marcus jumped off the board, giving James a slight wobble.

'Trust me... You're better off checking on that crazed lunatic in the kitchen.'

James tried going into the kitchen, but the minute his hand touched the door a voice commanded 'Out!'

There was nothing to be done. Irene had left, everyone else was busy and Maureen was nowhere. He sat down on the stairs, banished to the hall of his own home. This was a safe spot for him. As a young boy it was where he had always felt most secure because he could check on everyone in the house from there. He could listen to his brother upstairs hurling lumps of modelling clay around his newspaper-lined room, hear his mother in the living room complaining about the particularly difficult stage he was going through and just about make out his sister and father in the garden shed hammering bits of wood. He had always been going through a stage. They even seemed to overlap. His mother moaned about a bossy stage even before she had announced he was clear of the sullen stage. He had asked her once during breakfast if she could tell him which stage he was in, when it would end and what other ones he could expect. Knowledge of what was to come might make things easier. He thought there must be a progression of stages he had to go through to reach manhood. Reassurance was not forthcoming, only a curt, 'Obviously in the precocious stage.'

Now he sat listening to the empty noise of his vision being constructed in the living room by others. Would his father be proud of his ship? He would probably have compared it to his sister's home-made furniture or his brother's art. James had been the only dullard in a highly creative family. His mother had baked, sewed and knitted her way into people's hearts. His father and sister were carpenters and his brother actually made a living from painting. As he grew up, Christmas had been an annual agony for him. It was a family rule that everyone had to make their presents for everyone else. They all gave each other wonderfully creative gifts, except for James. Each year he had produced a succession of objects that always required an explanation before anyone could guess what they were. As everyone else gave hand-thrown vases, home-made chocolate truffles and specially composed pieces of music, he would hand out flat pieces of wood masquerading as spice racks—onions, garlic and chillies drying together in a pungent and undecorative heap. His dreadful presents were part of the Ting Christmas tradition, the laugh that kick-started the day's festivities as his mother's brandy-marinated apricots were passed round. The first Christmas after he left home, he rebelled and resorted to his credit card. No-one commented. They understood it was harder for James. Without saying anything, his father had seemed to respect his breaking free of the creative tyranny.

His thoughts turned back to Maureen and how she had rescued Christmas for him and turned it into an enjoyable family experience. She created presents for his family that were more than just bought, but didn't involve hours on a lathe. He could enjoy the presents he received without thinking the ones he gave were inferior.

Now, as he sat on the stairs, cradling his mobile in his hand, he wiped his fingers over the screen and thought of Maureen. The counter-surprise theory was not holding up to scrutiny. If she was doing that, she would not have created suspicion by vanishing—she would have carried on as normal.

He repeated the word 'perhaps' to summon up some explanations, but none came. He had tried 'perhaps she's just gone and got drunk', but not her, Maureen did not get drunk. She would drink and enjoy herself but never lose control. The worst he had ever seen her was many years ago. They had gone out for a drink and somehow managed to bypass dinner. Maureen's usual safe limit was blown away by an empty stomach. In their bedroom James had declared 'I love youse touse' at her chest and lunged at the girls. When she started feeling queasy, she shoved James out of the way and looked for the nearest receptacle as her cheeks ballooned like an overstuffed hamster's. His boots. They were old and easier to clean than the carpet, so she filled them. James looked on in amazement.

She was drunk, half asleep, vomiting and still did not spill a drop.

Maureen collapsed back on the bed and passed out, leaving James to stagger to the bathroom with the filled boots. His shoulders, always broader when drunk, caught the edge of the doorway and he fell into the bathroom, the boots spilling out onto the tiled floor. Too weary to begin cleaning up, he dropped them and lurched back to the bed.

Maureen would not be drunk. James decided activity was the best distraction. He walked into the living room to find Ulrika standing defiantly on the sprung platform. The ladle had finally been relinquished, but the look of fury had not.

'I thought this was a culinary journey, not an amusement-park ride. I spend hours in preparation so my staff can hurl food at your guests on a roller-coaster?'

'That's something of an exaggeration. The platform doesn't move,' James defended his creation.

Marcus moved in front of her with the port bow of the ship and put it in place along the front edge of the platform. Ulrika was unimpressed that work had not stopped at the sound of her voice.

'I'm talking,' she announced. Marcus looked at her, smiled and went to fetch the starboard bow.

'I will not be a gimmick.' Her voice grew shrill.

'But you knew about the theme. It was clear from the start,' James used calming tones to avoid an eruption.

'I was led to believe it was a culinary theme, not a scene from *HMS Pinafore*.'

'I made it clear.' The calm tones were not working.

Marcus slotted the piece in place behind Ulrika, deliberately pushing on the springs to make her lose balance. She turned, scowled at Marcus, and then resumed her stare at James. Stepping slowly to the port side of the ship, she raised her foot and kicked it, punching a hole in the side and trapping her shoe in the splintered plywood. Marcus stormed round to see the damage and raised his eyebrows in derision at her foot.

He walked towards the kitchen.

'Don't even think it,' Ulrika shouted, attempting to wiggle her foot free.

'Stop him,' she glowered at James, amazed that he had not already moved. It was too late: Marcus returned from the kitchen with a whole salmon. As he approached the vessel, staring into Ulrika's eyes with his tongue shoved hard in his cheek, he swung the fish round, and slammed it against her foot protruding through the bow.

'Here, let me help you,' he said without a smile, and swung the fish again.

James realised these two could completely destroy his plans. He rushed forward to intervene, only to be caught by the fish on the backswing and be winded. Marcus smashed the shoe again with enough force to release it from the ship. Catapulted by the sprung board and shrieking all the way, Ulrika jumped over the bow at Marcus' throat, knocking both of them to the floor with the fish between them. She grabbed his hair and started banging his head against the floor.

'Do you realise what you've done?' With each word she hit his head on the floor.

'My ship, you've sunk it!' Marcus' seemingly impenetrable cool exploded. He pushed Ulrika over and sat on top of her. Grabbing the head of the salmon, he shoved it in her mouth as she opened it to scream. Her teeth crunched down on it with determination. Swinging her head from side to side she bit the

91

salmon's head off its body and spat it out in Marcus' face. He squealed and let go.

James, recovered from his winding, stepped up, dragged his interior designer off his chef and called for David to come from the kitchen and assist in keeping the two apart. They clawed at James' arms in trying to reach each other.

'Take her over there,' James ordered David, who dragged his boss to the hallway. James held Marcus tightly and moved him away.

'That's it. You're both fired. David, you're staying to help, but you two, out.'

'You can't,' they cried in unison.

'I can. David, you happy to take over in the kitchen?'

'Yes,' David spoke for the first time. Ulrika turned and spat at him.

'Viper.'

It took some time to persuade them that James' words had not been a fit of petulance or a bargaining position. It was not their usual experience for people to mean what they said. For James it was proof that he should have done everything himself. This was his event, and for it to really work, he had to do it himself. This was the lesson he should be learning, he thought. Ulrika and Marcus stormed out, united by their common enemy and muttering barbed comments about amateur artists as they stomped to their respective vehicles. Their dramatic exit was marred by having to return and ask James to move his car so they could get theirs out of the drive.

Within seconds of their departure and his decision to do everything himself, James was regretting it. Given his attempt in the kitchen that morning, he could not take over the cooking himself. At least David was there to manage that. James gave him carte blanche and the keys to his car. A replacement for the battered decapitated salmon was required.

The ship was a different matter. James could accomplish that. He surveyed the damage and gritted his teeth. Surely he had absorbed something from all those years his father had spent trying to interest him in woodwork.

Before the fight had taken place, it looked like all the pieces of the ship were going to snap into place quite simply. The pieces now looked horribly complicated and unfinished. It would be best to line all the bits up where they were supposed to go and then look at repairing Ulrika's hole. He started moving the disparate elements around. He tried matching up the lines of painted rivets on the outside of the ship, but that did not work. Then he looked at getting the portholes evenly spaced. He managed that but the top looked more like a castle's crenellations than a ship's deck rails.

There were any number of carpenters he could summon with ridiculous sums of money. His sister would have it erected in no time with a self-satisfied smile. But no, delegating had got him into this trouble, his bare hands would get him out. He banged a piece into place next to the broken bow. It seemed to fit, portholes and rivets were lined up. It was a start. If he pushed it hard enough perhaps he would get that easy snapping-into-place noise that Marcus had generated. No such noise came but the support timbers creaked and splinters dug into his fingers.

James looked at his hands in frustration. Fingers like fat sausages. Chunky round useless hands. Hair crept up their sides, and small colonies sprouted on the fingers just above the knuckle.

As a boy he would have chopped his hands off if they had been capable of carrying out such a precise exercise on each other.

He had learned at an early age it was easier for him to get other people to do things than do them himself. At primary school he was the gang leader who organised everyone else. If they were building a den, James would be the one to dispatch some to hunt out building materials, others to prepare the ground, and more to do the building. He was always the brain, while his friends were the brawn. Occasionally there had been a few cries that he was being too bossy and not actually doing anything. He would bow to peer pressure, stand aside as leader and watch the gang fall apart faster than the den. Then he would be recalled and his gang would soon have the best den in the neighbourhood. Today there was no gang, just clumsy hands ramming the wrong pieces in the wrong places.

His strategic mind knew to leave the task, focus on something else and then come back with a fresh perspective. Ulrika's hole needed mending and it could be done easily. He found a piece of wood to cover it, sprayed it with the touch-up paint Marcus had left and began nailing it over the hole. The hammer blows shook the ship. There had to be a balance between the force required to get the nails in and the weight of blows the ship could take. He failed to find it. Getting carried away with the one nail that was going in smoothly, he finished it off with a slam, admiring the way the head fitted flatly on the wood. The brief satisfaction snapped when the other segment which Marcus had so easily slotted into place fell down. He hurled the hammer down in frustration. It bounced off the sprung platform and he had to jump out of the way, landing close to the mended bow and in danger of falling on it. He bowled his arms around like a gymnast losing control on the beam, determined not to topple onto the only correctly positioned piece.

Through sheer movement of air he regained his balance and stepped away. He was relieved, but not much: this constituted his second hands-on disaster of the day.

He was called away by the phone. It was Stephen.

'I went back to where I saw Maureen but there was no sign. Sorry.'

'Doesn't matter,' answered James wearily, 'everything's ruined. There's no point.' He explained recent events in the house.

'Can I come round and help?' Stephen asked. 'It'll be like the old days, building a den. You can direct.' In their gang Stephen had been the chief builder. He was good with his hands. James had always been jealous—Stephen would never have wanted to chop his hands off.

'Yeah, that would be great.'

Sometimes Stephen could just do and say exactly the right thing. He might lose it completely with women, but he knew how to be a friend.

'I'll have to drop the car off for Tanya, then get a cab to you so I can be there right up to the dinner. Don't worry, everything's going to be fine.'

James wished he could believe it.

•

Irene browsed in her favourite bookshop. Hidden away from the busy crowds, in the centre of town, it had Sydney's most formidable collection of foreign language books and the obscure texts that she adored. It was a regular port of call on a Reenies' day, so she decided to go anyway. Maintaining ritual was comforting but the bookshop visit was not the same without the sense of being indulged. Maureen would take her there like a grandmother taking grandchildren to a sweetshop. The best grannies would enter in the spirit of the event, and taste as many sweets as possible. Maureen did that for Irene, emerging enthusiastically with a stack of books bought on Irene's recommendation and a few others to prove she was not just doing it to please her friend.

Today there was no-one to hunt down in the general fiction, thrust a dry tome in front of and say, 'Now this you have to read.' Irene generally avoided the piles of new releases. There was nothing there for her taste. An author wasn't a real author unless they wrote in a different language and were dead. This time Irene did visit the new releases, because that's where Maureen browsed. Bright covers wrestled for her attention, none of them pinning it down until she recognised a picture of a thirteenth-century tapestry. It depicted an unknown knight riding a horse with chivalric pride. It was a curious choice of picture, she thought, until she saw the book's title, *Le Chevalier d'Étoile*. Picking it up, she flipped to the back and scanned the blurb:

'Jonathan Townsend brings this forgotten classic to vibrant life. Drama, passion, self-sacrifice and love in its truest form are set against the turbulent backdrop of twelfth-century France. This is no stale historical text, it pulsates with life and resonance. The first ever modern English retelling of one of the greatest forgotten stories of western civilisation.'

It was her life's work and someone had beaten her to it and left a verbless sentence on the cover. She quickly looked around. Embarrassment flooded her first. What if someone had seen her horror? What if someone who knew her was watching the scene? All the people who knew this was the book that she was meant to write would see it. She stood still holding the paperback. She was relieved Maureen was not there—one less person to share in her humiliation, but there was no-one to comfort her or prevent her from punching herself in the stomach by buying a copy. The assistant added a few extra blows.

'It's going to be huge. It was a monster hit in the UK. God, I wish I'd written it.'

Irene smiled. 'So do I.'

She retreated to the nearest alcohol-serving venue. This book required wine. There was no avoiding reading every page that she should have written. The sooner she started, the sooner the torture would be over. She would have to tell everyone it was wonderful, far better than she could ever have done—a sandbag of grace against the flood of shame. She looked at the cover, the very picture she had imagined all those times she sat in front of a blank piece of paper visualising the completed novel. Visualising the finished product was supposed to motivate her but it only made her think the book would happen anyway, whether she wrote that particular day or not. On those occasions, she went back to the text and made more notes. You could never make too many notes on a project of this importance. Being ill-prepared was the worst mistake she had thought she could make.

Jonathan Townsend probably had not worried about note-taking. Who the hell was he anyway? She had never come across the name in all her reading and no-one could have read more on the subject of this book than her. The waiter placed her glass of wine next to the unopened book.

'My girlfriend's reading that. I may as well be invisible when it's open. Says it's amazing. You'll love it.' He smiled, thinking he was being friendly.

'Where is Buzz.com and its blissfully human-free service when you need it?' thought Irene.

Humiliation dripped through her like a stone through water. This was not just being beaten to the top of a mountain, this was discovering someone else had got there and built a souvenir shop while you were still counting your tent pegs at base camp.

She remembered how she and Maureen had laughed at some model who claimed to have written more books than she had read. They had cackled with contempt. The model did not seem so stupid now. If only Irene had dedicated all the time she had spent reading to writing, she'd be looking at her name, not Townsend's, and celebrating with champagne, not commiserating with Merlot. She opened the book and read the first line. It was exactly as she would have written it.

She hated Stephen, she hated Sophie, she hated herself for the years of distractions. Most of all she hated Jonathan Bastard Townsend for not being too distracted and for having a wife to look after everything while he committed himself to Irene's task. She checked the dedication, 'To Stephanie, without whose...' It was more galling than the crisply invigorating text.

•

Stephen had not wanted to go back to Darling Harbour. He wanted Tanya to do well, and knew she would probably compete better without him there distracting her and demanding attention. He tried to couch his unwillingness in terms of support for her, but as he drove there, he knew what it was really about: the impending moving-in conversation. It had hung in the car like the scented cleaning fluids they used at the hand carwash. The Clean Team always asked him what scent he wanted: pine, floral or lemon. Every time he would request no scent at all, but that was not an option. Everyone had to have scent, just like every couple had to have the moving-in conversation. There was no avoiding it and no avoiding his agreeing to it. It was the next step, that was how it went. Tanya, so far, had been the sole object of his sexual desires. It would change with co-habitation, which was always the beginning of the end.

Perhaps if he had taken a Chinese wife, as still suggested by his grandmother, it would have been different. However, he had always gone for white women. Being third-generation Australian-Chinese, he felt little cultural affiliation with 'home', as his grandmother referred to Hong Kong. He did not want a partner raised in old traditions he knew little about. His parents had spoken English at home. They believed that thinking and speaking like 'true blue' Aussies would be a big help for their children in overcoming prejudice. They had been right, for phone calls at least. Stephen spoke virtually no Cantonese and had made no effort to learn. Irene, a fluent speaker, was the nearest he had got to a Chinese wife. When they had visited 'the relatives' in Hong Kong they had caused considerable confusion. Not only was he barely able to communicate with them, but his white wife had to translate for him. He suspected some of the older relatives were not very impressed behind their polite marvelling at her linguistic skill. Not only had he forsaken his own language, but he let his wife speak for him.

His parents took to Irene immediately, a classy smart white wife was all his father had ever wanted for him. His grandmother had taken more persuading. She felt she was being practical when she announced, 'White girls for sex, Chinese girls for children.' However she was won over by the birth of Sophie. The fact Irene gave up her job to raise her daughter helped even more.

Try as he might, Stephen could not blame his Chinese background for his compulsive infidelity. There was no cultural tradition he could refer to, unless it was ocker blokes refusing to be tied down. It was always the co-habiting that did him in. He had no thoughts of straying as long as he did not live with a woman. As soon as they moved in together he felt frustrated and hemmed in. That was when the wanderlust, as he called it, started. Logically he could see that love, companionship and trust were worth far more than getting his end away, but that logic was absent when confronted with the possibility of extra-relationship sex. If he got a whiff of possibility, suddenly it was all that mattered. The prospect of immediate gratification was more important than everything.

He could sense the wanderlust the second it kicked in. He could walk past a woman on the street and, like a smell unleashed from within his own body, it was there. It was also remarkably accurate in the women it selected. Without any obvious body language, the wanderlust knew he would get sex from the women. He wished it worked when he was single. He would have been able to have as much sex as possible and perhaps get it out of his system, but sadly wanderlust and its special instinct only came with co-habitation.

At Darling Harbour he tried to make his way to the competitors' changing rooms to leave an envelope with keys and instructions for Tanya. Without the relevant accreditation he was not allowed in the changing rooms and so put the keys in an envelope and entrusted them to a security guard who promised to tape it to her locker.

The corridors he had wound through looking for the changing facilities must have been right under the competition arena as he could hear a cheer go up. Perhaps Tanya was competing. It would do no harm to glimpse the competition if she had no idea, he thought. If he saw Tanya in action, it might remind him of all her wonderful attributes. He might see something that would let him know it would be different this time.

He retraced his steps, or thought he did. Walking down corridors, up steps and through doors which seemed familiar, he couldn't find his original entrance. He tried going back to get directions from the security guard. It seemed an even longer walk than before and the point of the security guard stopping him was now clear. He could walk straight to the changing room. As he rounded the next corner several female athletes wearing tracksuits came into view. The parts of their bodies that were revealed looked very muscular, even more so than Tanya's. She had a battle on her hands, he thought. He saw a sign on a door saying 'Female Competitors', and knocked. A voice called him in.

'Is that the Hot Stuff?'

As he entered sight and sound confused him. There was just one woman in there, standing in a drawstring bikini, heavily tanned and with a staggering set of muscles. Stephen gawped at her rippling six-pack and then the breasts that sat so unyieldingly on the chest above. She was sipping a glass of red wine.

'You got the Hot Stuff?' she repeated.

'I'm sorry, I was looking for the Taekwondo competitors,' Stephen replied.

'Wrong hall. This is the NSW Natural Bodybuilding Championships. Shit, I'm going to miss it. I need that Hot Stuff.' She looked at him, downed her glass of wine and laughed.

'Don't worry, it's a spray to make my veins stand out. I sent Gerard off to fetch it and he's still not back.'

Stephen was confused but could not take his eyes off the woman as she checked her poses in the mirror. Her V-shape back flexed out in great detail. She was not like the caricatures that got paraded on television. This woman had grace with her power. She caught him looking.

'What's your name?'

'Stephen. Sorry I was...'

'If you're going to gawk you may as well make yourself useful. We'll have to resort to slapping.'

'What?'

'My veins aren't popping enough. The idiot Gerard will have got lost and the wine won't do enough. I'm due to pose in ten minutes. Slapping might help bring the veins up.'

The explanation did not make much sense to Stephen.

'I don't think I can.'

'Come on.' She grabbed Stephen's hand with a firm

grip, opened his palm out and then brought it down hard on her own thigh.

'See. Now try it, same spot.'

Stephen slapped the girl on her thigh.

'Harder. I'm tough you know.'

He slapped again.

'Harder,' she shouted. He swung his hand down on her thigh and gave a resounding slap.

'Better. Now again, on my glutes.' She turned round and pointed to a left buttock so solid, the tight-fitting bikini bottom could make no indent. He slapped hard.

'Good. Other side.'

As he slapped his way around her muscles, he thought it was a job he could get used to. This woman's body was so firm, so rounded. Muscles he would have been proud of himself. He stopped slapping, realising he was actually being turned on. It was bad enough accepting Tanya's firm physique was arousing, but a bodybuilder's was a big step further.

'What's wrong?'

'Err, well I...I don't even know your name.'

'Merissa, now do my pecs.' He swung but there were breasts in the way.

'Just go around the boobs.' He slapped. She looked him in the eyes, curious to see his reaction.

'More fun than martial arts eh?' He smiled. She had

a pretty face. A little too much competition make-up, but a gorgeous smile.

'You have a fantastic body.' He was flirting. Minutes after wondering how he could stop the onslaught of his wanderlust, he was slap-flirting with a buffed muscle-freak.

'Got it, love.' A gruff voice made Stephen turn to the doorway. The man-mountain filling it must have been Gerard, given he had a bottle of Hot Stuff in his hand.

'Where the hell have you been? I had to get...'

'Stephen.' He held out his greasy hand for a shake but was rebuffed.

'Stephen,' continued Merissa nervously, 'agreed to slap me—I've no time left.'

'I'm here now, aren't I? I'll spray while you walk up.' He grabbed Merissa and yanked her through the door.

'Come and watch,' she shouted back at Stephen.

Gerard sprayed Merissa as they waited at the side of the stage. Merissa raised her eyebrows at Stephen as the closing strains of 'Simply the Best' accompanied the previous performer's final poses.

'How original,' she said and locked her arms forward, warming up for a traps pose.

'Shit.' She wiggled on the spot as her name was announced, waiting for the first bars of 'Man, I feel like a Woman' to blast around the venue, and then walked her puissant femininity to the podium. Stephen watched in amazement as the muscles that had been hard and defined in his hands suddenly ballooned. She became pure brawn. Her entire body appeared twenty per cent bigger. He understood the accuracy of the term pumped-up. Gerard watched and growled, 'Symmetry's fucked, has been since the accident.' Without explanation he turned away, looked down at Stephen, grunted and walked off.

Merissa worked the crowd. Every flex was perfectly on the beat. It was a choreographed ballet: each muscle working harmoniously in the corps that was her body. She ended, bang on cue, with a phenomenal V-shaped pose that made her seem more wide than tall. The crowd loved it. She walked beaming back to side stage. Approaching gently while still visible to the judges, she leapt at Stephen once out of their sight, wrapped her legs around him and then looked shocked.

'Sorry, I thought you were Gerard. Couldn't see 'cos of the lights.'

Unprepared for the joyous force, Stephen was almost knocked over. He could feel her wrapped around him. Her skin pushed against his clothes. After she realised her mistake, she made no attempt to release herself. Her legs squeezed his torso tight, far more strongly than Tanya ever had. She nearly crushed him in her post-performance high. He loved it.

'They loved you,' he said.

'It's down to the judges, but a bit of showmanship never goes astray.'

'I Want Muscle' blared out and the next contestant lurched to the podium.

'Are you staying for the results?' she asked as she jumped down.

'I can't, I've a real emergency to help out at.'

'Pity.' Merissa pressed herself against him. 'I wanted to say thank you.' The wanderlust had got it right again.

'You're an amazing woman, Merissa, and it's not that I don't want to, I can't.' Merissa pushed him back up against a wall.

'You might not have a choice.' She ground her hips against him.

'What about Gerard?'

'That bastard couldn't even be bothered to watch.'

Her solid thighs pinned him against the wall. She was persuasive, he had to admit. It was a wild opportunity for a unique experience he would never have again. This was different. He ran his hands over the pumped and oiled body. It was tight and solid with a bouncy quality that could mean serious fun. He could feel himself submitting to the desire of the moment as his fingers worked across her shoulder blades and under the bikini straps. They slid over the taut skin. He savoured the greased perfection until his

hands sensed a few bumps on her shoulder blades...
steroid spots. They brought him back from the brink.

He was about to say, 'I can't, I have a girlfriend,'
when Merissa leapt away from him.

'Gerard,' she said. He stood and glowered as Stephen
stepped around him.

4.00 pm

Nicole had driven so determinedly that her hands had cramped onto the wheel. Every time she moved her left hand to change gear, her knuckles groaned and clicked. It had taken an hour for an ambulance to arrive. The police came shortly after. The car driver had been unable to speak. The police officer had inspected the sides of Nicole's truck. It was scraped from Louie's efforts. She explained it had happened while parked at The Milk Bar. He looked at the car and back at the truck and concluded the marks were too high up to be from a collision with the car. Reluctantly he let Nicole go, having taken her details.

She realised the foolishness of helping Louie. It had only placed suspicion on herself and guaranteed she would not meet her delivery time. That meant a penalty and probably a loss on this trip.

The one comfort was that she was getting nearer to home. She could almost smell it. Each white dash that blurred into the next put her further away from the accident and closer to the sanctuary of Sydney. In Sydney she was just another trannie having dinner with friends, not a gender-bending truckie perverting the course of justice on country roads.

Visions of police interrogations flashed through her mind. Files being placed on a desk in front of her and the dreaded word 'Tom' announced with self-satisfied snarls by the interrogating officers. The fight at The Milk Bar, the pursuit on the road—it all pointed suspiciously to dangerous driving.

Her hands did not lose their white knuckles until she saw the Harbour Bridge. Once she crossed it, the harbour and the sprawling people-packed North Shore were between her and the accident. A thousand trails and scents, hundreds of trucks, millions of people with something to hide.

On the bridge she took the chicken-run lane on the outside. It was her favourite, giving her the comfort of familiarity, enhanced by another familiar bridge sensation, a traffic jam. A critical mass of cyclists had chosen her lane to make a lightning environmental protest. The traffic crawled along at slower than cycling pace. There was no exuberance from the cyclists. No whistles or shouting, just sullen point-making.

The traffic stopped altogether. Nicole wound down the truck window to breathe Sydney air. She was nearly at the stone pylon on the south side of the bridge. Close to her shore, but not close enough to relax. She looked out at the bridge and noticed, for the first time in all her crossings, people climbing iron steps between her lane and the rest of the bridge. This must be the way up, Nicole thought. Billed as Sydney's best tourist attraction, the Bridge Climb enabled the public to climb to the top of the great icon. The climbers were close, just metres from her face. A woman looked around and caught Nicole's idle gaze directly. She stopped, stared at Nicole as if caught in a criminal act, and then hurried up the rest of the stairs without any hint of recognition. 'She looked as guilty as I feel,' thought Nicole, but decided she must have been projecting her own guilt.

A horn brought Nicole's attention from the unexpected eye contact to the bicycles clearing and traffic moving in front of her. She drove off, her mind for a brief period distracted from her own troubles. She had to get to Mascot to deliver her load. She would then head straight for the party. There might be time to go home and get changed but the sooner she was in familiar company the better. And she wanted to know why Maureen was doing the Bridge Climb and why she looked so guilty.

•

The competitor Tanya confronted now was a far greater challenge than the big-boned schoolgirl. One of the American contenders, she must have weighed within 10 grams of the 70-kilo limit and been in possession of a set of very light bones. She was a full 10 centimetres taller than Tanya but had a similar strong build. Tanya sized up her opponent, calculated all the taunts she would have received at school for being so big and weighed it up against her own experience. It would be a battle of the bitter inner teenagers, she figured. Tanya had never competed against anyone from overseas before. They all worked to the same World Taekwondo Federation rules, but techniques differed. She saw that at the Olympic contest.

As the start signal beeped out, Tanya flung all thoughts out of her head, visualising a bucket of water being thrown out of a window. It was her super-fast technique for instant focus. This time, it was not fast enough. The water was still stretching to the window frame when she felt a blast to her ribcage: a foot precisely positioned on her red dot. She staggered and was immediately one point down. The referee allowed her to regain her balance before restarting the round. Tanya was ready for the second assault and lunged close to prevent the kick reaching its target. She tried a kick of her own, an imprecise stab landing on an arm. It scored nothing. The remainder of the three-minute round was a defence game. The two competitors circled each other, shouting, occasionally locking in, but striking no blows. The crowd grew dissatisfied, calling out 'we came to see a fight'. Anything less than 100 per cent aggression did not go down well. The end of the round sounded. Tanya had recovered well, but was still down one point. She had to gain the advantage in the second round or face a near-impossible task in the third.

The second round came. Tanya's American assailant knew not to try the same lightning strike again. They rained blows on each other but were always too close for effective strikes. The crowd was satisfied with the level of fighting but no points were being scored. Suddenly there was a shift of tactics. The American introduced a peculiar reverse twist to a kick with her right leg. Tanya struggled to determine where the kick was heading.

Without thinking, Tanya assumed the direction it would take and crouched to the left, avoiding the blow. The crouch gave her the momentum to leap with a jump kick. She felt herself fly upwards, imagining the impossible jumps achieved in martial arts films. For a fraction of a second, she was looking down on her giant opponent. The hair under her helmet looked badly bleached. Weakness, she thought. The American, registering the momentary attention to her head, guessed that was Tanya's target and moved to block it. She was wrong. There was a clear path to her chest. Tanya's foot flew to it on the descent. A point at last, and an appreciative crowd roared. The bout ended. Tanya's spirit was indeed indomitable and the score was evened.

By the final round, Tanya had the momentum but both competitors had a steely determination. The American, outfoxed in the previous bout, needed to gain the advantage. In the midst of regular sparring, she spun round, down and up. Legs and arms seem to surround Tanya. A split-second confusion as to how to respond gave her assailant all she needed and she felt a blow, but not on an expected target. The kick had come straight up between her legs and hard into her crotch. The pain seared through her as she fell to the floor, hearing the crowd's jeering disapproval mixed with mirth at her pain. Her hands held the area that had been the cause of so much pleasure a few hours before. Such a blow scored no points but severely disabled an opponent, and as it looked like an accident, the American did not earn a warning.

Tanya had to stand, but felt the need to stay on the ground as long as possible. The referee stood over her, exhorting her to stand. If she stayed down too long she would incur a warning. She stood, the cheers of the crowd doing nothing to stem the agony. She was wounded and it was only sheer determination that would see her through. Just as the bout was to recommence a voice called out.

'Stop the match.'

It came from the edge of the spectator area. Tanya was confused but grateful for the breathing space. Her opponent understood more than she did, pulling off her headguard and throwing it to the ground.

'Shit. No way.'

The three judges and the referee came forward to join the competitors as the man who had called out strode forward. Dressed in a suit and carrying a briefcase, he looked out of place.

'I'm a lawyer with the ATA, American Taekwondo Association. That last form used is copyrighted by our organisation.'

'This is bullshit, man.'

Tanya looked in total bewilderment. Plunging from a thought-free state into this provided a serious comprehension challenge. The lawyer continued.

'That move is available only to members of the ATA and cannot be used in competition by non-members. Ms Krell, you have not been a member of the ATA for thirteen months and so have forfeited the right to use that move.'

'We're not even in the States. This is bullshit. You can't do this.'

'We have asserted global rights. You do admit you used the move?'

'No, I do not.'

The referee tried to intervene in the argument, hoping to finish the round and then have the dispute resolved. The crowd were standing, unable to hear the discussion other than Ms Krell's intermittent cries of 'Shit, man.' The lawyer threatened to have the entire competition closed if the match was allowed to continue. The use of the copyrighted move had given Krell an unfair advantage. Even though a point had not been scored, the psychological benefit she had gained from sending Tanya sprawling on the floor could easily have led to another point. An advantage had been gained. He insisted Krell be disqualified and Tanya declared the winner.

'Is that not fair, Ms...' He looked to Tanya expecting some form of support. To her it seemed like the American had fought within the rules, even if at the edge of them. Winning by legal challenge did not seem like a victory.

'No, she played fair,' Tanya responded. Ms Krell looked astounded for a second and then seized the advantage. The match had not ended for her.

'See. Restart the match.'

The group on the floor had swollen to include the competition organisers and the president of the

Australian Taekwondo Association. Attempts to clear the mat failed. The lawyer refused to move aside. Ms Krell refused to move until the match was completed. The main argument soon became drowned as individual opinions were voiced, argued and eventually shouted. Tempers flared. One of the referees lost balance while stabbing his finger in the air, reinforcing his point. As he toppled his finger prodded the American lawyer, who immediately dropped his briefcase and assumed combat pose.

Like dominoes in reverse, the rabble of shouting voices was silenced as everyone locked into battle pose. Even Tanya, by sheer force of habit, stood ready to fight. The audience resumed their seats, ready for a Jackie Chan-style martial arts battle. This would be real fighting. No-one moved for fear of missing even a second of the impending spectacle.

Silent statues moved only their eyes in the competition area. A sudden action and everything would explode. Tanya spoke without the slightest body movement.

'I concede the fight.' It took a second for positions to relax. She bowed to Ms Krell and walked away from the mat. Regardless of how evenly the score stood, if a contestant withdrew, the opponent was the winner. The argument was irrelevant.

As she walked off, one by one the other contestants

began to applaud, a slow handclap that soon was taken up around the arena. She had demonstrated the honour and dignity that her sport valued. Her own victory was sacrificed so that Taekwondo could be the winner on the day. In the changing room she could still hear the applause. It had not been an easy choice. Months of preparation had come to this.

Self-sacrifice and nobility were easy options, she now thought. Standing your ground, fighting in the face of anger and opposition, that was the tougher path, the one that led to victory. Perhaps she was a quitter, a coward. Bullies were cowards, they were always told at school. Tanya had never been able to shake the doubt that behind her bullying might be a lack of bravery. It was that doubt that usually pro-pelled her, made her push herself further, until now. When it really counted she had not fought for what she believed in, her right to win, but had chosen the most convenient option for everyone else—it was a gutless self-sacrifice.

She stared at her locker door. There was an envel-ope taped to it. Opening it she saw the car key and read the message.

'More self-sacrifice,' she thought, realising she hated the stench of burning martyr, especially if it was herself.

●

Stephen walked past the open front door and into the living room to see James sitting cross-legged among the flotsam and jetsam of what was supposed to be his ship. He paused and smiled to himself. This was like the James he had first met. A boy sitting on the floor of their primary school hall waiting to be allocated to a class. Stephen had been late for assembly for the first day of Year 5. James was just starting at the school and, due to an administrative glitch, his name had not appeared on any class lists. He waited alone in the hall while the teachers tried to discover where he should be. Today he had the same forlorn look of not really knowing what he should be doing. He sat pressing the ends of the corresponding fingers on his hands together, one after the other.

'Chucked you out of class already?' Those were the first words that the friends had spoken to each other. Each time they were used, they invoked over thirty years of friendship.

'It's woodwork. I'm crap at it,' James replied. 'You any good?'

'Not bad. Teacher reckons I could be a carpenter.'

James looked up and smiled at his friend.

'Just like my dad.'

Stephen was already assessing the various ship parts and working out how they connected. Picking up each piece, he placed it face down on the floor in front of where it was supposed to go.

'Thought it best not to do the supporting boyfriend thing and cheer from the sidelines. I'd probably only put her off anyway...'

'You're making excuses,' James interrupted him.

'We should have this ship sailing in no time.'

'What's happened?' Stephen winced at the question, but James was the only person he could talk to about this.

'I got a bit lost after I dropped the key off to Tanya and sort of ended up with a bodybuilder sliding down my legs.' Stephen stood holding a piece of the ship in front of him like a shield.

'I don't think I want to know, but you'll always be my friend.'

'Mate, she was a girl!'

'Are you sure? With all those steroids, you know, it's hard to tell.'

'She was a woman. Kinda sexy, if you ignored all the bumps on her shoulders.'

'Gross...That's exactly what I did. How come it works for you?' James was distracted from the steroid spots by seeing Stephen slide the pieces into place as easily as Marcus had.

'It's a simple snap-fit. You just have to look at the bottom and at these posts.'

'Of course.' The posts were a revelation to James. 'I wondered what those were for.'

'Why isn't your designer doing this, anyway?'

'I sacked him and the chef.'

'Smart move!'

James pointed to the patch on the side of the ship. 'They did that before they started hitting each other with the salmon.'

Stephen dragged James up off the floor, made him take one of the ship's pieces and showed him how to slot it into place.

'It's so easy,' James groaned. 'I'm so stupid.'

'At least you're not getting turned on by body-builders...I was fine. Tanya was everything I wanted, but then I said "I love you" after sex.'

'Shit Stephen, how many times? Never tell a woman you love her straight after sex. During, that's fine, they won't hold you to it, but after...'

'I know...she went all quiet, didn't say it back and I went off to the shower. We're heading straight for the "where do we go from here/let's move in/who the hell is she" trifecta. I really like Tanya. I don't want to lose her and if we move in I will. Wanderlust will take over.'

'Don't move in!'

'But if we have the "where do we go from here"

talk and I don't say move in, it'll fall apart. If you don't go forward you go backward, and all that crap.'

'Doesn't have to be like that.'

'It's already started. A bodybuilder, for Christ sakes. She still turns me on.'

'I'm watching you, mate. You've been looking at my biceps, haven't you?'

'Phwoar!' Stephen lunged at James' arm and grabbed his bicep with both hands as he tried to flex it.

'Excuse me.' They both froze and looked at the person now standing in the doorway. Stephen's hands held onto James' arm, his lips puckered to plant a kiss.

'I've got a flower delivery for Mr Ting.'

'Er, yes of course,' James intoned deeply, while Stephen busied himself putting the final support rod in place.

'Where's the installation to go?'

'Against this wall behind the...erm...ship.' James indicated the far side of the vessel.

'OK, bring 'em in.' The delivery guy shouted to his colleagues to bring in the cornflowers.

'Not just flowers...an installation!' Stephen grinned at James.

It took three people twenty minutes to carry in all the flowers, and then the installation frame. Stephen stared in amazement as the entire floor of the living room turned blue. The frame was longer than the ship itself and had to be carried in three parts and assembled in place. It looked like three giant volleyball nets made of fine chickenwire. When the flowers had been brought in and the frame put together, the florist whom James had spoken to at midday walked in.

'Good afternoon, James. Everything going to plan? Don't worry, I'd have sacked Marcus too. His surname might be Toomy, but he's not called Marcus Too Much for nothing. I just presumed you'd be going ahead as indicated. Did I do right? I'd better get to work. Want to help? We'll get through quicker. Hello, my name's Rebecca.'

She addressed the last sentence to Stephen and held out her hand. There was a silence as both the men were unsure whether they were supposed to speak at all.

'Hi...I'll finish the ship, if that's OK with you, James?' Before James could answer him, Rebecca was off again.

'Fine. James, it's terribly simple. Now, we can fit three cornflower stems in each of these holes in the wire, see? So that's what we do, but as the heads are a lot wider than the stems, we can only do every other hole. Get me? So, like here...here and here. I'll start top left, work my way down and across like so. You start at the right, OK? Let's go.'

Rebecca set to as if there was a prize for the first person to reach the middle. James, nervous about the competitive space, went at a slower pace. The flowers, which wedged each other so perfectly when Rebecca stuck them in a hole, fell out of the wire when he tried. Rebecca looked at his slow progress.

'Hate to hurry you, but I do have a frill-necked lizard to make out of carnations by eight.' She beamed her encouragement to James, as another bloom fell on his shoe.

5.00 pm

By the time the chevalier had departed on his search for Queen Marguerite's star, Irene had finished a bottle of Cab Sav. She only noticed this when she brought the glass to her lips—thinking she had replenished it from the bottle without removing her eye from the page—and didn't get anything from it. Next she noticed her naked body in the bath. The bubbles had completely dissolved. The torture had been compulsive. Much as she would have liked to rip the book up, douse it with lighter fluid and roast it in the Weber barbecue, she couldn't. She had to read, knew she would read it to the end, so the quicker she passed through hell the better. Wine made the trip less painful.

The bathroom clock-radio blinked the time at her and she realised she had to hurry. She tossed the book as far away from the bath as she could. Pretending it was a gesture of contempt, she knew that really it was so it wouldn't get splashed as she got out of the bath. As she stood up, the full impact of the wine made itself apparent. She slipped and grabbed the shower curtain, which broke her fall enough to prevent any damage to her body, but ripped the rail out of the wall.

'Oh God, granny mat here I come!' Irene wailed, holding onto the side of the bath wrapped in the shower curtain. She was drunk. There was a big occasion and she had promised to behave. Promised not to start.

'That bastard,' burst from her lips. An automatic gesture that was not supposed to happen.

'Come on, Reenie. Action stations, sober up.'

Remaining seated, she removed the shower curtain and threw it on the floor, taking care not to throw it over 'her' book. Unplugging the bath, she switched on the cold shower tap and squealed as the cold water hit her head. She forced herself to accept the punishment. This was her fault, all her fault: the curtain, the cold water, the wasted life.

'I'll not punish others.' She clenched her hands and slammed them into the rapidly draining water. Turning the shower off, she grabbed the edge of the bath with both hands. Putting one leg over the edge onto the floor, she tried to keep as low as possible to avoid a rush of blood. She rolled over the edge of the bath and onto the shower curtain on the floor. On all fours she padded to the basin, reached up with both hands, pulled herself up onto her knees. After another pause she made it onto her feet to confront herself in the mirror.

'Oh Christ!'

Wet hair was plastered over her face, dripping down her chin.

'Thank God you've got a brain my girl, 'cos your body couldn't dance a conga, never mind a ballet.'

She felt steady enough to towel herself off and put her dressing gown on. She wrapped the towel around her head—it made her feel slightly glamorous. A killer coffee was in order before any attempt at beautification.

As she stood in the kitchen waiting for the kettle to boil, she had a bout of guilt. This was supposed to be Maureen's night. The realisation that something was wrong had filtered through unnoticed as she had been reading. Tonight was her chance to be the strong one and even the balance. Maureen was going to get support. There was a sneaking satisfaction that finally something was wrong. The kettle switched itself off and Irene determined that her friend would be supported whether she wanted it or not. This called for sobriety and a coffee plunger already a quarter full of industrial-strength arabica.

Downing one cup as fast as the heat and the intense taste would allow, Irene returned to the bathroom and the *Chevalier* on the floor. She bent down to pick it up with a second cup of coffee in her hand and spilt it onto the book. It ran over the glossed cover, sprinting to the absorbent edges of the paper. Irene tilted it in the opposite direction, hoping the coffee would run off the glossed spine. She miscalculated and it ran off the top edge and into the book.

Putting the coffee down in the bathroom basin to avoid further spills, she opened the book to see the blooms of coffee at the top of half the pages. It was a sight that normally would have filled her with horror, but then her eye caught the stain right through the middle of Jonathan Townsend's name. This felt good. She opened the book, cracked the spine good and hard and tossed the *Chevalier* into the empty bath. Taking two large slurps of coffee, she tipped the rest over the book in the bath. This was the best she had felt since seeing the book. She would not read the rest of it, she decided. 'As if I don't know how it ends!'

Serious tarting up was required. She applied her base moisturiser and then began to blow-dry her hair. As she tilted and turned her head to dry the underside, she glanced occasionally in the bath to make sure the book was still there, and hadn't risen, unblemished, to attack her once again.

As she mused about the coming evening something told her that everything was changing. James and

Maureen, Stephen and herself, even she and Maureen. Each relationship was up for grabs, as if the ribbons that held them had been loosened. As that thought came, the biggest uncertainty of all hit her for the first time. What if Maureen did not come back at all? What if she never saw her again?

Her breath quickened, the loose ribbons suddenly flayed wildly. Her head spun, making her grab the sink unit with both hands to steady herself.

'I'll have to stop drinking in the bath,' she said, attributing her dizziness to the easiest cause.

•

Rebecca met James far more than half way on the creation of the cornflower seascape. By the time she was two-thirds of the way across, he was just getting into the stride and no longer expecting every flower to fall out on the first attempt.

'Love, I'm going to have to leave you here. You've got the hang of it...eventually. Now with the orange and yellow gerberas, do what you want. Put them in little clumps. Now you don't want them all the same size, do you? No, it's a seascape, not wallpaper, so don't try making any pretty patterns will you? OK? Marvellous. Have a wonderful evening.'

James had given up trying to respond to her

questions. He managed to get a ''bye' in as she swept out of the door. The ship which had now been built in his living room looked exactly as he had imagined.

'Stephen, it's fantastic.'

'There are still some bits left here. I'm not sure what they're for.'

'That's my bridge.' He pointed to the small dais-like wooden box. 'See? It's shaped like the rear of the ship. It goes there and my wheel goes on there somehow.' He pointed to a mock ship's wheel attached to a post leaning by the window.

'You've thought of everything.'

'That plank,' James was on a roll, finally getting a vision of how the puzzle was meant to be now it was virtually complete, 'is the gangway and there should be some little steps for the other side. That's the trestle table which we'll eat off with...'

'I have brought dessert.' James' roll was brought to an abrupt holt by the latest visitor. The voice made him turn swiftly in panic. He saw Ulrika standing there, holding a large plastic container.

'I fired you...You can't do this to me, not now all this is going so well...Where's Marcus?'

'I need to talk to you...alone.' She turned her head slightly towards Stephen and raised an eyebrow.

'Fine. I'll go in the kitchen...'

'No! Outside.' Ulrika seemed to think it was still her kingdom. James nodded to him and he walked out.

'You'll have to be quick, and I've got to work while you talk.' James returned to his seascape.

'Look, I'm so sorry.'

James turned back in shock. It was not just the apology, it was the voice: gentle, quiet and without a trace of northern European chill. She hastily looked around to ensure no-one was watching. She caught Stephen peering through the window and waved him away.

'I'll come clean,' she said. 'The whole Ulrika thing's an act. It's so hard nowadays. I'm a great cook, but that's just not enough any more. You've got to stand out and I can't afford to open a restaurant with harbour views or a $5 million refit, so I've got to make it on personality.'

'Nice personality.'

'Everyone's nice. I need something different, so I'm the meanest chef in Sydney. I've got to be an absolute bastard. You're the only person who knows I'm not now.'

'So can I expect Marcus crawling in saying he's really nice too?'

'No, he *really* is a wanker.'

'What d'you want me to do? You nearly ruined a very important day.'

'I know and I'm sorry,' Ulrika whispered. 'I've made you that dessert from the *Paramount* cookbook you wanted. Let me do this dinner. I won't charge anything for my labour and time, just the other staff.'

'David has it all in hand.' James felt confident in his delegation.

'I know. I've been briefing him on his mobile. It was set on vibrate so you wouldn't hear it ring.' James felt less confident. He looked at the dessert. Considering her vicious reaction to the cookbook earlier, it was a major gesture.

'Please, Mr Ting.' She looked towards the door to ensure they were alone and bent her knees briefly. 'See, I've begged.'

'There'll be no tantrums.'

'Oh.' She looked awkwardly at him, as if a sticking point in complex negotiations had been reached. 'I'm going to have to have a couple, otherwise people won't believe I'm a monster. It's my thing. I need to do it.'

'No damage to my property.'

'OK, but you've got to tell everyone I kicked a hole in your ship and spat a salmon head at Marcus.'

James agreed. A delighted smile began to spread across her face until she heard the front door open. The smile disappeared and Ulrika returned.

'...this is my event and no-one is going to steal it

from me. Not David, not you, not anyone. Now, beg me to come back...BEG!'

James gave a half-hearted 'Please, Ulrika'.

'Very well...David,' she screamed, turning towards the kitchen and pushing Stephen out of the way, 'cease everything!' She then produced a whistle and blew hard, summoning her staff who had been waiting outside.

Stephen looked at James with an 'are you mad?' mouth drop.

'These are Jasper and Bethnee,' Ulrika announced. 'They will be serving dinner. I will permit them to assist you when I do not need them. Come.'

Jasper mouthed hello and Bethnee gave a silent wave as they followed Ulrika into the kitchen. As the door swung shut behind them, James could hear the ladle crashing once again on the single-sheet granite surface. There was something reassuring about the jolt the noise brought to his heart.

•

'You are in big trouble, lady.' Frank the depot manager had kept additional staff on for three hours at Saturday rates waiting for Nicole to deliver. He was not impressed.

'There was an accident. I had to help. I couldn't drive on.'

'No, you couldn't,' Frank replied, 'seeing as you caused it. Louie's told us all about it.'

'I didn't...It was...' Nicole was about to explain but realised it was too late. Louie had done her over: completed his trip on time, escaped a police investigation and blamed her when he got to the depot. So much for camaraderie.

'Speak to the police?' Frank asked.

'Yeah, they've got my details,' Nicole gave in. She wanted to give her version of events. Explain she had been trying to help, that she had sacrificed her timing for Louie. There was no point, Louie was probably waiting in the pub. Frank had too much in common with him and too much distrust of her to ever think she might be telling the truth. He wouldn't care if she was.

She had tried so hard to be good at what she did, work within the law, play everyone at their game, and this is where it got her. She was good for a laugh at The Milk Bar but if things got serious, the ranks closed and she was on the outside. She looked at her dirty nails. Her hands had that grimy feel that said when she washed them the water would be filthy grey. She wanted to clean them.

'It's not a game you know.' Frank had been waiting for a moment like this since she had been taken on. 'People depend on you to deliver. We've got to pay overtime because of your bad driving.' Frank worked up a rage, ignoring that he was the one being paid overtime. 'I know it's not easy, but if you can't hack it...'

'I don't need a lecture, thanks. D'you think I planned to spend over an hour sitting by the road hoping someone wouldn't die?'

'You'll be lucky if we use you again. We've made allowances for you, you know that, but there's only so far we can bend. Can't condone illegal activities.'

Nicole looked incredulous.

'Allowances? My delivery records are second to none. This is the first time I've been late at this depot, ever.'

'Leave it out. Louie said you were wired as hell this morning. Attacked him like a maniac for no reason.'

'That's a lie.' She could hold back no longer. 'Complete shit. He started it, lost and got so worked up he smashed his truck into mine. It was him, him.'

'Don't get hysterical on me, missy. Louie might have put up with your speed freaking, but I won't.'

'You're all in it, aren't you? Boys' club. Can't wait to get rid of me.'

'That's right, scream discrimination the minute you fuck up. Blame everyone else. Besides, from what I hear, you were in the boys' club, but resigned your... err... membership.'

'With you as club president, who wouldn't resign?

You telling me Louie's the model of good driving?' she asked bitterly.

'His record's clean, he delivers on time. That's all we ask. He hacks it when the going's tough and doesn't blame other drivers. You make me sick. You've never been a real driver, never will be.'

'Why not?' She pushed her face in his, defying him angrily. He looked with satisfaction at the maniacal determination and the furious spit forming at the edge of her mouth. He had proved his point.

'That would be saying. I'm not saying anything. Go on, get off.'

She watched him walk away, shouting to his 'lads' to get a move on. They joked, he laughed. His anger had melted the minute he turned his back on Nicole.

•

'Incredible.' Stephen was impressed, standing at the doorway with James surveying the completed ship. Five metres long, it dominated the living room. Like a ship constructed in someone's shed, there was no way the whole vessel could have been removed. The sides of the ship were classic ocean liner, black to the ground with a white band across the top. The portholes lined up and in one of them Stephen could just discern the face of a child peeping out. The deck dipped towards the middle more than a real one would, as if the boat was weighed down by a particularly heavy cargo. The rivets all lined up and there was even some rust dripping down from a couple of them. In the middle of the ship the gangplank went up, with strips across it to prevent slipping and a rope rail to hold onto.

'Wait,' James said, dashing upstairs and coming back with a captain's hat. He ran up the gangplank to the helm. The ship swayed gently as he moved forward.

'I know they don't really have one here, but I had to have my bridge.' James spun his wheel, 'Full steam ahead!'

The blue cornflower display was complete. It formed a vast backdrop of deep blue. The gerberas speckled through looked like wave tops or seagulls. James was particularly happy with this detail.

'Prepare to be boarded!' Stephen shouted, picking up two spare pieces of dowelling. He threw one at the ship's captain as he ran onboard.

'*En garde.*' Blade clashed with blade as the former friends, now mortal foes, fought for supremacy of the ship.

'You'll never take my ship alive,' James shouted, pushing his sword against Stephen's and forcing him back down the gangplank. The sword fight continued, cut and thrust, across the ocean to the living room door. With a double swirl of his blade, James knocked the invader's sword from his hand and stood poised with its tip at his neck.

'Prepare to die.'

'Hello?' A voice called out from the front door. Stephen was saved in the nick of time by the arrival of a small, grey-haired man with a suitcase.

'Xavier,' James smiled, 'my secretary said you were coming. This is very kind.'

'If I may have a room to prepare myself, I'll begin when the moment is right.'

James showed the new arrival to one of the spare bedrooms. When he returned he explained to Stephen. 'He's a performance artist. I've lined up a few sponsorships for him in the past. Remember that guy who was dressed as a platypus, strapped to a cross on the outside of the covered bridge over Pitt Street for a week?'

'Yeah...those kids started throwing doughnuts at him because they thought he was hungry.'

'That's him. He's one of Australia's top performance artists. He found out about this dinner and insisted on doing a private performance.'

'Another platypus?'

'No idea, but it'll be him keeping still as if he's a work of art. It's a very generous gift. If it was one of my clients, they'd be paying $15,000 for it... Shit! look at the time, we'd better get going.'

James was still working to the timetable of Irene bringing Maureen around at 7.00 pm. He approached the kitchen. Before he could even put his hand to the door, the voice rang out.

'No!'

He stood outside and shouted to the door. 'I need help setting up the dining area. Are Bethnee and Jasper free?'

There was no response. In all the time that Ulrika had been in his kitchen during the day, the only noises he had ever heard were her voice and the occasional slamming ladle. After a couple of moments and with no announcement, Japser and Bethnee emerged.

The four of them worked quickly to clear the ship-building debris. The room was empty apart from the vast vessel. Ulrika's assistants set the table on the ship, laughing as it swayed under their feet.

'Mr Ting, this is fantastic,' said Jasper. 'You must have a brilliant designer.'

'Actually,' he said quite proudly, 'it's my concept.'

'That's amazing. You're a genius,' the young man replied as he smoothed out the tablecloth on the ship's table. He said it with a genuine sense of being impressed.

'The boy can flatter,' whispered Stephen, 'Wait till he starts on your wife.'

The word 'wife', made James stop and turn. With

everything falling into place, he had managed to put the biggest problem of all out of his mind.

'Stephen, what am I going to do?'

'There's nothing else you can do. We'll just have to wait. Whatever's happened, she'll come home. Maureen is not the running-off type. Even if she's gone loopy, she'll come back.'

'I suppose so.' The satisfaction he had been feeling was suddenly hollow.

'Whatever she's doing,' Stephen said, 'she doesn't want anyone knowing, so it's best to pretend we don't know when she gets here.'

'You're right. You know, sometimes, just for a few seconds, I think you do understand women after all.'

'Don't get gushy on me. Look, the ship's great, but where the hell are we going to sit before dinner?' Stephen waved at the empty seafloor.

'Shit, the deck furniture! I got *Titanic*-style deck-chairs. They're out the back.' James headed for the kitchen door to get the chairs.

'*No!*' Ulrika screamed as his hand reached for the door.

James briefed Jasper and Bethnee as to where the deckchairs were and how to get to them. He whispered the directions as far away from the kitchen door as he could and watched them approach. They entered without a challenge from Ulrika. It infuriated him. How did she know who was approaching?

•

Michael had assembled the team of actors who were to form his troop, Urban Terror. In addition to Janine, he had been forced to use Justin's original Cut-throat Crazies, Sasha and Colin. Despite being totally confused by Michael's announcement that a new era in drama would be born that night, they did not want to lose out on the $100 they had been expecting. As soon as they arrived at Michael's apartment, he made them change into army clothes. 'Your personae must permeate your being before the performance.' Emerging in her fatigues, Sasha was quickly corrected when she referred to her costume. They were not costumes, they were uniforms. Costumes were what people who pretended to be characters in theatres wore. And they were not 'in character', but assuming personae. There would be no pretence tonight.

'We are creating a whole new school of theatre,' Michael addressed his troops. 'This is about being real. We *are* Urban Terror. This is a guerilla raid on middle-class artistic complacency.

Janine trembled. Michael was at his most inspiring in moments like this. 'Savour every moment,' Michael continued. 'Remember everything because in years to come historians will be poring over every detail.'

Janine reported that her friend, a researcher on *Arts Now!*, the cable-TV arts show, had expressed an interest in what they were doing. The program might be sending a camera crew to document the event. The two original Cut-throats were impressed—any chance of TV exposure was a big plus.

'We're not here to make some fake reality TV for the masses. If they come, they can document, but we're not staging anything for them.' Michael was not pandering to the mainstream.

'We're not staging anything at all,' added Janine. Michael nodded his approval. He was relieved someone understood his objective. As he assumed the persona of a unit commander, he had to screw down his nerves. This was his big moment. If he did it right, it would make the papers and television. Ting was the ideal target, given his pivotal role in the hostile takeover of the arts by commerce. Michael could see his perfect wave approaching and he was determined to catch it and ride it home.

'Now, I want you to remember these people, James Ting and his rich friends, are the enemy. Scum that need to be taught a lesson.'

'But they hired us, didn't they?' Colin had not quite got the gist of Urban Terror.

'I think you'll find we're in charact...assuming personae now, Colin,' Janine glowered at him.

'Sorry, Janine.' Colin stood to attention.

'There is no Janine here, just Unit Two. Our leader is Unit One, you are Unit Four and that is Unit Three,' Janine announced coldly.

Michael resumed his briefing.

'People pay to learn things. These people are funding their own education on what art is really about. When we reach the target house, Units Three and Four, I want you to proceed to the kitchen and hold all staff there. The bastards have got some chef and slaves in to serve them.'

'Hang on, Michael,' Sasha intervened. 'Who's in what unit?'

Michael slammed a fist down onto the coffee table and felt the sticky ring from a days-old coffee cup on his hand.

'No names. You are Unit Three, that is Unit Four. I am Unit One and that's Unit Two.' He pointed to Janine.

Units Three and Four rolled their eyes. Michael continued. 'Once the kitchen is secured, we have to silence James Ting immediately to preserve the reality of the situation. This is paramount. He's planned a surprise, according to my sources...'

'You mean Justin? How is he? He sounded dreadful

when I spoke to him this afternoon.' Colin's persona still had not seeped through his fatigues.

'Justin has served his purpose. Only Ting is expecting an invasion. If he manages to communicate that we are "paid actors", the operation will fail. Unit Two will gag him immediately with the duct tape.'

After the plans were run through and details recited until every unit knew their role, gun handling was practised. Michael issued them each with a machine-gun and showed them how to load the blanks, unload and reload. His expertise with weapons came from four years with the Territorials. Part time army training had funded his brief stint at drama school. It had been incomparable experience. For him, manoeuvres had been exercises in human observation. Dropped with members of his squad in the middle of the bush with orders to return to base camp by any means possible, Michael had destroyed all the maps, communication equipment and food, and watched the team disintegrate into terrified panic. Accountants playing tough and IT consultants thinking they were on a glorified paintball field crumbled as Michael left them defenceless against the raw power of nature. Assuming the role of one of the most panicked, he wet his pants and avoided discovery as the creator of the chaos. He had learned much from the experience, and was putting it all to use now.

'So are we expected to fire these things?' Unit Four was getting worried that some real harm might be done.

'If the plan is executed without a hitch there should be no need for any weapons use, but we must be prepared to use all necessary force to achieve our aims,' Unit One replied.

'What exactly are our aims?'

'What if someone gets hurt?'

'Silence!' Unit Two cried, totally immersed in persona. 'Orders must be followed immediately and without question.'

'Precisely,' the commander echoed, 'the aim of the exercise is to shock the targets out of their suburban, pain-free lives and back into the real world. Now lock and load.'

'I thought they were meant to play party games?' When Justin had explained the exercise to Unit Three, it was a bit of light-hearted fun leading into a few party games.

'The emphasis has been changed, but the subjects will find their brief is more than fulfilled.' Unit One knew exactly what sort of party games were in store but that information would be issued on a need-to-know basis only.

7.00 pm

On her way to James and Maureen's house, Tanya had put the events of the afternoon behind her. By breaking the deadlock and stopping the entire Taekwondo championships from falling into a messy pile of claims and counter-claims, she was the hero of the hour. Even the fat girl she had beaten in the previous round approached her in the changing rooms to tell her how wonderful she was. The girl asked if she was going to the party afterwards. It was to be held at House, the superclub close to the competition venue.

'I've got a dinner on, but I'll try to make it,' she lied, smiling at the girl. Nobility was difficult to shake off. Everyone was planning to see her there. She had no intention of going, but figured the place was big enough for people not to see her and still assume she was there, being noble in a corner. She did not want to be noble, she wanted to be aggressively determined. A winner, not a good sport. Respect was a bitter consolation prize.

Now she had to face the ordeal of Stephen's friends

and the ex. She did not actively dislike Irene, but there was no doubting she was scary. When she got going, her tongue could be vicious and Tanya was often a target. She brought back memories of the clever popular girls at St Angela's, the ones that got away with verbal bullying when she got punished for the physical kind.

Maureen was different. She was still one of the clever girls, but she had made an effort with Tanya. The first couple of times they met, she had been polite but reserved. She did not say anything rude, asked all the right questions and tried to make her feel at ease, but it stopped there. She waited to see if Tanya lasted more than a couple months before making any real commitment. She had obviously passed that test. Maureen had called her the previous night to wish her luck at today's championship. It was a nice gesture. Nice that she remembered. Nice.

The car before her changed its mind at a yellow light and slammed on its brakes. She did the same. As she waited to go, she noticed the sudden stop had jolted a bag from under the passenger seat. The lights changed before she had time to look inside.

•

By the time Irene arrived at the house she felt sufficiently sober and collected. She was determined to make it through the evening without any arguments, bitterness or tears. It was going to be a perfect evening: pleasant, civilised and peaceful. The panic of Maureen's disappearance would be resolved, and as for the book, it did not exist. She persuaded herself no-one else would have seen it yet.

The vision that presented itself in James and Maureen's living room took her mind off any worries. James' vague description of a nautical theme had not suggested the dazzling transformation.

'James, this is absolutely amazing. I'm speechless.' Realising what she had said, Irene turned to Stephen who was sitting in one of the *Titanic*-style deckchairs. She waited for the 'that's a change' barb. He looked back at her, aware that he had to choose whether or not to plunge immediately into their normal behaviour. There was a comfortable familiarity drawing him to say what they both expected to hear. Their eyes locked for a second.

'Yes, it's incredible, isn't it?' he stumbled out as an alternative. Irene smiled. He had made the first move. She would not spoil it.

'How are you, Stephen? Where's Tanya?'

As Stephen replied politely James eyed them nervously, afraid that one was luring the other into a trap to be sprung at any moment. It did not happen. They started talking about Sophie, having both received whingeing phone calls about her enforced stay with her grandparents.

'Music,' James cried. 'I've forgotten the soundscape.' He rushed over to the stereo, hidden away in a cupboard. The tiny speaker cubes discreetly positioned in the corners of the room wafted out Debussy's 'La Mer', with a few added seagulls cawing in the background. As if on cue, Xavier appeared in the doorway of the hall. Transformed, he was no longer a mousy man but a mermaid. Long hair draped around the front of his body in clumpy seaweed locks. A few shells stuck to his hair in a haphazard fashion as if they had snagged on his flowing tresses as he swam past. A tight-fitting flow of blue and green sequins contoured his legs and formed a fishtail behind him. But this was no fresh mythical sea creature. This mermaid lived in the real world. Some sequins were missing and a close inspection revealed fishhooks digging into her scales and a plastic bottle-ring attacked her tail. She stood with her arms full of dry seaweed, looking intently at the floor of the room as if searching for something lost.

Irene and Stephen looked to James, unsure how to respond to the latest presence.

'He won't react in any way to us. Probably finding a spot to keep still on.'

Suddenly, over the music, one of the seagulls gently calling in the background dived and shrieked. Everyone ducked and even the mermaid looked up as if under attack. Hers was not a safe world. Irene and Stephen looked at each other.

'Was that part of it?' Stephen whispered. Irene had no idea.

'No,' said James, trying to talk in a normal conversational manner. He gamely ignored the fact that Xavier was scattering the seaweed on the floor and making keening sounds as if trying to communicate with whales. 'The sound guy said the levels on the CD might be a bit off, but Xavier reacted wonderfully, didn't he?'

'If you say so.' Stephen shrugged his shoulders and took a swig of his gin and tonic.

'Irene, sorry. A drink?' James resumed host duties.

'Just a mineral water for now.' She asked about Maureen as James went out to the kitchen to order a drink. Stephen told her there had been no news since he had seen her in Darlinghurst.

'No!' Ulrika's voice screamed from the kitchen, once again sensing James' presence on the other side of the door. He shouted the order through and suggested Bethnee come through to look after the guests, rather than him shouting through the door every time a drink was required.

When he returned, the mermaid had found the spot she had been searching for so intently and had lain down right in the middle of the floor. Anyone approaching the ship would have to step over her. It was inconvenient, but James felt it made a spectacular addition to his theme. He walked back to the others, stepping over the mermaid with maximum nonchalance.

'That's it,' he said. 'Xavier won't move for the next few hours. You can go up as close as you want, but it's best not to touch...'

'Get out, everyone. You're fired, you group of nothings. You can't do anything. OUT!' Ulrika was having another turn in the kitchen. The door duly opened and Jasper, Bethnee and David trooped out and headed for the front door. The guests watched in silence as their dinner departed. At the door, David turned to James. 'Don't worry, it's just a fag break. We'll be back in ten minutes.'

•

When Nicole arrived in her truck, she was afraid she would be last. Having come straight from the depot, James let her shower and change in their spare room. Conversation was flowing, although not without difficulty due to the soundscape. At erratic intervals the 'off' levels produced seagull attacks, giant waves crashing, ships' bells and fog horns bellowing. There was no way of knowing when a sound shock might hit, adding to the tension they were all feeling. Tanya arrived as the soundscape suggested a wave had swept over the ship and carried a luckless sailor overboard.

'Welcome aboard,' said James, as the sailor's desperate cries were washed away in the ocean. She looked around. The whole gang was assembled, apart from Maureen. A cosy foursome waiting for their leader, she thought. They looked nervously at her, particularly Nicole, who had curled herself up on a chair and was holding her drink in both hands. After a second, Stephen jumped up, kissed her and asked her how the competition had gone. The other three echoed his question, relieved to have something to focus on.

'Don't ask.' She wanted to change the subject quickly. 'This must be for you, Irene. A peace offering from Stephen, I think.' Tanya handed over the bag that had slid out from under the passenger seat.

Stephen turned white. He attempted to grab the book before Irene could get hold of it. He was too late. He stared at Tanya, appalled at the horror that she was unleashing.

As she felt the familiar weight of the book in the bag, Irene knew exactly what it was. This was his lowest punch yet. Using Tanya to hand over the bomb after he had got her defences down. She pulled the book out the bag and saw what she expected, *Le Chevalier d'Étoile*.

'Irene, I...' She stared at him, her face growing hard and square. He looked terrified, as if an evil genie had been released, ready to lay waste to the land. She continued glowering at him as she held out her empty mineral water glass.

'Gin and tonic. Emphasis on the gin, not the tonic.' Her rage needed fuel.

James was perplexed. Everything was going so well. What could be so terrible? Answering his silent question, Irene held out the book.

'Shit...Stephen, really.'

'I don't understand. What's the problem?' Tanya had thought a book on Irene's favourite topic was a nice gesture.

Irene took her first inspiring gulp of gin. 'Well you wouldn't, would you. It involves words, thoughts, history, literature. Using your brain not your thighs.'

'Irene, it's not Tanya's fault. I can explain.' Stephen was horrified. The one time he had really tried to make an effort and it had exploded in his face.

'I know it's not Tanya's fault. She wouldn't know. You probably can't tell from the picture on the cover, unless of course you're familiar with medieval tapestries. Are you familiar with them, Tanya...? No, I thought not. Let me explain it to you. The title means, in English, the Chevalier of the Star. That's a horseman to you...not a jockey, a man who held up chivalric ideas. Honour, loyalty, celibacy.' She flung the last word at Stephen.

Tanya still looked puzzled, taking a step backward as Irene stepped closer.

'Irene, please.' James was terrified that Maureen would walk in. He was silenced by the empty gin glass thrust into his chest. There was arguing to be done and no avoiding it. He passed the glass to Bethnee for refilling.

'Still don't get it?' Irene smiled at Tanya. 'Let me spell it out. This was supposed to be my life's work. This was the book that was supposed to make me famous, which would be marvellous except for one thing which you probably missed...the name Irene is not spelled J-O-N-A-T-H-A-N. Somebody beat me to my own life's work and your lovely bonk, my brilliant ex-husband, decided to rub my nose in it.' She choked as tears began to stream down her face.

'How could you? Of all the blows,' she whispered. Stephen moved forward to comfort her.

'How could you,' she screamed. 'It's all your fault. You're to blame for me not writing it.'

Stephen snapped. The familiar pattern was in play and he could not resist his role. For a few minutes he had seen the view from her side of the battlefield. It was unbearable and so he retreated to his own side.

'That's right, blame me. Everything in your life is

my fault. How long have we been divorced now, eh? What were you doing since then? You know, perhaps if you'd written a page for every gin you've had since then, you might have written six books!'

'You'd like to think that. You'd like to think life without you has driven me to drink. Well, if I drink it's to get the taste of years of you out of my mouth.'

James realised only exhaustion could stop them. He pulled Tanya over to Nicole as if some form of normal conversation could be had and they might try to ignore the fury.

'He was determined to behave for you and Maureen, you know,' Tanya said. 'Perhaps if it wasn't for you two he'd never have these screaming matches.' She needed someone else to blame. With the horrendous atmosphere being bellowed out by the battling exes, the part of her that was glad to see them arguing felt guilty.

'What if Maureen arrives now?' Nicole stated the obvious.

'I don't know.' James was at a loss. He looked at his hands in despair. It was their fault somehow.

'You've got to do something,' hissed Tanya. 'Only you can.'

'Make them stop, James,' Nicole agreed.

'I don't know how. That's what Maureen does. Where is she?'

Nicole had been quiet up until now, barely speaking to anyone, unable to think of anything except her awful day. She had rushed to the house, expecting to find Maureen and blurt everything out to her. She was not there. It was all Nicole could do to sit still and wait. The others had noticed something was wrong. Even Stephen had expressed some sort of concern, but she could not say anything.

Irene's dull rage blocked access to her precious words. They always failed her when she needed them most. How could Irene express the pain he had caused? How could Irene make him understand only a deeply sick person could do what he had done? She screamed and sobbed simultaneously, raising her fist and issuing a war cry.

'Is this what you want? Want me down to your level?' She pushed him. 'Reduce me to physical violence?'

'I've never hit anyone in my life. How dare you imply that?'

'You've come close and you've driven me close. It's what you want, isn't it? The ultimate...' She tried to think of the word 'abrogation', but failed. 'Ultimate...'

'Lost for words?' He saw her struggling. He knew this was the low point for her, the defeat of her power. 'Want a break to check how clever you are in the dictionary?'

She screamed, 'Your way then,' and let fly a kick at

him. 'We can kick-box to the end. That's what you'd like, isn't it?' She kicked again and the ice cubes in her glass fell to the floor.

'Like Tanya's muscly body inflicting itself on you, do you?' She tried to kick again, put her foot down on the ice cubes, lost her balance and fell to the floor. Stephen looked at her lying on the floor.

'You should mop that up. Someone could kill themselves,' he said to Bethnee.

'I saw Maureen on the Harbour Bridge.' Nicole blurted the words out at the top of her voice.

They all stopped and turned to her. James helped Irene up off the floor and they moved round Nicole, who shrank back, nervous at having gained such ferocious attention.

'I was in the truck near the south pylon and she was climbing the bridge. Our eyes locked and then she moved on.'

'What time?' James asked, 'Why didn't you say anything?'

'It was about four, I think... and well...' Nicole sat down and burst into tears.

Stephen rolled his eyes, still panting from the row. Irene caught him and was about to start again.

'I'm being framed for an accident, accused of drug-taking and about to lose my livelihood.' Nicole poured out everything that had happened. As she spoke the atmosphere in the room settled, the fury of the fight drifted off in the music like a passing storm. All thoughts were on Nicole as she protested her innocence over and again.

'It's OK, we believe you. We all do. Don't we?' Irene glowered round at everyone. They nodded. Stephen homed in on her less commendable behaviour.

'You beat him up?' Stephen could not believe she could be so aggressive. She had always seemed irritatingly soft to him.

'Good on you.' Tanya was impressed.

8.00 pm

No-one spoke. Maureen's name was no longer a balm to soothe arguments. Stories had been told, day's events related, arguments had been held. Excuses for the empty chair were exhausted. There was only waiting and silence. They sat in the *Titanic*-style deckchairs staring at the motionless mermaid. Ulrika's spasmodic shrieks in the kitchen indicated the meal was nearly ruined. The absence became everything. No thoughts, no memories, just the question: Why isn't she here?

One by one they turned from the mermaid to James. He was the closest to Maureen, he should do something. He should know why she was not there. He sensed the accusation because he made it himself. The sting of blame was upsetting, but the truth which was struggling up in him was worse. Drawn up by the accusing looks, the thoughts he had dared not think for weeks were forming themselves into words and about to escape into other people's heads.

'There's something...', he hestitated. 'I haven't...
Maureen...' He stopped and looked at the door,
hoping even at this last moment she would appear
and save him from saying it for the first time.

Bridge Climbing

9.00 am

Maureen had taken the nine o'clock appointment for two reasons. She did not want to wait around with other people looking at her, guessing what was wrong with her. It also meant she could hide the appointment between leaving home and meeting Irene. If everything was fine, nobody would be any the wiser. There was no point worrying people with uncertainty.

That was in the future. Right now she was alone in the waiting room with the hum of the water cooler. This was how it always turned out. Twelve years of marriage, a great life with James, and the result: sitting alone in a waiting room. She could have said something to James. He would have been here for her, sitting uncomfortably, sleepless dread hanging round his eyes. It felt more like a burden for her than a means of support. She would have held his hand and told him it would be fine.

Perhaps if she had said, 'This is what I'm going through, this is what I need from you,' she would have received it. Communicating honestly was what everyone was supposed to do now, but it was not that simple. She had spent too long being sensitive to the needs of others. She knew when people needed an arm placed round them and a kiss to the top of the head. Telling them when she needed that was much harder. Her needs never made it beyond her throat, pushed back down the easier path.

'What do I really want anyway?' the coping side of Maureen asked contemptuously. For James to have noticed, was the grudging reply. She wanted him to have grasped the girls in his hands and immediately sensed something was wrong. Felt a slight pressure in a dollar-size spot on his hand and said 'What's this?' But he hadn't. No matter how hard she waved her breasts in front of his eyes, the girls were 'as pert and perky as the day we all met'. He never noticed.

They had made love at least six times since she noticed it. She remembered the last time they made love. Time and again his hand, his nose, his tongue had swept within millimetres. She even tried shifting so he had direct contact, so there could be no mistaking, but she never quite achieved it. Could he not feel it, smell it, taste it? She could see it through a bra, blouse and jacket. Everything hung differently on her body because of it. She looked in a face-mirror and could see it, hovering out of sight, and yet he did not notice anything with his lips practically on it.

Her lungs heaved and she gasped for air. Looking to the ceiling, she stared at the over-painted cornice, the pattern dulled by years of emulsion. There was a straggle of tape with a strand of tinsel left over from the Christmas decorations. She would not cry. There may be no need. She could cry later if she wanted to.

He had not noticed. She knew the pain James would feel if she had to tell him. He would hate himself for not seeing it and resent her for not saying anything. He relied on her to tell him everything. Normally she would, but just this once she had wanted not to have to.

'Maureen, come in. I'm so sorry to keep you waiting.' There was still hope. She could walk out in five minutes and her biggest problem would be a husband so enamoured of her breasts after twelve years of marriage, he never saw them as anything but perfect.

'I'm not going to draw out the suspense.' Claire Thornton had been Maureen's doctor for years. Of all the illnesses she had to diagnose, Claire hated this one most. It was the one condition she herself feared more than any. She worried about it and then panicked that the worrying itself might somehow bring it on. Irrational, but even doctors had to be irrational sometimes.

For Maureen anything other than opening the surgery door and shouting out the result was drawn-out suspense. Claire had taken a ridiculous amount of time to reach her chair. It seemed as if the patient was seated and comfortable before the doctor had even closed the door. Claire opened the file on her desk. The desk was not between them, but pushed to one side against the window. The doctor-patient rapport was better without a barrier.

'Why's she looking at the file?' Maureen asked herself. She must know. Surely she had prepared herself for the news. She must have done it a hundred times before. Perhaps she saw so many patients, she had no time to look at the files before the patient walked in. Perhaps she even had to look at the appointments book to check who Maureen was and why she was there.

Claire took a breath and grimaced slightly. Maureen knew. She could have walked out then and spared them both a difficult scene. It must be dreadful for her, she thought, bringing this kind of news. Maureen's heart was touched by that painful flicker round Claire's mouth.

'It's alright,' said Maureen. 'I know.'

'I wish it was better news...The results of the biopsy have confirmed what we feared from the mammogram. You have a malignant growth.'

It was said. It existed. It was no longer a possibility, it was a thing. She could feel its realness for the first time. Maureen moved her left hand to rest on the breast, and then stopped. It seemed too obvious. Her hand paused mid-air as she looked at it and glanced at Claire watching her.

It was the moment Claire hated most of all. The complete uncertainty that arrested ordinary motor function. Reflex actions were suddenly confused. She continued.

'We will have to operate. I'm recommending a surgeon who is very, very good. You can have every confidence. It looks like this is a fairly early detection, not as early as I would have liked, but I'm not panicking. There are several options nowadays. The surgeon will discuss them with you in detail, but in brief, some women only require a lumpectomy—a part of the breast is removed. Others require a complete mastectomy, where the whole breast is removed. It's often advisable to remove some of the lymph nodes from under your arm too. Judging from the biopsy, I suspect we may have to remove a significant portion of your right breast.'

Maureen put her hand down. She would have to say something. Claire needed some sign that she understood.

'This must be awful for you. Please, you mustn't feel bad.'

'I don't think now's the time to focus on my feel-ings, Maureen.'

'I suppose not. I just didn't want you...'

'Never mind how I feel. What are you feeling?'

Maureen searched for an answer. 'I'm feeling sorry for you...I think that's all I can manage right now.'

'It will take time. Have you spoken to James yet?'

'No.'

'Anyone?'

'No...I didn't want to raise any unnecessary fear. There was a chance...' Her voice trailed off. That was in the past now. The chance had been replaced by a lump. Her hand reached up again.

'It's OK, touch it,' Claire encouraged her.

Maureen's hand made contact with the breast and she looked again at the doctor. Tears came to her eyes. Her head began to nod from side to side as she bit into her lip.

'I'm sorry...No, please.'

Claire was crying too. She reached for the tissues in the second drawer of her desk, took one and passed the box to Maureen. They blew their noses in unison.

'Thanks...OK, give me the practicals. When, where, what.'

'There's time enough for that. I'll forward your results to the surgeon. Call the number on this card and arrange an appointment...and take someone with you. There'll be lots of information and emotions whirling around. You'll need someone to keep a clear head and ask all the questions you can't think of. You can't do this alone.'

'Yes, of course.'

'I mean it.' Claire looked hard at her.

'And in the meantime?'

'In the meantime, I want you to have a day of indulgence. Whatever you want, give it to yourself. Stop thinking of other people and be totally selfish. Max out your credit card, stab a few pillows, get horribly drunk.'

'Is this what all doctors say?'

'No, but it's what you need. I've got the inevitable leaflets for you. Many women have gone through this and are leading fantastic lives. There's a contact number...'

'Please, not a support group. You've been so good, I couldn't bear that now.'

'They are very good.'

'Will I have to mourn and write a letter to my breast?'

'Well...' Claire stopped, realising it was not the moment to push the benefit of writing to parts of your body. 'You do have to tell someone, hopefully James.'

'He...he didn't notice anything.'

'Are you meeting him now?'

'No, I'm...I'm supposed to be meeting my friend.'

'Good...However strong you think you are, you can't do this on your own.'

'I'll make my appointment straight...' The doctor interrupted her.

'There's no rush, cancer is slow. A few days make no difference and you need that time to prepare yourself mentally. Go indulge and call me at any time. D'you hear, any time.'

The day looked bright as Maureen stepped out onto the street. There were still enough of the night's breezes wafting around to give a pleasant cool draught, but they indicated a hot day ahead. Given the thousands of hot days there had been, Maureen always wondered why this early morning moment still had a buzz to it. A woman walking into the convenience store next to the doctor's smiled at her, a man walking out loaded with his Saturday papers smiled at the woman—a busy satisfaction.

It was too busy. Vans pulling up, cars pulling round, bicycles pulling out, the monorail rolling overhead. Trains trundled deep below. Too much movement everywhere. Which near-accident should she watch? Which cyclist to step back for, which cars to dash between at the lights, which newspaper-lugging smiler to smile back at? Busy-ness everywhere.

She needed a quiet space away from the happy

bustling. She did not want to buy this beautiful morning, or even be part of it. Trying to focus on exactly where she was, Maureen knew if she walked up the hill, she would reach Hyde Park. There she could hide from all the movement. A child ran past, carried away by the gentle gravity of the street's slope. This way, she thought, and set off in the opposite direction. Looking across the street (that's Elizabeth Street, she told herself) she saw green—Hyde Park. The lights took ages to change. She stood panting, waiting for the burst of beeps from the crossing to propel her across the road. When they did, she was as oblivious to the taxi hurtling round the corner as it had been to the red light. It screeched to a halt, the driver's shouts blending with his furious horn. She ran until her feet touched grass.

The sounds receded. What she needed now was the one spot that was as far away as possible from tourists at the reflection pool, street people stirring from a night's sleep, inner-city dwellers pounding their way to the swimming pool for their morning workout and the skateboarder paying a suspect tribute at the war memorial. The rose garden, she thought, and walked in a straight line to the part of the park across the street. Another busy crossing, a rise in noise and then she ran to the spot she knew would be quiet. No benches, no paths, no fountains.

Her breath grew calm as she lowered herself onto the grass and listened for the furthest-away sound she could hear. There was a faint cry of children over by the cathedral, a bird overhead. She waited for some noise from inside, some word to emerge from the subsiding panic.

'Get you!' They were not her words, but the words of a young woman cavorting across the rose garden with a man. She was in a minuscule black dress, he wore black leather pants with no shirt. The sunglasses and half-drunk bottle of water gave them away. Maureen sat there, catapulted into the tumultuous next day of her life and they had not yet completed the night before.

'I'm still flying. Gary was right, they're the strongest Es ever.'

'Woo, I love Eurodollars,' the girl giggled and fell over. The boy threw himself on the ground next to her. Maureen watched their perfect bodies. The girl had great breasts, an even tan and long slim legs. He had great breasts too, pumped from the gym and trimmed down from nights of frenetic dancing with nothing more than chewing gum for sustenance. They make a stunning couple, she thought as they began writhing on the grass.

'Jules,' she shrieked as the bronzed muscle boy

pushed her breasts together then stuck his nose in them.

'I love them, I love them,' he cried and they settled down to some serious kissing.

Sex and drugs, Maureen thought. What a great idea.

'Christ, your skin feels great.' The girl was lying on her back, rubbing her hands over the boy's smooth, blemish-free, lump-free chest as he knelt astride her, his face turned up to the sun. They had impossibly perfect skin. The boy opened his eyes and saw Maureen in his direct line of vision. He smiled and shook his head, as if laughing at himself, and then licked his lips at her. Maureen smiled back, surprising the boy with her composure. He raised an eyebrow and continued staring at her as the girl began fumbling with his pants. He held his hands above his head, showing off the curve of his muscled arms and chest, pretending to be enjoying the sun.

The drugs must have been good, Maureen thought. He closed his eyes again. Their whole bodies seemed to be coursing with pleasure, pleasure so strong he had almost embraced Maureen with it. He knew nothing about her, a strange older woman sitting a few metres away in a different world, and he still looked at her with desire. Desire for her admiration of him, probably, but desire all the same. The girl opened her eyes, pushed him over and jumped on top.

Her breasts bounced with a pertness Maureen remembered well from her twenties. She had always loved her breasts—they made her feel sexy in an earthy, roll on the ground in the rose garden sort of way. Without them, Maureen felt she might have been too prim, too classy, too intelligent. Her breasts had meant she could compete on a purely physical level.

It was the girl's turn to look at Maureen with an 'aren't I lucky' smile.

She threw herself upon him so every part of her body was resting on every bit of his, her breasts squashing out to the sides.

It was distracting, but their flagrant youth and stunning complexions provided no sanctuary for her. As she walked past they were oblivious to everything but their own bodies. The sun would soon add some red tones to their perfect skins, Maureen consoled herself.

10.00 am

Maureen watched Irene pick up her phone. She hastily grabbed her own from her bag and switched it off. Lurking behind a billboard which masqueraded as a public phone, she looked at the scene she was supposed to be in. Leaning back against the advertisement, Maureen was oblivious to the topless girl in jeans, smiling soulfully with her arms crossed over her bare chest. In the scene, as it was supposed to be played out, Maureen would join Irene, tell her the news, watch her tears and be strong. She could hear her own words of comfort,

'I'm not dying...the majority of women recover fully.'

And Irene, lovely Irene, would do her weeping for her.

Maureen knew the call would probably be to her. She avoided it while she decided what to do. Her life was sitting there with Irene and her nearly finished latte. There would be comfort and support. Everyone would rally round, her brain knew that, but the thought of people fussing irritated her. Allowing herself to be supported seemed too much effort.

What was the alternative? She could go in and pretend everything was alright. She could tell them later, after the operation. That was pushing things too far, she knew that. It was either go to Irene now and subject herself to supporting everyone else through her illness, cope brilliantly and be a model cancer patient or...or what, disappear?

One thing that had emerged in her quandary—she did not want to cope. There would be no performing with a cracked rib today. She wanted to be the opposite of Maureen—carefree, unreliable, self-centred. A day, as her doctor suggested, of reckless self-indulgence. There, she had made a decision about what she wanted. It brought a satisfaction, like the quiet naughtiness when she sneaked off to the cinema on her own some afternoons and never told anyone. Nobody in the world knew she had seen every *Scream* film, *Dude, Where's My Car* and whatever that last teen flick was.

She looked at Irene again, watched her casting round, looking at her phone, willing it to ring. She was getting distressed. Maureen knew that her simply being late was a cause for concern. The temptation to call her with a lie so she would not worry was strong, but she resisted, peeling the thought off her head, sticking it on the wistful poster girl like a redundant Post-it note. She walked away to seek outrageous indulgence.

11.00 am

Maureen was not impressed with her attempt at hedonism. She might have successfully walked away from her life, but she had not walked into anything other than a florist. She took a deep breath to absorb the overall shop smell and wandered around, sniffing closely at those flowers from which she expected a scent. There was not much—there never was anymore. The large slab in the middle of the shop where the florists made up their displays was busy. The water spray passed from hand to hand, ribbon samples flew off the rolls attached to the end of it. A mortician's slab, it dominated the room. The florists were tarting up corpses.

Maureen's morbid thoughts came from annoyance at herself. Her objectives were wild and dangerous and sniffing flowers did not meet them. She had tried, marching straight back to the park to demand the young lovers take her somewhere loud where she would flirt outrageously with the boy, make the girl jealous, and unleash the sexual power of an older woman. The plan was foiled by their absence. Flowers were a tame substitute.

Before her was a wall of blooms, a terraced stand with vase after vase on each row. A mad mix of colour. No arrangement, just random beauty. She bent over to sniff the bottom row, only to be disappointed yet again. Behind her a familiar voice rang out.

'OK, Marcus said you had a couple of options. Let's see them.'

It was James. Her life was pursuing her. Was there no escape? The most sensible option would have been to sidle out of the shop, but she was gripped with curiosity. James in a real flower shop. He did send flowers, but he usually ordered over the internet or got his assistant to arrange it. With a sideways step, she reached the end of the flower terrace. Glancing around while moving her head as little as possible, she saw his back was turned. She whipped behind the wall of flowers where he would not be able to see her, but she could manoeuvre to see him. The miniature sunflowers afforded the best view, so she crouched down to peep between them.

He brought the shop to a standstill. Standing on one side of the slab with the other customers, whose flowers had been tossed aside to make way for him, he was viewing what looked like a performance. The assistants were huddled together, holding huge bunches of blue cornflowers in front of them. The shop owner was running between them, scattering bits of baby's breath, and weaving her way along with a handful of red gerberas which she was forming into a wave shape. Everyone burst into applause. James went around to the performance side of the slab and removed the baby's breath.

'That's a relief,' Maureen thought. She hated the stuff. He left as quickly as he had arrived, phone in hand, earpiece in place, and saying, 'Yes to the cornflowers. I love them.'

Maureen stood up. Who was all this for? Her? Someone else? She grew angry. He could see the effect of baby's breath from the other side of the counter, but not the lump that stared him in the face during sex.

'Bastard!' she shouted, startling a woman selecting Australian natives from the display.

'Bastard.' She brought silence down on the shop.

'Bastard.' She walked out with the bemused eyes from around the slab upon her.

She felt something inside her. Further down her body than she normally felt, it was uncomfortable, a frustrating itch that she wanted to rip out. Standing on the street she felt like a panting werewolf, her hands in a claw-like open clench. She looked up and down the street searching for a victim whose throat she could slash open with her talons. But there were no talons, only well-groomed nails, naturally shiny and clean. They would have difficulty tearing through the throat of a jelly baby. The feeling died down.

She had felt a flash of anger in the shop, she had even verbalised it. That was a start, but it had petered out quickly. Sobbing hysterically in the street, causing strange looks, would be a healthier option than standing there feeling nothing, but her mind could only run to everyone else's feelings. James' shock, Irene's agony, her doctor's tears. Nicole...Nicole would be devastated, would remember their bra-buying trip to Melbourne and then attempt to hide her feelings without success. Maureen could even imagine Stephen's awkward attempt to say something soothing which would come out wrong and provoke a furious reaction from Irene. She would intervene in their fight and her condition would bring peace between them. They would settle their scores for her.

She smiled to herself. Breast cancer as a relationship-counselling tool. Only she could play out such a scenario.

The street was busy. She was in the way of people entering and leaving the florist, walking up and down in the hectic rush of a day off. She walked, unconscious of the direction, aware that movement made her less conspicuous. She had to focus. There were two objectives for today: work out her feelings and the indulgence thing.

So far she had felt anger, she knew that. It was understandable, it was explained, and so she could tick it off. Objective two: 'sex and drugs', the ultimate selfish pleasures she could pursue. Where could she find them? How much easier, she thought, if she was a man. She could catch a cab to Kings Cross, find a prostitute and do it. Quick, easy and suitably dirty. She imagined the squeaky PVC and gum-chewing noises hookers on TV always made and she cringed. There must be male sex workers somewhere, she reasoned and then realised what it was she should be looking for.

'A brothel.'

There had to be a brothel for women. She had seen a report a few years ago on *BBC World* of a South African one called Spartacus or something tastefully masculine. The reporter had chatted to the 'boys' and wandered round the faux Greek statues. She finished her report sitting on the edge of the bed and flicking the door shut with her toe. That finish had amused Maureen, so unBBC. Jane Standley had been the reporter. She had noted the name and always looked out for her. What would Jane Standley do, she thought, to find a brothel in Sydney?

Half an hour later, Maureen was sitting in a café feeling satisfied, a copy of the *Sydney Star Observer*, the free gay paper, on the table in front of her. In the back she had found several advertisements for male escorts and for agencies. All she needed now was a chance to call up one of the agencies and find out if they took women and if they didn't, who did.

Turning on her phone was a question of strategic timing. She realised that by now Irene would have spoken to James and they both were probably taking turns to call her phone every few minutes. She did not want it to ring. Her first act on turning it on was to scroll quickly through the menu to 'divert all calls'. Next she needed the courage to call the number. She looked around at the people in the café as they looked around at everyone else. She was the only one with a newspaper open at the escorts page. She entered the number into her phone and then discreetly closed the newspaper.

'Didn't find one you liked?' The waiter had returned with her coffee. It had been so long since she had ordered it, she had assumed she had already drunk it. The empty cup on the table was not hers but the previous occupant's.

'Pardon?' She smiled, trying to look innocent.

'Don't mind me, but I wouldn't bother with him.' The waiter flicked open the paper again. Maureen looked around to check that everyone else was still watching everyone else and not her.

'Him,' the waiter tapped on the picture of 'Rick: 6ft, hung, all scenes, actual photo'.

'Six foot in his stilettos, hung like a chipmunk, loves making a scene. That is an actual photo,' the waiter indicated the perfect fat-free washboard, 'but it's not actually of him. I should know, it's my ex. Learn from my mistake, steer well clear... He's supposed to be good.' The waiter was now looking at 'Aaron: hot, rugged, muscular, dominant'.

'I'm... I'm researching an article.' Maureen felt the need to proffer an excuse.

'Sure.'

The waiter was finally distracted by someone demanding to know if there was a chance of getting served. He rolled his eyes, slumped his shoulders and trudged back to his spine-breaking work. Maureen felt the whole venue had been witness to their discussion. She looked at the tables close to her and caught the eye of one in a group of four crammed around a table.

'Lucky you... you got a coffee.'

It was the waiter attracting their disdain, not her choice of reading material. She sipped her tepid long black.

As a table near the back starting complaining and the waiter answered back, Maureen seized her chance and pressed Call on her phone. The boy who answered was surprised to hear a woman. Maureen explained her situation as delicately as she could.

'I've never really done this sort of thing before.'

'That's fine,' the boy replied. It was a line he was used to.

'I'm looking for somewhere that takes women... real, I mean women born women.' Maureen silently thanked Nicole for educating her on the right terms.

'Well, some of our boys specialise in the whole pretending to be straight thing. I suppose they could...' the boy trailed off, realising perhaps it was not a good idea for a woman to visit a gay brothel.

'They'd kill me here if they heard me, but there's this fantastic new place opened for business women. Spent over a million on the refit. It's brilliant, every possible scene you could want. They've even got... please hold.'

Maureen held. This sounded very promising. She wanted luxury and indulgence and to hell with the cost or the repercussions. That word echoed around her head. A flash of terror shot through her as she imagined what would happen if anyone found out. She almost ended the call but steeled herself and held on for the receptionist's return.

'Sorry, that was the boss. It's called Heracles. Got a pen? This is the number. Tell them Maurice sent you.'

'Thanks, Maurice.'

'It's not my name, that's a code. Let them know you've been recommended. You'll love it, they've got a rotating...'

The line went dead. The boss must have returned.

James and she were never really 'experimental'. They had sex. It wasn't always in the same position, it wasn't always in the bedroom. She had paraded around once in underwear and high heels for him. James had happened to buy her some red-lace underwear and a pair of shoes she had wanted. She tried them on, walked up and down.

'So these are *your* presents on my birthday. What have you bought for me?' He laughed and shoved a $50 note in the elastic of her knickers as she attempted a lap dance. It had been a great spontaneous moment.

They did not plan sexual adventures but sometimes lay in bed talking about whether they should be doing more to invigorate their sex lives. James was happy and if he was happy with their sex life, so was she. She did not live to please him, and her orgasm was just as important as his, but it never occurred to her to say 'I'd like to try this'. There was something too clinical about planning your sex life.

12.00 pm

The 'Maurice' code had worked effectively at Heracles. The polite and reserved person on the phone suddenly became a mine of information, giving precise details as to the location of the establishment. It was housed in a former warehouse in Darlinghurst and could only be accessed through a narrow back alley. As she ducked down this alley she could have sworn she heard her name called out, but put it down to guilty paranoia. Just in case, she had not responded and had run as quickly as possible.

The warehouse did not look like a million dollars had been spent on it. It was unpainted, and only a close observer could tell that new windows with heavy tints had been installed. A very small plaque which simply said 'Heracles' sat above an intercom buzzer. Maureen had expected at least some sort of muscle-man motif. It looked too discreet and tasteful.

Concerns of good taste were soon dispelled when the door was opened and the million-dollar refit revealed itself. She stood transfixed, as if on the threshold of another world. The sun-washed and dirt-stained colours of the alley yielded to a burst of technicolour from the open door. At her feet stretched a carpet which suggested an ocean floor, its swirls of blue and aquamarine giving way to the russet tones of the Australian bush along the hallway. A blistering yellow stripe ran down its sides. Uplights set within the carpet illuminated the wall and the plinths which were spaced at regular intervals down the hall.

There were ten plinths in all, and on each was a twenty-first-century interpretation of a Greek god. Buffed and scantily clad, they were turned towards the door, each inviting Maureen in with his trademark smile. Lascivious Bacchus lured her from the left as 'wine' from the bunch of grapes he held aloft dribbled onto his chest and ran down his muscled body. Aries, clad in leather pants, commanded her with clenched fist, a copper armband above his bicep accentuating his powerful arms. Zeus, older and with a beard but no less perfectly formed, issued thunderbolts which flashed across the ceiling from his right hand. Apollo, Hermes, they were all there, beckoning her towards the door at the end of the hall which was dominated by Heracles himself. His head and chest emerged from the wall as his strong pleasure-offering arms embraced the doorway.

'Come in.' A young mortal in a Greek tunic invited her to cross the threshold.

'Sex and drugs,' she reassured herself, and stepped onto the aquamarine swirls. From this new angle she was fascinated by the carpet's ghastliness. As she was walked along the avenue of gods into Heracles' welcoming arms she could only think of the skill and dedication it would take to design a carpet so horrible. Brilliantly creative, it was bad taste elevated to an art form.

'If you'd like to take a seat here, Maurice will be with you shortly.' The waiting room was less spectacular than the hall. A few more classic Greek pillars with random male body parts on bronze rods adorned the edges. On the wall behind them Maureen could see flock wallpaper. She smiled, almost reassured to see the brothel stereotype in such a sumptuous setting.

'Tacky, isn't it!' Maurice had entered, a perma-tanned man who could have been anything from thirty-five to sixty-five. His clear skin was well cared for and worked on. His idea of growing old gracefully was to grow old as little as possible. He got away with it.

'It's just...'

'It's there to produce that exact smile. Our gods can be a little intimidating. We want our guests to relax. The flock wallpaper makes people comfortable. This place may be the best, but it's not *too* classy.'

'I didn't realise so much psychology went into it.'

Maurice smiled a smile that refused to allow the rest of his face to move.

'We like to think of everything. Now, some champagne while we discuss your needs. Lydia, isn't it?'

Maureen hesitated, unsure if that was the false name she had given. She thought it best to agree. The young man who had answered the door brought in a bottle and two flutes. Maureen noticed the label. Veuve.

'Yes, we offer the real thing here.' Maurice's mouth smiled again. 'Before we begin, let me assure you: complete confidentiality, no exceptions. We'd be out of business if we didn't. Brothels are legal in this state, you're not breaking any laws being here. We are a legitimate business, I can give you our ABN number if you wish. All our employees have superannuation and health benefits.'

It was beginning to sound a bit too respectable. She reminded herself she was still exploiting someone for their body, even if they did have a good dental plan. She felt a reassuring pang of guilt.

Maurice continued his introduction. 'All our men have monthly health checks and we insist whatever is done is done safely. Beyond that you're free to do what you want with whomever you want here. Your wish is our command. But, sadly, filthy lucre first. Could we have your card for an imprint?'

Maureen took out her card, and realised her real name was on it.

'Don't worry, it will be charged to HRZ Holdings.' Maurice had the sensitivity not to look at the name on the card as Maureen placed it on the silver salver the young man held out to her. Everything was above board, she tried to reassure herself, as the card disappeared through another door. She sipped her champagne. It might have been her nervous state but the taste did not match the bottle. It was a passable Australian sparkling wine. Maureen realised she should say something as Maurice had now finished his introduction.

'Well, I . . . '

'Normally I would invite some of our men to join us. We all chat for a while and you decide who would pleasure you most . . . However, I suspect you might like to look through the portfolios first, pick one, meet him and decide. OK?'

'Fine.' Maureen gulped more sparkling wine.

Maurice produced his white iBook and rested it on the table in front of him. 'Of course we have all types of men. What's your ideal type, Lydia?'

'I've been married for several years.' Maureen was at a loss as to why she had said that. It was irrelevant, but she had never really had to think what her type was. Even when she was single, she was never one to plough through magazine multiple-choice questions to find her ideal partner. Maurice, experienced in this, sensed her difficulty.

'Let's try another way. If one of the Greek gods were to carry you off for an afternoon of pleasure, which would you want?'

Maureen glanced out to the hall. She looked for the least imposing. They all seemed so vast. She wondered what did she actually want. What sort of man would be best for her right now? What physical attributes? She supposed she would want someone strong, someone who could take care of her. Zeus, she thought, would be the logical choice, but he seemed so big and too obviously a father figure.

'I think Hermes,' she said suddenly, without any reason.

'Excellent.' Maurice started tapping on the computer. 'The Messenger and also a symbol of fertility. Did you know that? Now, here's Michael. Been with us a couple of years. Nearly finished his medical degree.'

'No.' Maureen did not want to be examined.

They flashed through a few other shots, all of whom Maureen suspected could have played any of the gods.

'Stop,' she said suddenly, arrested by eyes that had a gentleness missing from the others. It was the nearest she would come to actually choosing.

'Cole,' Maurice informed her. 'Excellent choice. Shall I get him to join us?'

In the moment that Maureen was left on her own, the ludicrousness of the situation bubbled through her. She was doing something completely off the wall, she was being somebody completely different and it felt wonderful. It was like the first time she had gone to a bar as an under-age girl. All the other girls at her grammar school had been very cool. She was racked with nerves, particularly in view of the double whammy they were effecting. Pretending to be two years younger to get away with half fare on the bus and then adding four years to get into the bar. As she ordered her Tia Maria she felt terrified, sure that six police officers and the school principal would leap up from behind the bar. But there was a thrill of actually doing something bad, something that her mother would tell her off about if she found out. There had not been many of those in Maureen's childhood. A trip to the same bar a few years later had revealed there was little chance of her being challenged about her age. From the many schoolgirls and thirty something men hanging around them it had been clear under-age girls were the main attraction. She would have had to be in kindergarten before the staff would have refused to serve her.

Maurice returned with Cole and introduced him as if they were both old friends of his who just happened to be in the same place. Cole shook her hand firmly, smiled and looked into her eyes. He was in his early to mid twenties, but with the strange environment, and Maurice as a dubious example, any age could have been possible.

'What line of work are you in?' Cole took the lead in creating conversation as they sat down again. Maurice beamed happily as if true love had been created by his deft skill. Maureen answered and was about to ask Cole the same question when she realised the answer was all too obvious.

He answered it anyway, without her even asking. 'I'm a law student. A lot of students work here. It helps with the fees and it means guests don't have to put up with any really dumb conversations.'

Chitchat continued to be made, sparkling wine was drunk, and Maurice retreated.

'If you need me for any reason, ask Cole or anyone else. Have a wonderful time.' He shook Maureen's hand with both of his as if she were about to embark on a three-month cruise.

'He gets very emotional,' Cole whispered with a smile. 'Thinks he's creating something lovely and precious.'

Cole picked up Maureen's hand and kissed her wrist. She pulled away quickly. The meter had started running. The Greek gods and the portfolio search that had seemed more like selecting a wedding cake were giving way to the reality of the situation: she was paying a boy to have sex with her.

'Don't worry, we've all the time in the world and...' he looked around checking he was not overheard, '...we don't have to do anything if you don't want. Come on, I'll give you the tour.' He filled up their champagne glasses. Maureen was unsure whether to take her handbag with her.

'You can leave that here, Maurice will return it with your credit card. It'll be safe.'

Cole led her through the waiting room and up stairs carpeted in scarlet red. He explained that each room had its own theme, catering for a variety of tastes.

'We can have a go in all of them or just stay in one that takes your fancy. Drink up and you might start fancying me.'

'Oh, I do...you mustn't think...I really haven't done anything remotely like this before...You must hear that a lot.'

'I do and it's usually true. Let's have a look in here.'

Cole opened the door to a room of medieval splendour. Mock stone walls decorated with long purple pennants with yellow fleurs-de-lys. The canopy over the large four-poster bed featured the same pattern in reverse colours. A window looked out onto a painted countryside scene with a castle. In the background a lute played a medieval version of 'Careless Whisper'.

'Look,' shouted Cole as he leapt out of the window and disappeared from view. Maureen moved to the window and saw there was an area outside the room, as if the chamber was in its own castle. The stone wall effect continued, but with fake ivy meandering up the wall.

'You're supposed to call me and I climb up the ivy to consummate our mad passion. Depending on what you want, I can either be the prince from that castle over there come to rescue you, a poor kitchen maid, or the dashing commoner you really love instead of the prince you're betrothed to. Look in the box just by the window.'

Maureen open the box and laughed. It was a long plait of fake blond hair.

'I presume it's secure!' she called to him as she threw Rapunzel's hair down. He climbed up to prove the nail holding the other end of the hair could support his weight.

'Should I be pretending it's my hair and holding it up here?' Her hands moved to the side of her head as Cole made his way to the window. 'I could be the witch having just cut Rapunzel's hair off and about to punish you.'

Cole smiled. 'Believe me, sometimes...'

'Is it hard...I mean difficult...for you?'

'One rule, Lydia. We're not here to talk about me. This is about you. Every woman comes here for a reason. It's not always sex but I'm here to make sure you get what it is you came for. OK?'

He gently stroked the side of her face with his hand and cupped her cheek. This tenderness was confusing. Maureen had expected it all to be more matter-of-fact. She had hoped the wine would fill her with over-whelming lust so she could be carried away by desire, but desire for Maureen had never been purely physical. Something in her responded to his touch. He moved closer to her, smiling. She stepped away, confronted by his warmth.

'I don't think the Rapunzel fantasy's really what we want, is it?'

The next approach did not work any better, but relieved some of the tension Maureen was feeling. They walked down and down a spiral staircase into a deep basement. It was the dungeon. As Maureen explored various thumbscrews, clamps and cuffs that were neatly positioned around the dank-smelling room, she tried to establish whether they were implements for use or ornament. Cole disappeared briefly and reappeared as a section of the wall swung round. Maureen shrieked. Stripped to the waist and dressed in leather chaps, he was strapped to a giant wheel, arms and legs splayed out. His body faced the wheel, revealing his buttocks to Maureen for the first time. They were great buttocks.

The wheel began to rotate and Maureen burst out laughing.

'It's not supposed to be funny,' Cole cried. 'You're meant to flay me with that leather whip there. The one with lots of strips.'

Maureen giggled. 'I feel I should be blindfolded, throwing knives at you.' She made a drum-roll noise. 'Ladies and gentlemen, Cole will now defy death as Lady Lydia attempts the impossible.'

'No, spare me!' Cole shouted.

'OK then.' Maureen could not take the sado-masochism seriously. Her slave gently rotated to an upside down standstill.

'It's a wheel of misfortune. I'll have H for Harry, please.'

Cole gave up. 'So I take it that's a no to the ritual domination. Can you untie me?'

Maureen bent down to release Cole's hands but the movement set the wheel turning again. His hands were free, but pressed against the wheel there was not a lot he could do. As his head reached the top, he tried to clutch the straps which had once bound him to stop himself from falling. He failed and started to tilt back-ward, out of control. Maureen stood up in time to catch him under the arms. The wheel moved from side to side and Cole swung with it. He looked up into Maureen's eyes with an irrepressible smile.

'If I had a job description,' he said, 'this would not be in it. Lower me to the floor and then undo my feet.'

As she lowered him, Maureen noticed with relief he was wearing a codpiece under his chaps. Viewing his bum had been nice, but she was not ready for his genitals. Once released, he disappeared behind the rotating wall as quickly as he could and re-emerged, de-chapped, and wearing a T-shirt and underpants. He grabbed her hand.

'Come on, before I die of embarrassment.'

Their next room, back up the spiral stairs, contained a vast heart-shaped bed. They laughed out the previous scene lying on it. Just as they calmed down, Cole reached to the side of the bed, pressed a switch and it began to throb. Maureen rolled her eyes as Cole vibrated in front of her.

'Enough! Can't you do anything normal here?'

Cole switched the bed off, lay on his side and looked at Maureen.

'So?' He ran his hand through her hair. She did not move, but looked away. The eye contact was too much.

'Why don't I give you a massage?' Cole suggested. He unzipped the back of her dress. It was a simple straight sleeveless dress she had selected for easy undressing at the doctor's. Standing up she let it slip to the floor and turned towards the bed.

the girls

'Wow,' he said as he saw her breasts sitting in her bra. The smile which he had expected to cross her face did not materialise. Instead, she stepped awkwardly out of her shoes and lay face down on the bed. She could hear him removing his T-shirt and she prayed that his underwear would stay on. If this was going to happen, it would have to be slowly. He smoothed his hand over her back, gently undoing the clasp of her bra and moving the straps aside. She removed the bra, keeping her back to him.

His hands felt soft. They did not have the strength and firmness that she loved in James' hands. She was reassured by how different they were. This was a completely separate experience she said to herself, as she felt his lips touch her neck. The hands caressed her. She could feel a waft of air on her skin, a window draught, air-conditioning, his breath. Maureen did not know, she just knew his hands and lips were seducing her into a place of calm where repercussions were wafted away.

He lay beside her, his whole body pressed against her and she felt the youth of his skin and his muscles. His youthfulness cosseted her. Something about him was unwearied by existence, she thought. Something that would disappear in a few years. He was getting aroused, she could feel it. She had turned him on. She could arouse a professional. She was attractive, stimulating and sexy.

His hand reached up to her left shoulder and turned her over onto her back. Part of her resisted. Exposing herself, she could not resist the confrontation that would come. She gave in to his gentle pressure and turned to see his smiling face. Pleasure glowed through his skin. She tried to smile but looked away awkwardly. Looking at her breasts with obvious satisfaction, he raised his hand to her right one. She expected him to grasp it firmly in his hand and squeeze the nipple. That was James' first move. It did not happen. His hand went straight for her lump, his finger touching it gently. She gasped and looked at him. He had been looking at her face all the time. His hand had found the spot on its own. She tried to move but he shushed and moved to kiss her forehead. His head continued moving. She felt his breath on her nipple. She expected him to take it in his mouth and again he confounded her by moving his mouth to the spot and kissing it.

Her mouth could only release a small gurgling noise. How could he know? How could he do it? He moved his body on top of her, focussing his hands on her breasts. Tears came to her eyes. She realised now, James had been avoiding that very spot. This was how James had used to hold her, with the fearless need to touch everywhere. James had noticed, he... Her thoughts stopped as a feeling wafted over her. This was it, she thought, she was finding a response. This was how she felt. She searched to put this feeling in words. If she could define it, then she knew she was feeling it.

Gratitude. She was feeling gratitude. She wanted to repeat 'thank you, thank you, thank you', but did not dare break the silence that held them. The gratitude brought a sinking inside. Something retreated like an eel into murky waters. She had glimpsed her emotions but realised there had to be more to them than pity for her doctor and thanks to a sex worker.

He moved off her body to give his hand access to her underwear. His fingers played with the top of her pubic hair. She tensed, worried about what would happen. The sensation was lovely but guilt was now flooding the gratitude. He was good, she did not want to hurt him, but could not brook the idea of pene-trative sex. His hand moved down and he nuzzled into her ear and whispered, 'Don't worry, I understand.' His fingers moved further into her underwear, gently manipulating, dispelling all her confused thoughts with pure physical pleasure. There was no penetration, just orgasm. Perfect.

As they lay on the bed, still in their underwear, Maureen had to ask Cole how he had known. She was tempted to maintain the easy silence, but she needed to understand. He could not explain it.

'I have a knack. I just know what the women who come here want. Don't know how. I grew up with my mum and four sisters. I suppose that put me in tune, I don't know. Quite a few women with breast cancer come here.'

Maureen felt stung. 'Oh, is that what I got, the breast cancer special?'

'Everyone is different, even if they have the same condition. You got the Lydia special.'

She felt petty, almost jealous. Cole continued.

'They come for different reasons, some come after their treatment because...' He stopped, realising what he was about to say. Maureen pressed him to finish. He looked awkward.

'Some come...I'm sure your situation's different, but some come because their husbands can't touch them.'

Maureen appreciated his sensitivity.

'I thought James, that's my "situation", hadn't noticed but after this afternoon I realised he had. He's always loved my breasts.'

'I can see why. They're beautiful. You must get a lot of men talking to them.'

'My God...I hadn't thought. I might *actually* miss that.' Maureen looked at her feet. 'I wish it had been my ankles. Is there cancer of the ankles? I've always hated them, they're so fat. I wouldn't mind chunks taken out of them. But my breasts,' he reached over and cupped one of them for her, 'they were one thing about me I wouldn't change. They're the one part that make me feel downright sexy.'

Maureen recounted her visit to the doctor. It was easy talking, now. She felt no pain, no cramp in her throat.

'You're very calm. I think most people would freak.'

'Well, I've had time since the mammogram to prepare myself,' Maureen lied. Like a junkie covering their tracks, she knew how to explain her calm coping self rationally.

'I'm on a day of extreme indulgence. I've run away from home in pursuit of sex and drugs. Those are the big indulgences, aren't they?'

'You've done one.' Cole still had his hand on Maureen's right breast. It felt natural, comfortable. 'How are you doing drugs...? Have you ever done drugs before?'

'I'm not that respectable. I've spent the whole of the '90s in the arts industry. You can't do that and not come across a line of coke.'

'Really?'

'Maybe,' Maureen lied again. 'D'you know where I can get some ecstasy? I hear Eurodollars are very good.'

Cole laughed. 'Quite the expert.' He paused, making

a quick risk assessment. 'I may be able to help you. I'll have a word downstairs. Wait here.'

When Cole left the room, Maureen put her bra and dress back on. She could still feel Cole's hand. The imprint had a comforting security. In the mirror, which lined the entire wall opposite the heart-shaped bed, she tidied her hair. Fortunately there had not been too many throes of wild passion to disturb it beyond repair. She decided, looking at herself, that she felt good. She had been dangerously self-indulgent, and it looked like the other half of her objective might be met too. The word 'guilt' was banished from her mind. She was banishing a lot from her mind.

She stared at the mirror, looking for clues to her feelings. Hers did not look like the face of an angry woman, not frightened or bitter either. 'Perhaps,' she mused aloud, 'this is me, this is normal. Perhaps I'm not missing anything. I cope naturally.'

She smiled at the reflection to convince herself she was right.

Cole returned with a small plastic bag containing a deep yellow pill. 'Not a Eurodollar, but a CK. Pretty good.'

'Is that it?' She took the bag with curiosity. No matter how many low-downs on drugs she had read in the *Sydney Morning Herald*, there was something dangerously novel about this little pill.

'Now, if I let you have it, you must promise: don't take it anywhere you could get stranded on your own. They're strong, so only take half and see how it goes. Remember to drink lots of water.'

'Do I chew it? How quickly does it work?'

'Don't chew unless you want a revolting taste in your mouth. Just swallow and around half an hour later you should start to feel things. Try not to do it on your own. Get someone to share it with you.'

'I don't suppose...'

'I'm working my other job in a few hours. They wouldn't be too pleased.'

'Won't it have worn off?'

'It can last several hours for some people, for others it wears off after two or three.'

'How much do I owe you?'

'It'll be added to your bill. You'll probably get charged for an extra bottle of fake Veuve. Very discreet.'

'I suppose time's up. Thank you, Cole.' She hugged him and he gave her a small kiss on the lips for the first time. Before he let her go, he turned her round to face the mirror again and his hand slipped down the top of her dress to the right breast.

'Now the meter's stopped running, I can tell you how sexy you are and you can believe me. I'd have loved to have done much more with you. Your husband's very lucky.'

After she paid her bill and received her handbag, credit card and tax invoice, Maurice led Maureen back down the Hall of Gods and begged her to return soon. The shock of the carpet and Zeus' thunderbolts flashing overhead struck her again. She had forgotten the opulent tackiness. Cole had transcended that. He had made her feel that none of it was sordid or desperate. She held on to that thought as she walked towards the door past all the gods' dusty bottoms.

2.00 pm

The excitement of having been wildly unpredictable subsided as Maureen contemplated her next indulgence. Spontaneity was hard work. Standing at a busy intersection, she was in the way as the lights changed. The crowd surged forward and carried her along before she could decide which direction she wanted to go in. The pill in its little resealable plastic sack sat in her bag. She toyed with the idea of returning to her spot in the park, taking the ecstasy and seeing what happened. Nothing might happen. Several hours might disappear in blissful indolence as she sat there, thinking how vibrant the flowers were. No, she had done flowers and had to put them out of her mind. Someone walked into her from behind.

'Sorry,' she mumbled, and moved to the side. Guilt smashed into her like a truck. Maureen had been unfaithful. She had never even come close before. Men had been attracted to her. She had been flirted with, she had been flattered by their attention, but she had always made it clear she was married. No man had really pressed the point. It had been a source of irritation. Why had no-one ever tried to seduce her? She had laughed about it with Irene once, pretending it was a joke.

Irene had suggested she was too confident, too open and too happily married. 'They can see they'll get nowhere, you're complete without them. They've got no power over you.'

Did it count as infidelity if you paid for sex? Did it count if there was no penetration, just an orgasm? There was none of the special intimacy she associated with sex, but there was intimacy of a different kind. The feel of Cole's hand on her breast returned briefly. Its warming comfort was ebbing away. With every pulse, she felt herself getting hotter. Her hair began to prickle and then she suddenly felt cold. Goosebumps erupted on the side of her chest.

Was she using her lump as an excuse to be irresponsible? Was she that shallow? Was this really what her doctor had meant? Perhaps deep down she was taking the news in her stride. There may be no adjusting for her to do. She was Maureen. Maureen was good at being a human. Looking for an emotional response was like running through room after room in an empty house, searching for furniture that did not exist.

The only feeling she could identify was guilt. It clouded her view. She looked at the phone and imagined all the beeps indicating her messages and the horror at how many there would be. Something stopped her pressing the On button. A voice said she was not OK and her finger listened to it.

She looked around her. She had only made it a few metres from the pedestrian crossing. In front of her was a steep downward hill that gave onto a view of the city. To the left were the towers of the business district. Straight ahead was the Harbour Bridge, just the top of the arch, but it amazed her that it could be seen from there at all.

It always surprised her that no matter how big all the other buildings in Sydney got, the bridge still stood out. There was something reassuring about it. It linked the city and was the major road north and south, yet it had a quality of being there for its own sake. A vast monument to itself that served no particular function.

The Harbour Bridge stood there, not communicating, just existing—a serene moment in her busy mind.

'That's what I'll do,' she thought. 'I'll climb it.'

2.45 pm

The Bridge Climb Centre looked like the set of a James Bond film. Behind the front counter staff in uniforms and baseball caps busied themselves, ushering groups of people up steel steps and along passageways. Headsets were everywhere—incessant communication in the highly organised melee. Somewhere, hidden from the public view, HQ kept an eye and ear on everything. The ordered confusion looked like someone had called 'action' the second Maureen walked in.

This, according to the tourist information Maureen had read, was the only means of climbing the arch of Sydney Harbour Bridge. Anyone could walk, ride or drive across its roadway, but going over the arch was strictly for organised tours.

Groups of twelve departed every ten minutes and never seemed to return, as if they had all been selected to blast off into space and start a new colony. Maureen assumed they checked out on the other side of the harbour.

She was offered a spare place in a group departing in the next fifteen minutes.

'It will be you and nine people on a team-building exercise from Santa Barbara. Is that OK?'

Maureen had no objections to team builders from Santa Barbara.

Sitting in the waiting room, she tried to spot potential team builders from their accents. A group of people clustered around the drinks machine debating loudly whether Australian Coke was the same as in the US. They were listening constructively on this important issue, hearing each others' arguments and repeating what had been said before putting forward their counter points.

A few others were hounding a woman holding an armful of walkie talkies. She was doing her best to answer all the questions and make her delivery, but was stopped by repeated queries about toilet facilities, safety on the bridge and photo opportunities.

'You will be fully trained and briefed before departure,' the woman repeated.

A television set in the waiting room was playing video footage of various international TV celebrities on the bridge. It consisted mainly of travel reporters enthusing from the top as the wind ruined their once-manageable hair. It was all amusing until murdered UK TV presenter Jill Dando appeared. Given the time since her murder, the tape must have been old. One couple guffawed from the corner.

'Sorry, we're English,' they offered as an explanation.

A uniformed staff member called the 3.00 pm group into the 'briefing room'. The details of what would be happening on their adventure were outlined. There would be an hour of training before departure, with every aspect of safety and protocol covered. Their most immediate task was to fill in the medical and indemnity forms which had been sitting on the bench as they walked in and which they now all clutched on their knees.

'After that,' Troy explained, 'we'll be breathalysing you. It's like driving: you can't climb if you've got more than a 0.02 alcohol reading. If you had a drink with lunch, that's fine. If you knocked back a couple of schooners half an hour ago, you can't go. We're very strict on this, no exceptions.'

The team seemed comfortable with this. They had taken a collective decision that none of them would drink anything before six during their course. Maureen was not so comfortable. She felt like a sinner in a born-again church. It was a couple of hours since she had downed the fake champagne. She did not feel drunk, but the alcohol might be lingering. Perhaps if she announced she'd had a drink an hour or so before, she might get a later departure. They might just refuse her all together.

'Control yourself, Maureen,' she thought, remembering she was actually planning far worse than a couple of glasses of sparkling wine on her climb.

As Troy left them to fill in their forms and prepare his breathalyser, he gave them a parting instruction.

'Introduce yourselves to each other. You'll be spending some time all tied together so learn a bit about one another.'

The team builders looked around. This could possibly be a test for them. All eyes turned to Maureen, the one person they did not know. A few felt they had sussed the situation.

'Hi, I'm Kelvin,' the guy next to Maureen introduced himself, triggering a cacophony of self-introductions.

'Now repeat them all back,' Kelvin joked. Maureen smiled. She had spent enough time trying to distinguish ballet dancers dressed in the same outfits with the same hairstyles and same bodies to learn names fast.

'Let me see. Kelvin,' she pointed at him, 'Blake, Jolene, Corinne, Enrico, Ray, Misty, Yolande and...' She paused dramatically at the last name as the team willed her on with wide-eyed amazement, 'last but by no means least, Hubert on the end there.'

They cheered.

'Wow, that was awesome. Have you done one of those memory courses?'

Corinne was in raptures of respect. 'What a first impression!'

'Are you a motivator?' Blake asked.

'No, I'm an administrator, for...never mind who for, it's not who I am.' She knew what they wanted to hear. This crowd was easy work for someone with Maureen's comprehensive people-pleasing skills.

'Go girl,' Jolene shouted over more applause.

Enrico explained they were all from a team-builders' training course. They were all learning to be work motivators and group-dynamic technicians.

'We call it a build the builder course,' Misty offered and they laughed at their own in-joke. 'Australia has been the final leg of training. It was a group holiday with a few surprise exercises thrown in.'

Kelvin told her that they had been up to Far North Queensland and thought they were heading out to view the rainforest from a helicopter. Once the helicopter had set them down by a river for lunch it took off. They had to make their own way back. It had taken three days of kayaking, ration-splitting and mutual support.

'It was just like *Survivor*, only no bitchin', and no voting each other off.'

'It was awesome.'

Troy returned. The breath tests showed all lungs were alcohol-free until Maureen's. She put the straw between her lips and blew as gently as she dared, clenching her throat as if she could stop alcohol escaping into her breath by sheer muscle control.

She had to cross the bridge. Once she had decided to do this, it had developed a significance of its own. Crossing over the top of Sydney Harbour Bridge would be a journey to a new phase of her life. It would put the expanse of the harbour between the old and the new. On the North Shore she could go forward, travel on without looking back. She envisaged stepping off the bridge onto the other side and everything becoming clear. She would be filled with the emotional responses she sought.

To have all this confounded by a breath test seemed harsh.

'Glass of wine at lunchtime?' Troy asked. Maureen smiled and shrugged.

'You scrape in. You'll be fine by the time we're up there.'

Through the next door and onto the main set. They were made to stand in a circle on spots drawn on the floor. Staff looked over them, instructing them to tell each other where they were from and what they had eaten for breakfast. The team all decided to introduce the person on their left instead. Misty introduced

Maureen and got the breakfast wrong. She had eaten nothing. Maureen correctly assumed Kelvin, on her left, had eaten waffles along with the rest of the team.

The looking over by the staff served a purpose. They were being sized up for the grey jumpsuits which would be issued to them. They could put the suits on over their clothes or remove most of them in the changing cubicles. Lockers were provided. Given the heat of the day, Maureen decided to remove her dress. She climbed into the baggy jumpsuit and was about to zip it up when she looked at her bra. The thought of the sea breeze blowing as close as possible to her skin was appealing. Remembering the young couple in the park that morning, she wanted as little as possible between her skin and nature. The couple had seemed to glory in the feel of the sun on their skin. She wanted that feeling too and so, before conflicting considerations changed her mind, she removed her bra, zipped up the outfit and stepped out of the cubicle. She placed her clothes in a locker with her undergarment carefully hidden in her dress. Reaching into her bag, she pulled out the tiny plastic sack and hid it in the palm of her hand.

As the rest of the team emerged from their changing cubicles, she was relieved to see the outfit fitted everyone as badly as her. They looked like costumes from a low-budget '80s science-fiction series. Maureen was pleased they were most unflattering to the legs. The grey material bunched around the shoes and gave everyone fat ankles. The two muted tones of grey, they were told, were so they would blend in with the bridge and not be a distraction to drivers.

From there the team learned how to attach themselves to the rail which ran right around the bridge. They were issued with hankies on elastic for their wrists and cords to clip to sunglasses. Nothing was allowed to fall off them as they climbed. Instructions were given clearly and repeatedly, with a few jokes and breaks thrown in to prevent information overload.

Maureen was unable to concentrate, more concerned with the pill in her hand than pushing her sprocket wheel round the bridge rail. It seemed like there would be no opportunity to take it. She contemplated slipping it out of its bag, nonchalantly popping it onto her tongue and mouthing the word 'heartburn' to anyone who had noticed, but that would seem ridiculous. The whole situation was ridiculous. She would just have to ask for the toilet. Before she could, their instructor announced it was their last chance to go to the toilet, and everyone who wanted to should go immediately.

Maureen headed to the ladies as directed. Unfortunately so did all the other women in the group. Banished to a cubicle she was alone with the pill, but with no means of swallowing it. She would have to do it without water. Taking the pill out of the bag, she wondered how she might break it in half as described by Cole.

'We'll see you outside, Maureen,' a team voice cried. It could have been Jolene, Corinne, Misty, or Yolande. The shock of the voice jolted her nervous hand and the pill fell on the floor and rolled behind the bowl. Maureen panicked. Dropping to the floor, she tried to see where it had stopped, but her head would not fit between the bowl and cubicle wall. The other side of the toilet was no better. She had to hug the bowl, stretching round with both arms, her breasts squashed and her head pressed to it. Her nose sensed the bowl had not been cleaned in the last hour. Her hands searched the floor blindly trying to find the pill. Eventually a finger brushed against something that could have been it. She picked it up and brought it round to the front. She looked at the object. It was her pill, along with a little fluff. She blew as gently as she could to remove the dust.

Time pressure was now on, although the noises from a couple of toilets down suggested she was not the only person still there. Maureen attempted to break the pill with her nail, pressing down hard in the palm of her hand, but her nails were too short and the pill too small. Revolted by the levels of hygiene to which she was plummeting, Maureen realised she would have to put this thing that had rolled around a toilet floor in her mouth. Visions of heroin junkies wallowing in their own filth flashed through her mind.

There was no decision to go ahead, no lifetime spent in a second of deciding whether to do it, only determination to see through whatever it was she was seeing through. She had just one goal now: to emerge from that cubicle with half the ecstasy in her stomach.

She bit into the pill. One piece remained between her teeth, the rest seemed to crumble. With her fingers pressed to her front teeth she was stuck, unsure how to move her hand without losing most of the pill. As she contemplated this, the piece that had successfully broken into her mouth began assaulting her tastebuds viciously. She had never tasted anything so disgusting—the oral equivalent of an acrid stench. Her tongue reeled. Her fingers began to slip, her mouth dried up and she had no option but to close her lips and consume the entire pill at once.

The taste was overwhelming. She had to have water. Dashing out of the cubicle she dived for the basin tap and put her mouth to it.

'Are you OK?' Misty had just emerged from her cubicle. 'You look even more nervous than me.'

'I'm fine, just a bit thirsty. We'll be fine. I'm sure there's nothing to worry about.'

As they returned to the group, Maureen tried to picture the contents of her stomach. There was no avoiding the completion of her sex and drugs mission now. She felt a shiver of anticipation, wondering if perhaps it was starting early.

If concentration was hard before, it was impossible now. Clambering over the practice bridge steps, being fitted with a radio receiver and earpiece, it all washed over her as she reacted to every nuance her body gave out. A slight shiver ran down her spine, making her dread that she was about to spin wildly out of control. A gurgle from her stomach and she was terrified of an allergic reaction. Some terrible toxin could be eating its way through her stomach lining.

Kyle, their tour leader, announced it was time for them to depart and opened the doors onto the street. After an hour of training it was almost disappointing to emerge on the street just next to where they had entered. Having changed clothes, attached and de-attached themselves to rails, and climbed practice steps, it felt like they should step out into a different world.

As they walked around to the bridge, Kelvin drew Misty aside.

'So what d'you think?' he asked. 'Is she a plant?'

'Dunno. She was kinda weird in the toilet. Ran out of her cubicle straight to the tap like her mouth was on fire.'

'Was it a role-play exercise?' Kelvin was attempting to establish if Maureen was part of their final exercise. This section had been billed as a reward for their achievement, a day off, but he reckoned they could not be too careful. It could easily be another secret test of their team skills.

'I don't know,' Misty was confused. 'It's too much of a coincidence that a stranger just happens to join our group...'

'But it's too obvious. They'd be more subtle, wouldn't they?'

'Perhaps they want us to think it's too obvious and decide she's a genuine member of the public.' Misty was delving into the labyrinthine minds of their course organisers.

'Remember the kayaking? That was supposed to be a few days R&R too,' she added.

'Let's get either side of her on the climb. We'll be able to assess the situation.' As he said it, Kelvin moved up the group of people to be next to Maureen. He noticed she had placed herself exactly in the middle of the group and concluded she wanted to be where she had maximum contact with the entire group. As an afterthought he added to Misty, 'Let's keep this to ourselves, OK?'

She nodded at him. If this was to be their final

assessment, it might be a good idea to establish a team within the team to make sure they finished ahead.

The first sight that confronted the group was not the bridge but the support girders holding up the road leading to the first stone pylon. They were walking on a gangway hanging underneath the bridge. Maureen marvelled at the geometric precision of the receding lines and angles. After several minutes walk, the pylon seemed no nearer but the distance behind them had grown as if they were in a time warp, walking the same step over and over again. Maureen clutched the rail and paused. Was this it? Was it happening? She felt quite normal apart from the effect of the overwhelming geometry around her.

'Does this feel like a time warp to you?' she asked Misty, behind her. Misty hesitated, unsure how to answer. Maureen suddenly felt guilty. Perhaps she was hallucinating. There might not be any girders around them. It might just be a short walk along a path.

'Yes, all those girders,' Misty responded. 'You do lose your sense of distance. It shows how our perceptions can be dictated by our surroundings. I think we need to sense the truth inside ourselves and let ourselves be guided by that. I know we will reach that pylon.'

'Quite.' Perhaps Misty was on drugs too, thought Maureen.

They did reach the pylon. Once there, Kelvin turned

around and started to talk to Maureen about where she lived and why she had come on the Bridge Climb. Maureen answered cautiously.

'I just felt like it. An afternoon to spare, a beautiful day. I saw the bridge and thought...I'll climb it.'

'Spontaneity is admirable. I admire spontaneity.' He nodded knowingly and then looked over at Misty.

'Maureen decided on a whim to climb. Isn't that great?' he said.

'Yes, I admire that.' Misty smiled at Kelvin and then turned her head, her entire facial expression intact, to their admirably spontaneous co-climber. Maureen looked between the two of them, unsure whether their behaviour was really strange or if she was experiencing things that were not really happening.

Kyle called the group's attention, first through their radio receivers and then loudly through the air. His heart was pounding. It was his first solo group on the bridge. Once through the pylon there was no going back. He was responsible for their safety and for ensuring they had a great time. Training had been extensive and he had been over the bridge more times than he could remember, but this was his first time in charge. At twenty-one, it felt like an awesome responsibility— the biggest moment in his career to date. He repeated the instructions on climbing the stairs once they passed the pylon. They would be climbing through the lanes of traffic on the bridge. Only one person was allowed on each staircase at a time, no stopping on the stairs, no waving at the drivers.

'This is the scariest part of all. If you can get through this, the rest of it should be OK.' His words had come out wrong. They were supposed to reassure the group that they had nothing to fear from their climb. Instead, a few gulps from them indicated they were bracing themselves for an ordeal.

'Really, it's not that bad, honestly.' His calming words were having the opposite effect. He gulped and stammered.

'It's OK,' shouted Kelvin. 'We're a team, we'll get through it together. Right?'

'Right?' shouted the others.

'You can do it, Kyle,' said Corinne.

'You have our trust,' encouraged Hubert. He glanced at Corinne, thinking that perhaps Kyle was a plant and they would have to work out how to get down from the top of the bridge themselves when he lost it. Corinne smiled and nodded. Weeks of team building had enhanced their silent communication. Ensuring the others could not see, she put a finger to her lips. They had sussed the game and would keep it their little secret.

Corinne turned and smiled to Maureen, mouthing 'OK?' at her. Maureen smiled back. It was getting very warm, she thought. The walk had brought a slight sweat out on her brow. Her stomach gurgled more strongly than before and she sensed a slight queasiness. Probably the next false alarm, she reasoned, having experienced such alarms at two-minute intervals since taking the tablet.

She realised it was not a false alarm halfway up one of the staircases. As she stood with hands clasped on either rail, her brain swung inside her head and her feet felt heavy. The wind, the sun, the noise of the traffic were overwhelming, and yet utterly beautiful. Nature and artificial construction blended into one marvellous experience. The sensual delights of steel and traffic fumes were interrupted as she looked towards the lane of traffic. She knew they were not supposed to, but she had to look. She felt no guilt. It was marvellous. What did she care if the rules were bent slightly? Guilt soon slapped her in the face as she looked straight into Nicole's eyes. She was sitting in her truck in a traffic jam. Their eyes locked. Maureen suddenly felt obvious, as if Nicole was saying, 'I know you've taken drugs and been to a brothel. You might have cancer but that's no excuse.'

Maureen broke the gaze and hurried up to the next stairway. Kelvin was waiting for her.

'I called you, but you didn't hear me. Are you OK?'

Maureen paused, trying to sense the answer to his

question. She realised it was a profound question that could be answered on many levels, like the steps she had just climbed. It was too hard to think of an answer, she had to experience it. It came.

'Had a wobbly moment there,' she put her hand to Kelvin's arm, 'but I'm fine. Isn't this marvellous?'

He patted her hand. 'I'll climb to the next level, you follow me.'

'Next level?' Maureen questioned. Surely it could not get any better than this, she thought, and then realised Kelvin was still operating on a physical plane. She laughed.

'Of course. Onward and upward.'

Once they had finished climbing the stairways and had emerged as a group to stand at the beginning of the vast gentle slope that was the arch of Sydney Harbour Bridge, Maureen realised she had been wrong. It could get better. With every level she climbed, the flush of euphoria in her body doubled.

'It's like being on the moon,' she cried out and took large slow steps. 'One giant step for Maureen.'

'The view is magnificent,' Misty tried to agree. Maureen beamed at her.

'You know I'm so pleased I'm doing the climb with you all. You're wonderful people and you've made me feel really at home. It's so hard, you know, a new person coming into an established group. It would have been easier for you all to stick to your own cliques but no, you and Kelvin...Kelvin, I want you to hear this too. You two are making this really special for me. I...well, I do have an ulterior motive for this...'

Maureen was interrupted by Kyle calling for their attention. He had been for some time and it was not until Misty tapped her and pointed to their supposed leader that she noticed. Kyle was informing them they were to begin their ascent.

Maureen heard none of it. The wind level meant communication over more than a few metres had to be made through the radios. She had removed her ear piece, wanting to be at one with the wind, the sun and the steel. The wind raced over her body, pressing the suit to her skin. She could feel it blowing through her skin.

'I think,' she murmured to herself, 'it's working.' She thought of James. It would have been so good to share this with him. When they reached their first resting place, she turned to looked toward her home suburb. He would be there.

'That's where I live,' she said, pointing vaguely in the direction of Woollahra. 'My husband.' As she said the words, home seemed far away. She was alone with her new friends.

'D'you think we make all our journeys on our own?' she asked. Misty looked at her quizzically. Maureen continued, 'We're here together and yet there's something terribly isolating, as if we're all climbing separate bridges on different harbours, connected in some way. I mean, I'm physically touching you and Kelvin here,' she grabbed their hands in hers, 'but we're all climbing for different reasons, aren't we? We can only support each other physically and by knowing we're together at the same time as we're alone.'

Misty turned to Maureen and looked into her eyes. Her desire to win whatever game was being played on the bridge had blown off in the wind that had carried Maureen's words to the world.

'That is so beautiful. You mean we are alone, but not alone. Kelvin, did you hear that?'

Kelvin nodded. He squeezed Maureen's hand. 'We're here for you, hon.'

It might have been the wind or a speck of dust, but Misty wiped something from her eye. This woman seemed to have blossomed on the bridge. They continued their ascent. Her wisdom was not something she and Kelvin could keep to themselves, everyone had to share in it. With each step Maureen was leading them onto a higher plane. Misty spread the word back in the group as Kelvin spread the word forward. This woman was worth listening to. She was not a test, Misty thought, she was a gift. Someone special to make this experience the emotional and spiritual highlight of the course.

Kyle made them pause again. They turned to face the city.

'It's never seemed like such a complete thing before,' Maureen said. 'It's a whole city, a living entity.' The view of the city skyscrapers was more complete than from anywhere else. Other views were from lower down or from the towers themselves. She felt more distant from her life than ever. Somewhere in that whole another Maureen was probably going about, soothing Irene, listening to Nicole, forgiving Stephen and... what would she be doing for James? They had been together so long she could not sense what she really did for him or him for her. She looked down to the harbour and ferries making their way into Circular Quay. He moored on her. Her thoughts became words.

'Sometimes we're like the posts down there in the water. Props people moor their boats to. Lone posts in the sea that provide support, something solid in shifting tides. It can be lonely. We forget props need support too.'

The whole group was looking at her. Those that could not hear her words were having them repeated by those within earshot. No-one spoke other than to relay her words to the group.

'Feel that wind and sun, feel it cleansing...' she

saw their faces looking expectantly at her. 'You're looking as if I'm here for you, but I'm not. This is my journey for me. I have to cross this bridge. There's something on the other side for me.'

She paused, remembering what this whole day was for. Perhaps in this wonderful enlightened state she could discover her feelings. She waited and discovered joy and power, overwhelming power. This must be it, she thought, this must be why she was here, to feel her own power. People used the power of their minds to conquer their bodies all the time. She thought of Tanya's saying about the mind being wasted on thought. She was right. Maureen had been wasting her time thinking things through, striving to express feelings instead of allowing them to flow and using her power.

'I can beat this,' she said, as they began their ascent to the very top of the bridge.

Kyle was concerned. He had been briefed that this was a team-building group but he had not expected this guru woman to deliver lectures at every pause. They were supposed to admire the view and ask to have their photo taken. Instead she had them enthralled. He sensed control slipping from him. He could ask headquarters to send out a supervisor to help him, but he was determined to manage. The group could not disengage themselves. They were all attached by steel cable to the rail running all the way round the bridge. There was no danger, he reassured himself.

Walking up to the top, Maureen turned her body to face the wind. With every gush of air pressing to her body, she felt her lump dissipate. The overwhelming presence which had dominated her for weeks was scattering to the wind. Her mind pushed the cancerous cells through her body to the surface for the wind to sweep away and dump out at sea. The material of the suit was her only impediment. She could feel the wind and the sun through it, but how much more could she achieve if it was not there. She had to be at one with the elements for it to work. There could be no barrier, nothing in the way. They were at the very top. The highest point of her journey was the moment. She could complete her task and walk down the other side. Crossing the bridge, she would step down on the far shore, reborn and rejuvenated. Her breasts firmed as if her age was reversing. She would be like the girl in the park, celebrating youth.

At the top it was customary to get the group to pose for a photo together. Kyle had his digital camera ready. Everybody got one group photo for free. Plenty of individual photos would be taken and displayed on the screens in the souvenir shop for them to order prints to take away with them. It was an important part of Kyle's job to ensure everyone had some great memories to buy and keep forever.

'OK,' he shouted, 'I want everyone clustered together. This is the big shot. Let's do a practice cheer.'

They cheered dutifully. It was not enough for Maureen.

'This is the highest point of our trip. We must totally express ourselves.'

The next bout of whooping and cheering was carried aloft by the wind. The flurry of arms waving happily gave Maureen the moment she needed. Crouching down she undid the zip of her jumpsuit and pulled it down to her waist. She slipped her arms out deftly.

'Ready everyone?' Kyle shouted.

'Ready,' they replied.

'Say bridge.' The group shouted 'bridge', threw their arms up and Maureen leapt up as far as her steel tether permitted. Her glorious naked torso sprang out in the middle of the group. She felt like a firework exploding. The photo was taken. Kyle looked on in horror. The others turned and looked silently as Maureen turned her face to the sun.

Eyes closed, she stretched her arms out. The wind blew across her breasts. Her nipples hardened. She had never been freer or more powerful. It was a moment of pure Maureen. She cared for no-one, cared nothing for the eyes that were turned on her. She relished the freedom of not caring. This, she realised, chemical though it may be, was her first truly carefree moment. Her disease-ridden, people-supporting life was miles below her and she gloried in reaching the highest point she could reach. She stood up on her toes and then beyond, going *en point* for the first time in years. As she climbed higher and stretched, she realised she could go no further. This was it, the peak. She gripped the moment tightly, determined that the wind would blow her lump away, determined to make the moment of carefree joy last.

It could not. She felt an infinitesimal lessening, realised she had reached as high as she could. She gloried in the fact and tried to burn the feeling into her mind. She had to save every aspect. Her toes became sore and gradually she returned to normal standing. Lowering her arms, she still did not want to open her eyes and return completely to the world. She had to. She could feel Misty raising her outfit and slipping her arms into it. She opened her eyes and smiled. All astonished eyes were on her. Kyle still held the camera in front of him, having not moved from his shock at the photo he had taken.

'I discovered I have breast cancer today. Here.' Maureen touched her lump. It was still there. She paused, disappointed but not surprised to find it was unaltered. 'I wanted to find out what I was feeling and somehow I . . . I thought this was all so magical, perhaps it would . . .' She stopped. It sounded so ridiculous. 'I'm sorry.'

The group looked at her. Misty cried and Kelvin closed his eyes. One by one, they moved closer. Misty and Kelvin were the first to put their arms around her. The others, trapped by their cables, did their best to get as near to her as possible. They hugged in silence, heads pressed together. The wind picked up hair from different heads, meshed different colours and blurred the outlines. In the middle, Maureen felt this should be her moment of realisation, but it was not. She felt her tears and, even in her chemically-distorted state, she recognised the familiar feeling of gratitude. Her mind tried to claw back that peak moment, but already the memory was fading.

Kyle had to break up the moment. Headquarters were wondering why there was a delay on the top of the bridge. Four groups were now backed up on the ascent, waiting for their moment of glory. He explained to the hugging team that they would cross the top of the bridge, over the roadway and go back down to the Sydney side. Maureen gasped.

'No! We have to go down the other side. We can't go back, not now we have come so far.'

Panic seized Kyle's throat and made his stammered explanations sound like his voice had broken that morning. After Maureen's display he felt there was nothing to stop her stripping off completely, freeing herself of the harness, leaping over the top of the security rail and streaking towards North Sydney.

'It's just not possible,' he attempted to explain, 'the north side of the Bridge is not set up for visitors. You're locked into...' he paused, thinking perhaps it would be best not to mention being locked to the security rail.

'Please,' Kyle was reduced to honest pleading, 'this is my first group. We're already behind schedule. I'll get into trouble as it is.' He dreaded the moment when he would have to hand in his digital camera and his supervisor would see the cause of the delay. He could attempt to wipe the photo but if he lost the other ones, there would be trouble about ruining people's memories. He wondered if heading straight over the bridge to North Sydney and vanishing would be better than climbing back down to HQ. His pained gulping and wide open eyes implored the group to behave.

Corinne saw this as an opportunity to establish some leadership and show the team she knew what the real game was. She and Hubert had assumed Kyle was the plant, and she had worked out from the way Kelvin and Misty had locked themselves into place on either side of Maureen that they thought she was the one to watch out for. Corinne realised that their final test was not a set-up, but a real-life situation. The games were over. There was a genuine choice between mad mutiny or re-establishing order. It was for Corinne to bring the team back to safety.

'We should support Kyle on this,' she spoke out. 'He is the expert. I respect and understand Maureen's views, but our group safety is the main concern.'

'We can negotiate the other side,' said Kelvin. He was unsure if Maureen was a plant. If she was, this was an exercise in striking out collectively to achieve the impossible. If she was not a plant, she was the most wonderful person he had ever met and if she wanted to go the other way, he would do his best to help her. 'We're a team,' he shouted. 'We can do it for Maureen.'

Kyle groaned. He could see the leader of the next group heading up the bridge to see what the problem was. There was nothing more humiliating.

'Please. If we don't go now, we'll all be marched down as fast as possible. One of the other guides is coming.' No pretence at leadership was now possible for Kyle.

'Come on...move.'

This was crunch time for the team builders: return to safety or strike out with Maureen. There was something heroic in her need to reach a different shore, as if a different future awaited all of them on the other side. From where they stood, North Sydney looked like a smaller version of the main city behind them, but Maureen had invested it with mythical status.

Corinne was the first to speak. 'Maureen, you said you wanted to cross the bridge.'

'Yes,' Maureen replied, 'I need to know we've crossed, gone to the other side.' Down from the peak she had reached, over her intense bout of gratitude, Maureen was lost in the pleasantness of standing with the marvellous view, the winds and the luxury of communicating what she wanted at that moment.

'But look.' Corinne pointed across the bridge along the narrow gangway that would take them over the traffic and down the other side. 'That's the other side of the bridge too. We will be crossing the bridge, from left to right, not south to north.'

'Yes,' Hubert jumped onto her argument. 'We will all cross the bridge but in a different way. It's like going into a room and the door closing behind you. You spend hours grouching that the door's closed and you can't get out, but you're so busy grouching you don't see the window was open all the time to let you out.'

'Win, win,' shouted Misty.

'Win, win,' replied the team in unison.

They began to move. Kyle crossed first and hurried his group across with flailing arms. One by one they crossed over until it was Maureen's turn to go. She looked longingly to the north, but the rail to which her safety harness was attached was taking her to the other side. Not the other side she wanted. They didn't understand—this was the apogee of her escape. Walking back down the same side meant she had to return to Maureen's life, face her reality: needy friends, worried husband, fat ankles and her breast. Locked into her rail she felt like a comet, doomed to stay on her trajectory and return to her starting point.

She crossed over, with the hands of Misty and Kelvin touching her on either side. On the descent, the city which had seemed so far away was now all too close. Her orbit had not taken her very far. She had not even managed to cross the water, had not even escaped the affluent set of inner-city suburbs that usually contained her.

'You have been an inspiration,' Misty turned and said to Maureen as they walked down. 'So honest, so open. You're gonna beat this, I just know it.'

Maureen smiled. They really were lovely people. Even as sadness crept in, she felt closer to this group of people than to anyone. They had shared an intense experience, bonded in a way she had never bonded with new acquaintances. She reminded herself it could just be the drug she had taken. It could all be artificial.

'At sundown, silk flowers have no scent,' she said.

Kelvin agreed, assuming it must have some relevance to what Misty had said. It sounded wonderful anyway.

'You're so calm about this, Maureen. I can't begin to understand how it must feel...I mean it must be... like of all canc...diseases...' Kelvin could not bring himself to say what he was thinking. He was thinking it would destroy her as a woman, desex her.

'I'm really not that together. I'm sure I'll fall apart soon.' Maureen sensed his difficulty and wanted to ease it. She smiled, reassuring him that it was alright and then turned away. Still on the bridge, and she was back to Maureen, supporting a man she barely knew through her own disease. The comet was hurtling back to Earth even faster than she had feared.

By the time they reached the pylon and clambered down the steps through the lanes of traffic, Maureen felt like the comet had passed through her mouth. It was parched. Not only that, but she could not stop clenching her teeth. Whenever her mind stopped focussing on it, which was every minute, she found her molars grinding away. She craved chewing gum. Normally she never touched it—a revolting habit, one step up from smoking, but now gum and water were all she could think about. To her relief, Kyle announced they were about to pass a water fountain. Unable to jump the queue because of the safety harnesses, she waited her turn impatiently. Each person seemed to drink deep and long, tormenting her with their access to liquid refreshment. Finally she was able to pounce on the fountain, swallowing in deep gulps over and again, feeling its coolness flow through her body.

Eventually she stopped and saw Misty watching her. Perhaps she had been a little too desperate. It was only at this point that she thought her recent behaviour might have seemed a little untoward. She was suddenly conscious that her every move on the bridge might reveal her mind had been altered by drugs.

'You forget how hot it can get. I was parched!'

'Climbing's hard work,' Misty agreed.

The cool water made Maureen's head spin. She grabbed the rail with her hand. Her other hand went to her head. Even though they were effectively under the bridge in darkened shade, everything became very light. The world was paling and Misty was shouting, as if from the other end of the walkway.

'Maureen, are you OK? Maureen...Kelvin.'

She felt something support her from behind. Her world was subtly varied shades of white. She could just make out Misty.

'Maureen!' Misty hurtled towards her at high speed, making her jolt. She stood right in front of her, staring into her eyes.

'Kyle, call for an ambulance.' Maureen could distinguish Kelvin's voice.

'No,' she interjected. 'I'll be fine.' The last thing she wanted was a paramedic announcing she had overdosed on drugs. It must be an overdose, she thought. That's what happened to junkies.

'It's OK, just a dizzy spell. I'll keep walking.' She moved off slowly. The movement helped her recover. Blood began to flow normally. She felt rather than heard a ringing in her ears, but it abated as she moved. She felt well enough to raise a hand and wave. The section of the team behind her cheered.

Leaning to Misty, she asked, 'Did I say anything?' Misty told her she had said nothing, but had probably passed out with the heat and excitement. Maureen tried to work out if Misty was being politely euphemistic, not mentioning it was obviously a drug-related incident. She might have even put it down to Maureen's 'condition'.

'Kyle, I'm fine, I hope you didn't call for an ambulance or anything,' Maureen said.

Calling in to report something going wrong had been the last thing on Kyle's mind. He suddenly realised that perhaps he should have. This woman might think it a dereliction of his duty of professional care.

'Er, well no, you seemed to recover OK... You'll be fine. Just take it easy when you get home.' Kyle dreaded the assessment forms which were handed out to all climbers on their return. Maureen herself was not convinced. It seemed like he was hiding something. Perhaps the police had been called and they had instructed him not to arouse her suspicions.

As they returned to the building they had started from Maureen could see they were hidden from those departing. She was apprehensive, convinced that Kyle had lined up the narcotics squad to pin her to the floor as soon as she walked back into the centre. She contemplated making a run for it. She would have to just abandon her clothes and bag to their locker. But she would not get far running the streets in an ill-fitting grey suit and a security harness. Evading arrest would be added to her charges. As her options closed in around her, Kyle drew up to have a quiet word.

'I'm sorry about before. I panicked. They didn't train us for people going topless, wanting to climb over to the other side and then fainting. I don't want to lose my job. Please, you don't have to say anything really positive but could you just not mention anything that happened on your assessment form?'

'So there's no ambulance, police or anything waiting for me?'

'No,' Kyle replied, puzzled.

Maureen grabbed him and kissed his cheek.

'Of course I won't say anything bad. You've been wonderful. You handled a very difficult situation mar-vellously. Believe me, you've no idea how well you've done.' Relief flooded her with happiness. She spoke out to the rest of the group just as they were about to enter the door.

'Before we all break up, I'd just like to say what a great group you've all been and thank Kyle for his wonderful work. What a team member!'

'Go Kyle!'

In her cubicle, Maureen was slipping her shoes back on when she began to feel tired. She had been on a journey. It now seemed terribly long and yet so quick. Four hours had passed but it could have been four days or four minutes. However long it was, she was not ready for it to end. Sitting on the bench in her cubicle, she dragged out the moment before she pulled the curtain back. The time wasting was brought to an end by a sudden cheer and her name being called.

Following the sounds she was confronted by a bank of TV screens above the counter in the souvenir shop. On each screen was the same picture from the top of the bridge. With the magnificence of the harbour and the towers of the city in the background the team huddled together cheering and waving their arms. In the middle of them Maureen saw herself, bursting out topless, arms thrust out towards the sky. Like a stripper jumping out of a cake, she thought.

Embarrassment was total until someone pushed a printed copy of the photo into her hand. She looked at it in more detail. It was spectacular. An unrestrained joy was splashed across her face. The team builders in the photo created a chaotic symmetry around her. Now she felt less like a stripper and more like a flower blooming. It was a remarkable scene. The incongruousness of her naked breasts in the middle of a standard tourist photo made it all the more fascinating. She examined the picture. Her face looked young and her lump was invisible. She peered closer, looking for some trace, some dimple, some shadow, but there was nothing. It was as if at that moment it did not exist.

The team insisted on a group drink in the pub across the road. Maureen was given an orange juice to get some goodness inside her. She gulped it down, only to discover a terrible cardboard taste. She grimaced and sent it back. The next glass tasted the same. Corinne tried it and could find nothing wrong. Maureen suspected that the ecstasy had killed her taste buds. This would be her punishment, food and drink would taste like cardboard for ever. The team's excitement at their wonderful achievement bounced around her. She sat silently smiling, signing the photos that were placed in front of her.

She too had achieved. She had been as unMaureen as she possibly could. Sex, drugs, reckless exposure. She felt the satisfaction of real accomplishment: a day off from herself. What in the world could have been more difficult?

The answer came quickly—going home. Going back to face James and reality. Remembering who and what she was made her remember for the first time that today was their little anniversary. She was pleased she had actually managed to forget, just like James always did. Remembering the anniversary meant remembering why they had stopped celebrating. It was the day she had lost their baby.

They had been married four years and had decided she would go off the pill. There would be no fuss or tests, they would just see what happened. She was pregnant within six months. A few weeks later, the morning of their little anniversary brought a searing pain, and it was gone. The pregnancy was over. 'It' never even reached a gender. After that day, it never would; he or she would have meant a human being, not part of her body. 'It' was easier. She had quietly resumed the pill, waiting until she was ready to face the risk again. They did not discuss it. James felt bad for her and did not want to raise painful memories. Maureen felt too guilty. It was she who had lost it, not she and James. She had jerked too fast, stretched too far, not developed properly. Perhaps, if the baby had gone full term, she might not...

'Is it true that women who don't have children are more susceptible to breast cancer?' She asked her silent question aloud and got silence back. The exercise was over. Emotional sharing on the bridge was one thing, confronting questions in the pub were another. No-one responded. There were a few awkward coughs and everyone avoided eye contact. Gradually the team returned to their regular conversations.

Maureen had to go. The looks of panic, discomfort and resentment she saw in that silence were something she would have to get used to. She attempted to leave unnoticed, humiliated at having marred the end of their wonderful day. Close by the door, Misty touched her shoulder.

'I don't think it's true. Nothing's really been proved... Don't mind them,' Misty indicated the team, 'they think the exercise is over but it never is really.' She kissed Maureen on the cheek and let her slip out quietly.

Maureen flagged a cab, got in the back and gave her address—not by choice, but because it was her inevitable trajectory. She had done what she set out to do, but what had she actually achieved? She was no closer to knowing what she felt. Surges of feeling glided through her but were always undefined. The eels surfaced briefly.

Irene would probably be at the house to join James in the 'where have you been' chorus. In her head she played out every line they would say, then what she would reply, followed by what they would say back. Then the script ran out. She had no idea what would happen next. There was a dread about what was to come. But the dread (she could feel and define that much) was more than about what to say. It was a rumbling, something dangerous rising from the deep. It scared her. She had no idea of how to control it or how to pretend she was in control. For the first time in her life, she had no script for herself, just a terrifying blank page.

Party Time

Maureen peered through her living room window. Existence, which was supposed to have continued unchanged in her absence, had altered dramatically. In place of her living room was an ocean. Her friends sat round with glum expressions. 'I'm dead,' she thought. 'This is my wake.' She looked towards the living room door and saw her reflection framed by the doorway.

There was something secure about seeing her image there. It was what these people were looking for. James started to speak. Maureen saw he was stumbling and knew she had to resume her role in this life. Destiny held a familiar comfort.

'There's something...' James said, 'I haven't... Maureen...'

He stopped and looked at the door, hoping even at this last moment she would appear to save him from saying it aloud for the first time.

'I think someone is supposed to shout "surprise", aren't they?' Maureen said to prove she was alive.

'Surprise,' they mumbled incoherently.

'James,' she came over to kiss her husband, smiling to mask the fear that she would taste different, 'this is incredible. You remembered, you did all this. I must admit I was expecting something, but not this. What fun...Irene, I'm so sorry. I thought I'd disappear to make organising things easier and add a little element of surprise myself. Nicole, yes it was me on the bridge. I had to do something to fill in the time. You looked so shocked. Had a bad run? Stephen—I'm sure you helped on the construction here, thank you, and Tanya, how did Taekwondo go? Any medals to show off?'

'But your phone?' Irene and James said in unison.

'You have no idea how liberating it is, switching your phone off for the whole day. Sheer bliss! You should all do it, just for one day...have I time for a drink?'

'No!' Ulrika burst out of the kitchen and through the hall. 'To table now. I cannot wait one second more.' She looked Maureen up and down. 'Good of you to join us'. She tutted and returned to her domain.

'She's a gem,' Maureen cried to James. 'I must change. Down in a second,' and she vanished up the stairs.

'What the hell's going on?' Stephen put their collective confusion bluntly. 'I thought you were going to announce a divorce or something.'

'You'd like that, wouldn't you?' Irene replied.

'Everything seems fine,' Tanya interrupted before Stephen could retaliate.

'Is she really OK?' Nicole asked James. 'What were you going to say?'

'Nothing...She seems fine, but...'

'Come on.' Irene stood up and beckoned to Nicole to follow her upstairs. 'Girl talk time.' She looked at Tanya and hesitated.

'Not my strong point,' Tanya replied. 'I'll stay here.'

'Quelle surprise,' Irene muttered, heading to the door.

On the bed lay Maureen's photo from her Bridge Climb in its presentation folder. Irene and Nicole eyed it as they sat on the bed, waiting for Maureen to return from the shower, neither wanting to be the first to peek. Nicole gave in, opened it up, squealed and closed it again.

'Oh my God!' she mouthed to Irene, putting her hand to her chest melodramatically. Irene peeked and shrieked. They sat facing each other, both trying to open their mouths widest in shock, like they had caught the head girl smoking behind the bike sheds. They looked again.

'It's a great photo. They look fantastic. She's still got it!' Nicole commented.

'Not for long.' In their surprise, they had not heard the shower turn off and Maureen return.

'What d'you mean?' Irene sensed something behind Maureen's chirpiness.

'Boobs don't last forever…they'll be round my navel in no time.'

'Maureen, sit down and tell us what is going on. Disappearing, topless pictures on the Harbour Bridge. Are you having an affair?' Irene wanted to get to the bottom of it.

'No, everything's fine.'

The shower had felt lovely—cool and refreshing. Her skin, more sensitive than normal, was tingling. She felt good, happy to be on familiar ground after pushing herself into new territory all day. She did not want to spoil the party. She could not say anything to the girls before she spoke to James; she had to wait for the right moment. Excuses flowed effortlessly.

Downstairs James sat back in his chair, relaxed at last. For once he had read Maureen's mind. He knew everything. The lump he had been avoiding had been tested and everything was fine. She would not have breezed in like that if there was a problem, he reasoned. Even Maureen could not be that good at putting on a brave face.

The girls were safe; relief swept over him. His wife was back, their friends were around, the living room was a sensation and there was more entertainment in store. It was going to be a wonderful evening.

'Rocks off the starboard bow.' His satisfaction was interrupted as the soundscape plunged into music James only knew as the theme from *The Onedin Line*.

Stephen was trying to shift blame for the book onto Tanya. James interrupted, not wanting the topic raised again.

'Whoever's fault it was, it's a sure-fire way of getting Irene to tear the walls down. Don't talk about it, OK?'

'Fine.' Tanya scowled at Stephen. It was bad enough being sidelined in the row, but to then be blamed for it was stretching her endurance. This sniping at each other was too couply. It was not what they normally did but the urge to carry on was strong. His accusation was so unfair, like the trouble she used to get into at St Angela's.

Ulrika waited at the bottom of the stairs for the Reenies and Nicole to appear. As soon as they did, she ordered them to the table.

'I will wait no longer. Bethnee, David, serve the entrees,' she screamed. 'Jasper, stay in the kitchen. I have need of you.'

The girls hurried down and James' party finally boarded his ship. At last, it set sail with a full complement of passengers chuckling with delight as they discovered its gentle rocking motion.

'James, you are so clever.' Maureen was touched by the effort he had gone to. She remembered her anger in the flower shop that morning. It seemed so petulant now. The gleeful giggling around the table, the promise of a fun night, made her feel like the wicked witch bringing her curse to the party.

Bethnee and David mounted the gangplank with plates of entrees in hand, wobbling slightly as they strove to find their sea legs. As each entree was positioned, they whispered, 'A trio of seafood pan-fried in dill butter on a bed of steamed watercress with savoury millefeuille crown,' to the recipient. Each guest heard the same description, whispered with a reverence drilled by Ulrika all afternoon.

'A toast,' declared Tanya, holding her glass of water aloft. 'To James and Maureen and the day they first met.' Sitting quietly was not going to make the evening go any faster, she thought. Everyone raised their glasses. Stephen attempted to kick her under the table. She knew it was his and Irene's anniversary too.

'Salut,' said Irene, raising her glass to her hosts at either end of the table. '*Oui puisque je retrouve un ami si fidèle, ma fortune va prendre une face nouvelle.*'

'We'll just assume that's aimed at me and let it pass. Cheers.' Stephen felt under siege from all sides.

'See if I can get it.' Nicole was with Irene. 'If I find a love so faithful, my fortune will take a new turn.'

'Not bad,' smiled Irene.

'You can't let it rest, can you?' Stephen shook his head patronisingly at Irene.

'Actually, it's the opening line from Racine's *Andromaque*,' she beamed at him, 'where the hero finds his long-lost best friend and is so happy to see him again he feels his destiny must be brighter. I was celebrating Maureen's return to us. Our future can only be better with her presence.'

'One, nil,' Nicole coughed into her napkin.

'Thank you, Irene. You always know the perfect thing to say!' Maureen took the interpretation at face value.

'So, how's the entree?' asked James, eager to move on. Murmurs of 'delicious' went around the table.

'Maureen, what on earth were you doing in Darlinghurst this lunchtime?' Stephen thought he was starting pleasant conversation.

'Darlinghurst?'

'Yes, I saw you disappear down a back alley.'

'Must have been my evil twin running drugs, couldn't have been me.' Maureen realised that it must have been Stephen calling her name.

'It was you...What?' he turned to Tanya who had kicked him under the table, 'What? What's wrong. You saw her too?'

'No, Stephen, I was focussing on the Trinity and you were driving.'

'But I'm sure.' Another kick. He raised his eyebrows

at Tanya and she responded with a grunt. She had sensed there was something strange about Maureen's disappearance. Everyone else had seemed to accept her absence so readily. Perhaps they needed to believe everything was fine.

James said nothing. All he could do was look at Maureen with delight. His worst fears had been allayed. It was so like her to go for the test on her own, find out everything was fine and not worry anyone. In bed tonight he would take her breasts in his hands like he always used to. He would ask her about it, safe in the knowledge that it was all sorted out. Perhaps he should have been there with her, he thought. But then she coped better on her own, that was the Maureen way. His hurt at being left out was lost in the relief at not having to deal with it. He loved her with a passion, he would do anything for her, but emotional support was not his strong point. He got so little practice.

Maureen swayed delicately in front of the corn-flower sea. She had never looked more beautiful. Her skin was lucid and she had a vague almost serene look. The day on her own, her good news, a bit of self-indulgence had obviously done her good. She was looking at Nicole, reacting with alarm at her predica-ment. He decided he should rejoin the table talk.

'So you really punched this guy out at The Milk Bar?' James asked.

'Yes, it happens all the time. The other drivers send a guy over who doesn't know. He gets angry, throws a punch, I beat him up and the lads all give me ten bucks. It's an ongoing bet, but Louie's done me over completely now.'

'So you punch guys out for the money?' Stephen was impressed but offended. 'It's not their fault if they're not politically correct enough to deal with you.'

'So she should just let them beat her up, because they're thick?' Irene retorted.

'No, but she should make allowances. I mean it's not easy for me, does that mean you're going to beat me up?'

'Let me get my ten dollars before you answer that, Nicole,' said Irene. They all laughed, except for Stephen.

'She rubs their faces in it and then kicks the shit out of them for not understanding.'

'Christ, Stephen, they're not school kids. They're grown men and he's more than got his own back. My driving career is stuffed and I've still got a truck to pay off...and besides, I don't have to explain myself to anyone, not them, not you. I'm comfortable with who I am and what I am. I'm Nicole, it's that simple.'

'No, you're not. You're Tom trying to be Maureen,' Stephen retorted. A groan of disbelief went round the table.

'Shit, Stephen.' James looked at him, wondering

where the delightful friend who had helped him all afternoon had disappeared.

'Come on, let's be honest. You want to be Maureen.'

'Stephen, please.' Maureen could see everyone getting uncomfortable.

'You see how gooey she is around James, and Christ, look at her tits, she had them modelled on yours. It's obvious. Took a picture of you in and said "I want to look like her" as if she was getting her hair styled.'

'That's the limit. Really Stephen, apologise...' said Irene

'No.' He folded his arms.

'It's out now. I always knew it, at least it's out,' announced Nicole, tossing her fork onto her plate.

'Anyone would think he's still your husband,' Tanya said to Irene, annoyed that Irene got her outrage in first, and even more annoyed that she agreed with her.

'Someone has to keep his worst excesses in check. You don't seem interested,' Irene replied.

'Look what you've done now. We can't have a normal conversation without you turning it round to your body,' Stephen shouted at Nicole.

'I'm not into controlling my partner. He's not a child,' Tanya said.

'Isn't he?' Irene retorted, pointing at him waving his arms and shouting at Nicole.

'Please,' James said to no-one in particular as two

arguments raged across the table between him and Maureen. Words flew off at angles, colliding in the middle of the table in a heap of babble. James looked desperately at Maureen. His plea had been to her. This was her role: soothing and healing.

She stared back at him, the vagueness which had seemed serene now was a barrier between her and the cacophony around them. She could hear the words, she knew what was expected. Even the arguers glanced at her, waiting for her intervention. It was their cue to stop. Without it no-one knew if it could end. The soundscape, which had been drowned out by the shouting and finger-stabbing, resurfaced with a deafening boom of a fog horn. It continued until the voices stopped. As it finished Maureen looked at James and announced into the silence. 'I have breast cancer.'

•

Michael and Janine, now identifying as Units One and Two of Urban Terror, were waiting on the street corner of the target house. The whole squad could not fit in a taxi with all their guns and equipment, so Units One and Two had taken the first cab and were waiting for Units Three and Four (Sasha and Colin). After twenty minutes a car pulled round the corner and went past them. Sasha screamed stop, the cab screeched to a halt and reversed down the road to the commanding officers.

'Where have you been?' Unit One demanded.

'You said we were supposed to take a different route to avoid suspicion, so we went via my house because I'd forgotten to set the video.' Unit Four was having problems extinguishing all vestiges of Colin.

'I don't think Hezbulla delay their actions to set the video,' Michael said testily.

The crack squad stood on the street corner, guns waving around as they argued about whether terrorists did everyday activities like setting the video.

'If we were terrorists, this would be part of our everyday lives,' Sasha pressed the point. 'It'd be just like a normal job and you would be thinking about things like the video and the washing-up.'

'Especially if you had a walk-on part being broadcast for the first time,' added Colin.

'I'm just being realistic,' continued Sasha. 'Terrorists use the toilet too. They don't just do terror, you know.'

'You want the toilet now?' Michael was getting exasperated.

'Their point may have some validity, Commander. For complete realism we should be assuming the whole lives of terrorists, not just the dramatically satisfying parts.' Janine was committed to complete verisimilitude.

'I accept your point, Unit Two, but as commander

I would probably punish troops arriving late for action with death. As leader, more than anyone, I must live and breathe our cause. This is not play-acting. We're making the most important statement that any of us have ever made. Remember that.'

'Besides, I went to the toilet while Colin was setting the video. You did do Channel 9, didn't you?' Unit Three always turned off when Michael started on his theoretical kicks.

'Attention,' cried Janine, asserting her Unit Two character.

No-one on the street appeared the slightest bit concerned that four terrorists were standing around with guns and stabbing at each other with their fingers.

'Synchronise watches.' Units One and Two managed that procedure, Unit Three did not have a watch and Unit Four didn't know how to alter the time on his.

'We're due at 11.00 pm precisely. I want no arguments. We are in deep personae now. This mission depends entirely on split-second timing. My orders must be followed precisely and immediately. Now, let's move into position across the street from the target house. Unit Two, you have the address.'

Unit Two had left the address in her civvies but did have a mobile phone from which she could call Justin to confirm the street number. They moved off to reconnoitre the target house and ready the invasion.

Michael's nerves were taut. He could rely on Janine, the perfect second in command. She understood his vision: the redefinition of theatre away from concocted entertainments to real experiences. As virtual reality games became more and more realistic, so drama had to follow. To do that it must leave the theatre and invade homes. The other two were a liability, but he could carry them with sheer force of will: they were actors after all. Michael was Urban Terror now. He carried the burden of leadership and the knowledge of what lay ahead. He focussed on his goal: scaring the wits out of these complacent bastards; giving them a taste of real emotion, raw and unedited.

His entire plan depended on gagging James Ting before he could say anything. It would not be hard to identify the host, but they only had a matter of seconds to do it.

9.00 pm

James stared at Maureen. She had fooled him. Pretended so brilliantly, hidden what he thought no-one could hide. It seemed so cold. The truth brought what he had dreaded all along: visions of his mother. She had died of lung cancer when he was sixteen, a progression from a late diagnosis of breast cancer. She had gone into hospital to have 'a little problem' fixed, and died six months later with one hair-free armpit and cough that followed him everywhere. The first he had learned that her condition was serious was walking into hospital and seeing her sitting up in bed. Her loose front-buttoned nightdress, a blue-checked pattern she had worn as long as he could remember, was undone at the top. There was a flat bandage where her breast had been hacked off. As he stared at it she said apologetically, 'It was more serious than they thought.' She had lied to him too.

Maureen knew what he was thinking. In his eyes, she could see herself turning from his wife into his mother, from sex object to mutilated old woman. His look reminded her of how the girls were her lush sexuality, her cornerstone of desire. Once they had tried making love without him touching them. It was supposed to be a tantalising game and a catalyst for exploring new ground. They had given up within minutes by mutual consent. Why deny yourself a joy that was so good for you?

What would she be without one of the girls? They were like their children, separate entities which James would mourn in their own right. There was no avoiding the reflection of that flat scar in James' eyes. He looked puzzled, hurt and horrified.

Maureen felt someone touch her hand. Another hand touched her shoulder. Irene and Nicole had come round to support her. She broke the stare with James.

'I'm sorry...I only found out for definite today. That's why I didn't meet you, Irene. I just...'

No-one responded. They needed the Maureen they knew.

'Sit down, girls. It's not a death sentence. It's a fairly early diagnosis. We don't know how much will have to be removed, but there's every chance of a full recovery. Things have changed a lot in recent years. Real advances.' The last sentence was addressed to James. She was attempting to shake him out of his staring. She needed something from him, some support in her supporting everyone else. He said nothing.

'Now, we're all going to have to be strong and, naturally, I'll need your support.'

James came to.

'Will you?' he asked.

'Of course.' They looked at each other again.

Nicole gripped her hand again, stretching across the table.

'We're here for you, both of you. All of us.' There was a chorus of agreement. Tanya smiled awkwardly. She felt out of place, a door-to-door saleswoman calling during a funeral.

'I'll have a meeting with a surgeon in the next week or so. He'll run through the options. Apparently there are several. Then we schedule surgery. There's tests and follow-ups, more decisions about what I...' Maureen stopped. Perhaps this was too much detail. She used to be able to judge exactly what people wanted to hear, but now she was not so sure.

'Enough time for that.' She could see Stephen had put his hand under the table and was probably touching James. She was pleased.

A flutter of relief passed through her. She had said it. They had heard it. Life was continuing.

'Do you want us to leave? Perhaps the two of you should be alone.' Tanya broke the silence in the hope that the answer was yes.

'No. Thank you, Tanya. I would rather you all stayed.

271

Tonight is a celebration. I want to celebrate.' She raised her glass.

'To life.'

Everyone echoed her toast, except James. He drained his glass.

'That was delicious. I'm ready for the next course.' Maureen turned and smiled to Bethnee, who had retreated as far away from the ship as possible. She came forward to collect the entree plates.

'Tell Ulrika that was splendid. Now, how did you get on this afternoon?'

Maureen turned to Tanya as her best hope for conversation. She could not look at Irene or Nicole. There were too many tears already on their side of the table. James was like marble. Stephen would only say something dreadful without meaning it. Tanya, strong and controlled, was her only hope. She read the pleading in Maureen's question.

'Well, it was a bit of disaster.' She recounted her experience. Maureen sat back, listening. Everyone focussed on Tanya's story. Even Irene clung to her words, allowing herself to be drawn back to normality.

'So they can actually copyright certain moves?' she asked, determined to do her bit in the rescue. Slowly the conversation returned. Stephen talked about the bodybuilders, omitting details of Merissa, but entertaining them with stories of Hot Stuff, red wine and pumped up veins.

The effort of recreating the conversation exhausted Maureen. The coping reassurance that was once so effortless was draining. Now the conversation flowed without her determined guidance, she could leave it. A couple of minutes alone were all she needed and then she could carry on. She took her moment and slipped off down the gangplank to the downstairs toilet next to the kitchen door. She could hear it swinging as the main course was being carried to the table.

She was back to Maureen playing the role she had to play. The day off was over. Her hands clenched. They were claws when she thought of the way James looked at her. He was so lost in his memories and his fears he could barely see her. She felt his pain as always but wanted to shout 'What about me?' She longed to focus her attention entirely on herself like she had done during the day, but it was impossible with other people around. She could not help her energy being taken up by those she loved and she could not help resenting them for it.

Solitude was the only escape, but it was lonely. She would have to return to the ship. She opened the door just as Jasper was returning to the kitchen, having delivered the last dishes to the table and removed used plates. The door almost hit him in the face and the plates wobbled in his hand.

'I'm sorry,' she said.

'Lydia!'

'Cole!'

It was the first time Jasper had seen the guest of honour. She froze, expecting to be horrified that the sex worker she had paid that afternoon was serving food in her own house. She was not. She was delighted as he held his one free arm out.

'I didn't connect. How are you?' He stood back, holding her shoulder and looking into her eyes.

'I still don't know... Could you just hold me for a moment?'

He turned her around so her back was pressed to him. His free hand moved down her dress and cupped her breast.

'Thank you,' she whispered. The feel of the shameless hand reminded Maureen of herself.

At the dinner table no-one wanted to ask if Maureen was OK. It seemed too glib, but her continued absence meant something had to be done.

'Perhaps James, you should go and check?' Irene suggested.

'Did you take the E?' Jasper whispered in the hall.

'Yes, on the Harbour Bridge.'

He laughed and plates in his hand rattled. 'I'm Jasper, by the way.'

'Maureen. Nice to meet you.'

'Are you OK?' James voice called out as he rounded the door into the hallway.

Maureen looked at him as if she had been waiting. Jasper froze.

'What the hell's going on?' James demanded.

The rumblings that Maureen had felt during the day surged up. She decided to shout and let the anger out.

'He's doing what you haven't. He's touching my breast, not part of it, not the nipple, the whole cancerous thing.'

'This boy's your lover?'

'No, he's a sex worker. I hired him this afternoon to make love to me. It's pure coincidence he's here.'

James took a step back.

'Who are you?' he asked, meeting the new fury in her eyes.

'He noticed, James. He noticed and he touched and he made me feel good and...I don't know who I am.'

As discreetly as possible, Jasper removed his hand from Maureen's breast and stepped backwards into the kitchen with his plates.

Maureen wanted to gouge out James' chest with her bare hands. He had not touched her, he had avoided everything and now he had ruined her one moment of pure Maureen.

'How could you do this to me?' he said.

The day which was supposed to be about her was now about him: his pain, his bewilderment. In her anger she could still feel his pain, but she resisted the urge to comfort.

'I won't say sorry.'

'Look at what I've done for you. All this...' his hand weakly indicated his wonderful creation, '...for you and all the time you were screwing some boy?'

'Poor you, poor poor James. How you must be suffering!' The words had a cruel familiarity. They looked down at the square black and white tiles of the hall floor, set out in a diamond pattern. They had chosen the tiles themselves.

'The dinner will be getting cold.' Maureen walked past him and back into the living room.

As she entered, Irene picked up her fork and started eating. The guests had been sitting in silence, pretending not to listen to the argument. The rage that had exploded in the hall was like nothing they had experienced. Irene decided the best they could do was pretend nothing had happened.

'So, Tanya, tell me more about the Taekwondo?' she asked, hoping it looked like conversation had been continuing. Tanya took the cue.

'It's about control, creating an equilibrium, between the mind, body and spirit.'

'Sounds almost like a religion,' Nicole said pleasantly.

'In a way,' Tanya replied as Maureen squeezed past her chair.

'She has to control her body completely. It's amazing, like she could stop herself being ill or anything,' Stephen added, causing another kick from Tanya.

'It's OK, really. I understand,' said Maureen. The journey across the sea floor and onto the ship were enough for her to regain control. 'I felt like that this afternoon, like I could just push it out of my body.' She felt a waft of wind from the top of the bridge. 'Bodies are amazing. It's like we try to control them all the time, when really they're who we are. I thought, when I found out, I wish it had been my ankles. I'd happily cut my ankles off, but I suppose the parts we hate are as much us as the parts we love.'

In the unreality of whether the hall scene had actually taken place, James wanted to reach out and help Maureen. Somewhere in his rage was a new sensation of being needed. Within the confusion and anger he could see she needed this evening to work, whatever else might happen. She needed this dinner party to work and she needed his help. Together they could make something even more impressive than his ship. It was a start.

'I'd cut off my hands,' he said. 'They're so clumsy, they can't do anything.'

'But...' Maureen was about to say how she loved their strength, but it was not the time for vague comforts.

'If I could disconnect my brain sometimes, I'd love it,' Irene added. 'You can think too much, sometimes.' She glanced at Stephen and held his eye for a moment.

It was down to the other three to say what body part they hated. Forks clinked on plates and mouthfuls of salmon were chewed. Nicole broke the silent stand-off.

'I still miss my penis,' she said.

'Oh Christ,' Stephen groaned, earning a 'shut up' from everyone at the table. Nicole was the only one to do what they had discussed. She had achieved the ultimate body control.

'I hated it so much, there were times when I pressed a knife to it myself. Then, when it wasn't there anymore, I missed it. I didn't want it back, but I'd wake up in the morning, put my hand down and get a shock, because in my mind I could still feel it. Sometimes, in my dreams, it's still there and it's like seeing an old friend. I don't hate it any more, it's not making me something I'm not.'

'At school, the girls said I had a boy's shoulders,' Tanya went next. 'They found out how boyish when I punched them. I hated anyone mentioning them, hated having to get school blouses that hung loose round my waist and neck just so they would fit my shoulders.'

They waited for Stephen's contribution. He continued eating as if oblivious to the pressure. He looked up to see all eyes on him.

'So I'm perfect, what can I say...? I suppose you think I might have wanted to change my skin, but I never have. I think my father did. He always wanted us to be as Australian as possible, but I love my skin. There's nothing quite like smooth Asian skin.' He looked at Tanya and Irene for agreement. Irene shrugged, unable to disagree.

10.00 pm

By the time the course was finished, Maureen had effected another rescue. They took a break from the table. For James, there were two Maureens in the house, the charming hostess at the table and the mad banshee in the hall. He preferred the hostess, but thoughts of the banshee consumed him.

Maureen and Irene crouched down to look closely at Xavier as the motionless mermaid lay on the floor.

'I hope he has a good chiropractor, lying with his head like that for hours on end,' Irene said and then added without pausing for breath, 'everything OK?'

'I don't know,' Maureen smiled and whispered, 'we've never been here before.' She stood up and surveyed the wall of flowers.

'It all looks so different, it's hard to believe this is where I live.'

'I don't know what to say,' Irene attempted.

'None of us does...I...'

She could not have finished the sentence even if she had wanted to. Ulrika demanded loudly that the dessert be served. Finally, a lifetime after his own attempt, James sat down to 'Soft Meringue with Muscat-poached Fruit and Vanilla Marscapone'. It was as delicious as he had imagined it would be.

The rich indulgence of the dessert was a blessing. It was the excuse they needed to cram everything into the 'tomorrow' box and squash the lid down. At last, James could look at Maureen and see the woman he had spent the day worrying about.

Ulrika had condescended to come through and congratulate James on his choice. It had seemed a nice gesture until she hurled the block of his attempt at marscapone onto the middle of the table. It had been in the freezer since the morning and still boasted the blue flecks from the kitchen wipe he had used to strain it.

After the dessert, they risked moving away from the table again and back to the chairs. Irene was calm, she had stopped sniffing at everything Stephen said, trying to get wind of a trap. Every now and again she glanced at Maureen, trying to see in.

The movement from the ship broke the conversation and a silence descended. They all spoke at once, afraid it might take hold and leave them with their thoughts. James' voice prevailed.

'So, Tanya, exactly which Taekwondo move was copyrighted?'

This brought back the unifying experience. Words and comfort returned. James took advantage of this to go to the kitchen and congratulate Ulrika on a magnificent meal. As he walked towards the kitchen, Bethnee and David came out to clear the table.

Jasper was wiping Maureen's granite bench top as James entered. His body was stretched across it, chest pressed onto the surface.

'Where's Ulrika?' James asked.

'Here,' she answered, walking in through the back door.

'I just wanted to congratulate you,' James said, watching Jasper wring out the kitchen wipe he had caressed the bench with. His hands were deft and precise. They used the cloth for its proper use, not for making dessert.

'I need no feedback. I know it was magnificent. Jasper, go out for your break now. Here.' She tossed him a packet of cigarettes and Jasper walked out. She looked at James. 'I have never been upstaged. I am supposed to be the star of my dinner parties. Tonight everyone was more crazy than Ulrika.'

James shrugged his shoulders. She looked to the back door.

'Here,' she slid a cigarette lighter across the bench top, 'he'll be needing this.'

James hesitated. Jasper was the person he had really

come to see, but talking to him would destroy the illusion that he had not seen his hand on Maureen's breast.

Outside Jasper was leaning against the wall, looking into the dark of the garden. James held up the lighter. Jasper took it and put it in his pocket.

He shuffled his feet and they both coughed.

'I should be giving you a hiding and telling you to stay away from my wife.'

'It's...' Jasper started to speak, but James ignored him and continued.

'But it was all her doing. She hired you.'

'Don't be hard on her.'

'I don't need excuses from you. Was she...?' James struggled. Part of him wanted to talk about how great sex with Maureen was. This was the first man who would know what he meant when he talked about that look, that clutch, that 'beautiful little dip'.

'I think she needed something that was just her, something that wasn't shared.' Jasper attempted an explanation. He waited for a response, none came so he continued. 'She needed to be touched on her breast and that was all I did. We didn't make love.'

'No. You're supposed to be in love to do that.'

'We didn't have penetrative sex.' Jasper broke client confidentiality. Maurice would not be happy, but this was an unusual situation. He had not actually broken the news to James, Maureen had done that. He thought he might be able to help.

James could not work out what it was he was expecting from standing in his own backyard discussing his wife with a prostitute. He wanted to ask what it was like. He wanted to know every detail: sticking his hand in the wasps' nest over and again to ensure he knew every different sting.

More than anything he needed to know if this boy had been inside his wife. Was he lying when he said no? He might be protecting his client.

Jasper continued, as if answering the question James could not ask.

'We lay on the bed, I touched her breasts and caressed her. I did touch her…but there was no kissing. She wouldn't kiss.'

'Is this good?' thought James. It was more confusing—no sex, no kissing, but intimacy. It would have been easier if Maureen had gone the whole hog—a passionate tongue-entwining, thrusting encounter, an aggressive lust he could relate to. That would have been betrayal, clear and simple, but what Jasper described made it harder to understand.

'I can't work out if she's even been unfaithful!' he said in frustration. 'What the hell was it all about?'

'It was about her,' Jasper began.

'I didn't expect an answer.' James cut him off, and then relented, 'Go on.'

'I think she needed something that was just about her, something wildly irresponsible that she didn't have to share with anyone. By paying me, it was just hers.'

'So why not do the full thing?'

'Guess she couldn't completely escape her love for you.'

'Now you're fucking *me*. You're good, I'll give you that.' James felt himself giving in to the argument and resisted.

Jasper looked him in the eyes. 'I can fuck you, but it'll cost.'

'I don't think so.'

Jasper shrugged his shoulders. 'I'm telling you what happened and how I saw it. It's obvious she loves you, but she's confused, scared she's not attractive anymore, terrified you'll look at her and see an ugly hole. For the first time in her life she's having to think about what she wants and it's not easy.'

'I think I know my own wife,' James growled.

'Do you? You didn't know what she needed more than anything was for you to touch her lump.'

James grabbed Jasper's shirt collar and pushed him hard against the wall.

'Don't you dare,' he spat. His hands firmed their

grip on the shirt collar. James could feel his blood squeezing through his fingers.

'Hit me if you want, but it'll do nothing to help Maureen. Is this what she needs? You've organised a bloody circus and all *she* wants is to be held. She comes home from the worst day of her life and she's looking after everyone else's needs. She's in there and you're out here making this all about you. It's not about you, it's about her, you selfish pig. I was trying to smooth things over because I care about Maureen. I thought she needed you, but frankly she might be better off without you.'

Tears crept into James' eyes. He was losing his anger. He wanted to be passionately jealous and wallow in his hurt pride. He wanted to take it all out on this boy, but it was sliding away. Maureen was what was important and he resented having this boy make it clear. As his fingers loosened their grip, even that resentment could not hold. Jasper meant well.

'I need to know you've been telling me the truth. You told me everything?' he asked.

'Yes.'

James gave in to his tears. Jasper let him cry without comfort. He calmed down after a few moments of sobbing, too confused to reason everything out.

'I thought you were having a cigarette break,' he

said to Jasper. Normal conversation was the closest he could come to an apology.

'I don't smoke. I think Ulrika set us up.'

'I do love Maureen, she's...she's the most incredible person I've met.'

'She is.'

James was about to answer when a loud crack came from inside the house. The shudder it created down James' spine was familiar.

'That'll be Ulrika's ladle on the granite bench top. I swear she's determined to smash it before the day's out.'

'I suppose we should go in,' Jasper suggested. He held up the lighter and flicked it on, looking at James' face in its little light.

'No visible tears.'

'Thanks...I think,' replied James.

Ulrika was summoning them back. The bench top was intact, but she wanted to serve coffee and petit fours.

'Why don't you come and join us for coffee, Ulrika?' James suggested. A verbal thank you for her intervention with Jasper would be too much. An invitation would suffice.

10.55 pm

'Christ, how much longer? I'm sure I've got a worm slithering up my leg.' Unit Four was irritated with having had to crawl on his belly across the road, underneath a truck, and then lie still on the Tings' front lawn. Unit Two put a finger to her lips. A false move at this stage could ruin everything.

Unit Three was on her back, doing leg stretches. Having lain down so long, and knowing that the operation required a top-speed sprint to the kitchen, she did not want a cramp ruining progress.

Unit Two felt in her pocket. The duct tape was ready. Her role was crucial. Michael's vision depended on the speed with which they could identify Ting and she could gag him. As they had waited across the road, Michael had made her practise on Unit Four. First she tried tearing off a strip of tape and applying it to Colin's mouth, but that had taken too long. She tried applying the roll directly to his mouth and stretching it across, but she could not find the end in time. Finally she had perfected the technique. With the end of the roll folded over, she whipped the tape from her pocket, pulled out a stretch, clamped it onto the mouth and then tore the piece off. From pocket to sealed mouth in three seconds. Michael was satisfied. Colin was less than satisfied. The constant taping had exfoliated one layer of skin too many.

Unit One was sweating. He had never perspired like this in his life. It was a warm evening and they were fully dressed, but even so he was over-damp. The pressure of control, the need for perfection and the sense of destiny all agitated. Excitement and fear waged a wet war across his back.

11.00 pm

The conversation had survived in the living room without James. The girls were sitting in the chairs. Stephen and Tanya were leaning against the bow of the ship.

'Why d'you keep siding with Irene?' Stephen asked, swilling wine around in his glass.

'Didn't realise I was your personal cheer squad,' Tanya replied. 'Besides, I've had nothing but glowers since I brought that book in.'

'Don't start on that. You nearly triggered World War Three.'

'Why are you snapping? What happened to you today?'

'This whole body-sharing thing's too much for me. I'm not your emotional bonding type.'

'It's not what I was expecting. Poor Maureen.'

'Poor James.'

'She's the one going to having her breast removed.'

'Exactly...look, I'm sorry this has all thrown me and earlier, well, I knew we were going to have the "where are we going?" conversation before the night's out and...'

Tanya smiled. She could relate to his feelings on that.

'I guess we have to be honest, mate. I just don't know.'

'Yom Chi, that's the tenet of...' Tanya did not have time to say 'integrity' before she was interrupted by the noise of gunfire. Two balaclava-clad people burst into the room. Behind them another two ran to the kitchen.

'Everyone face down on the floor,' shouted the first from behind his mask. 'NOW!' He held his gun up and fired. The noise ricocheted round. Nicole screamed, Maureen and Irene gasped at each other and followed the instructions. Tanya moved to attack, thinking a lightning strike could get him down. Stephen grabbed her hand and pulled her to the floor. It was no time for heroics. Ulrika raised her ladle, only to have it ripped out of her hand and thrown to the floor by Unit Two. Defenceless, she lowered herself quickly.

James' look of horror was different from the others. He had forgotten about the entertainment. His hilarious *pièce de résistance* could ruin everything they had worked so hard to maintain. He moved towards the assailants, holding one arm out. The original Captain Bloodbath would have been inappropriate. This full-scale invasion was even more so. It was not what he had ordered.

'Don't, James!' shouted Maureen from the floor. 'Do as he says.'

'Him!' Unit One pointed at James. Unit Two pounced with the duct tape, sealed his mouth before he could speak and tied his hands behind him with more tape.

'Mmmm.'

'Shut it.' Unit One pushed James into a chair. Unit Two pointed a gun at his head.

'Right, you,' he pointed to Irene. 'Sit there.' She took up a seat. He directed everyone to take a seat except Nicole. The terror of her afternoon charged back. She was being singled out for a reason.

'Stand up,' the man shouted. She could not move.

'Stand up!' he shouted louder, coming over and shoving her with his foot.

'Leave her alone, you thug,' Irene shouted. Unit One turned from his position next to Nicole and pointed his gun at Irene's head. He took a step, leaned close so the end of the barrel was two centimetres away from her forehead.

'Don't worry, it'll be your turn next.'

'What about that one, Commander?' Unit Two indicated the mermaid on the floor. 'She hasn't moved.'

'Get up, bitch!' Unit One screamed. There was no movement.

'It's a dummy,' said Maureen. 'Part of the nautical theme. Ship, sea, mermaid.' The commander leaned close, and shoved the mermaid's arm. It was heavy like a real one, but he could see no signs of breathing.

James looked at Maureen. His eyes were wide, trying desperately to say that it was all an act. He attempted to smile and shake his head chirpily behind the duct tape but every gesture made him look more desperate. Maureen closed her eyes briefly and nodded. She discreetly pressed the palm of her hand downward, suggesting he try to calm down.

'We are Urban Terror,' the commander announced as he pulled a sobbing Nicole to her feet.

The staff in the kitchen were caught completely unaware as Units Three and Four burst in. Unit Four ushered them to the far corner, while Unit Three checked the door to ensure no-one followed them in.

'All clear,' she said.

'Thank God for that,' answered Unit Four, pulling his balaclava off. 'This wool's giving me a rash. Janine practically ripped all my skin off. Hi!'

He turned to the hostages and introduced himself while Unit 3 removed her balaclava and placed her gun on the marble slab.

'Mmm, those look good. I'm starving.' She indicated the petit fours. She looked at the terrified faces.

'Wow, you're really scared! We were convincing! That's great, isn't it, Colin?'

'Have I got a rash?' he asked, holding his chin up to the light.

'What is this?' Jasper asked.

'Oh, it's just some entertainment Mr Ting organised. We're supposed to keep you at gunpoint until Michael and Janine shock them out of their bourgeois cocoons into the real world.'

'I don't think they need that right now.' Jasper was concerned.

'Mr Ting's expecting it... Well, it's not exactly what he was expecting, but that makes it all the more fun,' Colin replied.

'But this is so not a good time.'

'Look, either we force you to stay in here at fake gunpoint or we sit around and have a glass of wine until it's over. Is that a Margaret River Sauvignon? Very nice.'

In the living room, Nicole was on her feet, tears streaming down her face. Tanya sat braced, waiting for her opportunity to pounce. Irene held Maureen's hand, gripping it increasingly tightly. Ulrika clenched the other one.

'What do you want?' Stephen asked.

'I want you to wake up. You're all sleeping in your comfortable middle-class lives,' Unit One announced, only to be puzzled at the wry amusement that came across their faces. Perhaps he was not being convincing enough. He fired another blank into the air. Nicole jolted and the smiles stopped.

'If it's money you want...'

'Your money's killing you. A cancer that takes over your lives and you, you're all terminal cases. No, keep your poison. I'm here to make sure you know what it is you are dying from.' The appalled looks he now saw were much more satisfying.

James attempted to speak. If he could make them fire at him, everyone would see this was all fake and everything would be revealed. He got up out of his chair, but Unit Two pushed him back down without a shot.

'You're rich, you're idle, in your comfy little office jobs.'

'But I'm a truck driver!' Nicole interrupted, 'That's my truck outside.'

Unit One was thrown briefly but recovered. 'And Marie-Antoinette was a peasant because she had a toy farm with pre-washed sheep. Your games make me sick. So we're going to play a sick game of our own. This is a dinner party and at dinner parties we play charades, don't we?' He produced a folded piece of paper and gave it to Nicole.

'You know the rules. Any cheating and Mr Ting here gets it. You've got five minutes. If you lot don't have the answer by then, she gets it.' He pointed his gun at Nicole again. 'And then we play again until one of you gets one right. Starting now. Read it.'

Nicole opened up the paper and read. She sobbed, putting her hand to her mouth. Faces looked at her in expectation but her mind was blank. All she could think of was getting *Jaws* as a boy, running around pretending her arms were the shark's mouth. She could think of nothing for this title.

'Come on, Nicole, you can do. What is it?' Maureen was trying to coax her into thought. 'Is it a book or a film.'

Nicole glanced at her instructions, made the sign for a book and then tremblingly held two fingers up.

'Two words,' shouted Tanya, determined to make a contribution while she could.

'Thanks,' said Irene. 'We hadn't figured.'

'The whole thing,' Stephen announced as Nicole's shaking hands attempted to make a circle. She stood still.

'I can't do it. It's too hard. I can't.'

'Shut up!' Unit One interrupted.

Nicole pointed to Irene, Maureen, Tanya and Ulrika.

'Female ... Girls ... Ladies ... *LITTLE WOMEN*!' screamed Ulrika in a decidedly non-European accent and turned to the judge. He shook his head.

'Three minutes.'

'Come ON, Nicole,' shouted Stephen.

The command jerked her into action. A vision came. She lay down on the ground briefly and then jumped up and ran over to where she had been lying, moving her arms like a train.

'*The Railway Children!*' offered Irene.

'No.'

Nicole shot over to where Xavier was lying on the ground and made as if to run over him like a train.

'*The Little Mermaid!*' said Ulrika, resuming the accent.

'That's a film,' corrected Tanya.

'It was a story first, idiot,' Irene corrected her.

Nicole was pointing again. This time at Maureen and then James and pushing her hands together.

'Couple, pair, wedding,' said Irene.

'Row, bust-up,' tried Stephen. Tanya kicked him again but Nicole rolled her hands over and then started pointing at Irene and Stephen. This caused confusion.

'One minute,' shouted the judge.

'Christ, Nicole, give us something we can work with.' Stephen looked nervously at his friend who was shaking his head furiously, trying to stand up and being pushed back into the seat each time.

Ulrika made no more contributions, worried her accent was giving way under pressure. She glanced at her ladle lying on the floor near the commander. If only he would step forward far enough, she could jump for the ladle and hit him. The game continued. Nicole held up one finger and pulled her ear.

'First word sounds like,' they chorused. She pointed to one of the painted bolts on the side of the ship.

'Twenty seconds.'

She made as if to tighten the bolt.

'Bolt.'

She shook her head and pointed to what she was tightening with.

'Sounds like.... Wrench...wench, bench. Watkin Tench!' Irene thought she had it, but Nicole danced on the spot trying to communicate another word for wrench. She did more bolt tightening.

'Sounds like spanner?' asked Tanya. Nicole jumped up and clapped.

'Spanner, banner, Anna...*Anna Karenina!!*' screamed Irene.

'Yes, yes.' Nicole touched her nose and pointed at her in glee. Irene jumped up and hugged her.

'You bastard,' she shouted at Unit One. 'That was

impossible.' He moved forward to pull the two women apart.

It was enough of a distraction for Ulrika to seize her moment. In a smooth movement, she leapt for the ladle, picked it up and cracked him on the head.

'Shit.' He fell onto his knees. Unit Two, unprepared for this insurrection, shot across the room and stood pointing her gun at everyone, moving it from side to side.

'Don't move. Michael, are you alright?'

'Shit,' was all he could say, doubled over on the floor.

'Unit One, are you OK?' she repeated.

Everyone stood up and James became more animated than ever.

'Mmmmm, mmmmm.'

They moved slowly towards Unit Two, like a pack rounding on wounded prey.

'You can't kill us all. Fire on one and the others will get you.'

Unit Two took a step back, nearing the mermaid. Nobody moved. The silence was disturbed only by the noise of the soundscape and groaning from Unit One.

It could have been the loud seagull caw that suddenly echoed around the room, or her own nerves, but something made Unit Two stumble forward. Maureen thought she had seen a flicker of movement from Xavier, but when she inspected him later there was no hint of anything having moved.

Tanya leapt metres across the room. Irene saw her flash past her shoulders. Unit Two's gun flew across the room and suddenly she was on her back, pinned to the floor with Tanya's thighs on either side of her neck. Stephen rushed over to James and removed his gag.

'Don't do anything, they're actors!' he shouted, terrified some real harm would be done. Tanya turned, the fire in her eyes was ready for a kill. Made to feel afraid, she was ready to punish to the full extent. Stephen watched, fully aware that a subtle flex of her powerful thighs and the person's life would be over.

'They're actors, let them go!' James shouted.

'What?' Irene turned to glower at James.

'I hired an actor to be Captain Bloodbath and his Cut-throat Crazies and stage a pirate takeover of the ship. He fell ill and I presume this is his replacement.'

'My head,' moaned Michael.

Tanya still had not moved.

'Help,' gurgled her victim. 'I can't breathe.'

'Tanya, back off...Let her go.' Stephen tried to coax her down. 'Control, remember the Trinity. This is not a real situation.'

The girl's face was beginning to turn blue. Tanya realised she wanted the excuse to kill someone. It was a unique opportunity to perform the ultimate act of violence and get away with it. She was not taking out her frustrations, but seizing her one chance. It seemed so unfair that the situation was not real. She had saved them. She had taken control and the prize should be hers.

'Tanya, please,' pleaded Stephen. She turned to him with her jaw set hard. She felt cheated by the pretence.

'Remember the tenets: Yom Chi, and whatever.' Tanya relaxed her legs. Unit Two gasped for breath.

'Of all the stupid ideas. This one puts you right up there with numbskull Stephen. We were terrified. How dare you.' Irene was working up a rage. Maureen calmed her down.

'This isn't over. The war continues.' Unit One, overcoming the searing pain in his head, fired blank shots into the air. 'You may have the power, but we have the determination to do what it takes.'

Janine was staggering to her feet, still choking.

'Unit Two, move out...now.' The command jerked her into action and she ran for the door. Michael fired another shot and ran after her. As they left Units Three and Four emerged from the kitchen, petit fours in hand.

'Is it over?' they inquired. 'Was it fun?'

'Just leave,' Maureen said to the remnants of Urban Terror. 'You weren't to know how horribly inappropriate this has been, but even so it hardly classes as entertainment. Go, all of you.'

From outside they heard the sound of a large vehicle starting up. Nicole ran to the window.

'My truck, those bastards are taking my truck.' She turned to the remaining unit members.

'That's nothing to do with us,' said Colin. 'We're just actors. Michael's probably still in persona.'

'Yeah, he'll come down the road, bring the truck back and we'll all laugh.' Sasha gave a stage laugh to break the hideous tension of the faces glowering at her.

'We'll wait outside. Leave you to your petit fours.'

'They're delicious,' added Sasha, and they crept outside.

Once outside they looked at each other in disbelief. 'I had no idea he was that bad. He's totally flipped,' said Colin.

'He is coming back, isn't he?' Sasha asked.

'If he's not here in ten minutes, we're off. Otherwise we'll be hostages.'

In the living room brandies were passed around. James apologised as many times as he could. Nicole paced around. Ulrika went to the kitchen to check on her staff.

'But what about my truck? Christ, can this day get any worse?' The question rang out and brought silence.

'Sorry,' she added.

'We'll wait ten minutes to see if he brings it back, and then we'll call the police. OK?' Maureen suggested.

They began to talk, massaging their terror into outrage, disbelief and finally near-hysterical laughter.

'Nicole, what was all that business with the lying down and the train?' James asked. 'The spanner was inspired, but I didn't get that.'

'I was doing the end, where she throws herself under the train, only it's a bit hard when you've got to be Anna and the train.'

'Oh!' James paused, and then everyone cracked up.

'I was at gunpoint, I wasn't thinking clearly, so sue me!'

'A toast,' called Maureen, holding her glass up. 'To what is, without a doubt, the worst surprise party I have ever been to!'

'The worst!' they toasted.

The truck had not returned. Nicole went outside to see if it had been abandoned further down the road. She wanted to give up, throw her hands up and say, 'That's it. Trucking's over, move on.' She wanted to be philosophical but could not. The thought of her loan payments and the difficulty in finding work rolled over and over in the tumble drier of her stomach. Maureen's news and Stephen's accusations were in there too, getting wrapped around the other thoughts and appearing occasionally. The street was empty, with a big gap in front of the house where her truck had been. She had left the keys in it. At the time it seemed sensible. People didn't steal trucks in Woollahra, they couldn't even drive them. They could ram their way around the streets in four-wheel-drive tanks, but a heavy goods vehicle, even when it was just the cab without a load, was a different matter.

Maureen came out to join her.

'Any joy?'

'No. The two idiots in the kitchen have left. I don't believe this. It's just so...'

She started to cry. Maureen took Nicole in her arms.

'What am I going to do? It's...' She paused and pulled away. 'What am I doing? I should be supporting you.'

'It doesn't matter what I'm going through, this is still dreadful for you.'

'I can't just wait. We've got to look. I'd feel better if we were actually moving. It's like when I'm driving and behind deadline, I feel it'll be OK as long as I'm still moving. The minute you stop travelling, the panic sets in.'

'I think we all need to do something,' Maureen answered. 'We're going to find your truck, if it takes all night. We'll keep moving.'

'But what about you?'

'I need something else to worry about right now. You're the easiest option.'

'Oh Maureen,' Nicole sniffled at her friend.

'Stop it. I'm being selfish, using you for my own ends. Let's get the others.'

No-one argued whether this was the best plan or not. It was a plan, that was enough. They had spent too much time wondering where Maureen had been to go through it all again with Nicole's truck. Nicole persuaded them not to call the police yet. After the road accident she now stood accused of, the less she had to do with the law, the better.

They crammed into James' car. James drove, Maureen and Nicole shared the front seat.

'Which direction did they go?' asked James.

'Left,' said Stephen.

'It was right,' contradicted Irene.

'Left,' he repeated.

Maureen intervened. 'Nicole's truck was facing left. They didn't reverse and so must have headed straight off.'

'Logical,' said Irene, turning to face Stephen. He was sitting in the middle of the back seat, Irene on one side, Tanya on the other.

'Let's just drive,' pleaded Nicole.

They headed for the city centre, figuring most destinations would be reached through there.

At the first main-road intersection they reached, another car had slammed into a bin. James pulled up and Maureen asked what had happened. The minute one of the shaking passengers said a truck had shot past, James took off, causing the wheels to screech and drowning out Maureen's attempt to ask if there was anything they could do to help.

'No time for roadside assistance!' he shouted and sped on with renewed vigour.

'This is ridiculous,' announced Tanya. 'We've no

hope of finding them. We would be better off leaving it to the police.'

'Really?' questioned Irene. 'Can you use your Taekwondo body control to project your mind and see where they are?'

'That's not how it works.' Stephen elbowed his ex-wife in the ribs.

'Pity,' she mumbled to the window. 'Might have actually been some use.'

'Pardon?' Tanya asked.

'Quiet in the back, we're trying to concentrate.' Maureen controlled the back seat like a seasoned parent.

•

Michael's experience driving a truck in the army had not been extensive. He could get the vehicle moving, but controlling speed, brakes and an infinite number of gears was a different matter. Janine was torn between the exhilarating reality of the experience and the terror of careering around the streets of Sydney in a stolen vehicle.

'Michael, perhaps we should head back. I think we've terrified them enough.'

'They nearly killed you. That's what they're like. Give them a dose of reality and they smash you to the floor and squeeze the air out of you. The least threat and they're deadly.'

'They didn't know it was a performance. Of course they were scared.'

'It was fantastic. Did you see their faces? Real terror. We did it, Janine.'

'Look out!'

Michael had shot through another red light. He had not seen it in his excitement, and would not have been able to find the brakes in time to stop anyway.

'Savour the moment, Janine. There won't be another one like it, ever. We were terrorists.'

'What are we doing now? Where are we going?'

'Wherever this truck takes us.'

Another near-miss confirmed Janine's fears that Michael was now in persona as a truck driver but had not rehearsed sufficiently. She felt a vibration against her leg—her phone was on silent from the raid. It was Sasha, wondering what was happening.

'We're on Cleveland Street, not sure where we're going... Don't know, Michael's living in the moment.'

'Give me that.' Michael took the phone and started crowing into it about how fantastic the whole experience had been.

On the other end Sasha was making eyes at Colin and mouthing the word 'loopy'. She hung up.

'He's just driving around. I think Janine's a bit freaked out. What should we do?'

Sasha and Colin discussed the pros and cons of telling the Tings where the truck was. It was now beyond drama and getting into scary legal territory. This was not what they had envisaged when they agreed to be Cut-throat Crazies. Getting the Tings' number from a virtually voiceless Justin, they called and gave them the truck's last location.

•

'We've been down this street before,' announced Tanya. 'We're getting more and more lost.'

'I know exactly where we are,' Irene answered.

'Let it drop,' Stephen said. 'And can you move your leg over. I'm getting cramp here.'

'Should have thought of that before,' Irene retorted.

'Before what?'

'Before everything.'

'You're mad, d'you know that?'

'Bet you say that to all the girls. You must be mad too, Tanya. We all are. All Stephen's women—that long line between you and me. Lunatics, the lot of…urgh!'

Irene's last word was changed to a yelp as James jumped on the brakes at some lights.

'This is hopeless,' wailed Nicole. 'We'll never find it.'

'We will,' soothed Maureen, as James' phone rang. She answered.

'That was Ulrika. Apparently the two from the kitchen called to say the truck's on Cleveland Street.'

It was not far from their location. James did an instant U-turn and headed straight for the street. They were just about to turn into it when a truck shot through a red light in front of them.

'That's it!' shouted Nicole. 'That's my truck!'

James sped up to get as close as possible, but there were several cars in between. A few blasts on the horn did nothing to move them.

'They're heading for the Anzac Bridge, down Wattle Street. Come on, James.' Maureen pressed her hand to James' leg. He looked at her. She was looking to him to help support her friend. It was their first physical contact since her brief kiss on arriving home. He had missed her touch.

'We'll get to them,' he smiled and reassured her with a pat on the hand.

'Both hands on the wheel please.' Irene was driving from the back seat.

As the car turned from Wattle Street, Maureen noticed a last-minute lane change by the truck.

'It's not the bridge. They're heading straight across.'

There was a car moving alongside James' car, stopping them from overtaking and getting ahead. They had to slow down and force their way in behind. The lights changed and the car began to slow down.

'Don't lose them,' shrieked Irene.

'The one driver in this town that slows for a yellow light and we get stuck behind them,' Stephen commented.

James swung out and stepped on the accelerator, shooting through the light as it turned red and just keeping Nicole's truck in sight.

'You go, James!' Stephen slapped him on the shoulder.

'Don't distract the driver,' Irene brushed Stephen's arm off. Tanya leaned over and pushed Irene's hand off Stephen. Irene pushed her hand back. Tanya retaliated. They both attempted to reach over and slap each other. Stephen moved forward, James braked and their hands both hit Stephen in the face.

Irene smirked and even Tanya could not resist a smile as Stephen's boyish face pouted, 'That's not fair'. They were stuck at the next light while Urban Terror had charged ahead. James hit his fist on the steering wheel.

'Damn.'

'We can still catch up,' Maureen suggested. 'They'll be heading for the Harbour Bridge. We'll be able to get to them.'

James saw the slap in the rear-view mirror and then

saw Maureen glance across at him. She was thinking the same thing. Given the tense atmosphere as they careered around central Sydney following Nicole's truck, the last thing they needed was yet another major row in the back. There was only one thing for it.

'So, Tanya, when's your next Taekwondo competition?' James asked as he pulled off. The car was sluggish with six people on board.

'There's a few club fixtures early next year,' Tanya answered automatically, wondering why everyone was so interested in her sport at the most inopportune moments. She detailed the progression of events on next year's calendar. Everyone calmed down as James and Maureen took turns to say, 'Really?'

•

In the truck, Michael was now out of persona and panicking as much as Janine. He had no idea how or where to stop. They had passed over Darling Harbour and were heading to the city. In the small hours of Sunday morning, with drunk people wandering around, it seemed like a bad idea. He continually turned left, hoping to find somewhere to stop but soon found they were heading towards the Harbour Bridge.

'No!' shouted Janine. 'We can't, you've got to pull over. Down here...the left, the left,' she yelled, indicating a turn-off road that led down to Cockle Bay, a trendy entertainment area. Then she spotted a bank of taxis in front of them, letting passengers out.

'Stop. You're going to hit them.'

Michael tried to brake but accelerated instead.

'Turn,' shouted Janine. Without thinking, Michael turned to the left. It seemed open but it was no road, it was the pedestrian walkway next to the bay. People scattered like dropped marbles. Janine covered her eyes and Michael groaned, 'Oh, shit.'

•

By the time Tanya had reached the national champion- pionships once again, they were on a fly-over above Cockle Bay, heading towards the Harbour Bridge. Nicole looked down at the water, despondent at having come so close to her truck but losing it once again. Heading north over the bridge felt like heading back to the unsafe territory of that morning. As she gazed moodily out of the window, she spotted a truck cab charge over the pedestrian walkway and leap off into the bay.

'My truck,' she wailed. 'They've driven it into the water!'

'Quick! Turn!' said Maureen.

James swung the car round just in time to change lanes and head away from the Harbour Bridge and down towards where Nicole had seen her truck drown.

When Nicole and the others got to the water's edge, Urban Terror had disappeared. The open windows of the truck let the water pour in, but also let them climb out. They had swum as far as possible, crawled out and run as hard and fast away from the scene as they could. Janine had tried to sit down, relieved to be alive. Michael had dragged her to her feet.

'We can't stop now. There's no going back. This is real, not some scene where the director shouts "cut". C'mon.'

Adrenalin was driving him on. They had broken free of art now, they were living life for real. Real fugitives, they must disappear into the seamy underworld of the city, never to return, he thought. They ran through a water feature on their way to obscure their wet footprints.

•

Nicole followed the water trail as far as the fountain and then could see no more. Too many drunk people had decided to cool off in it. Wet foot imprints surrounded the fountain making it impossible to see which way they had gone.

She returned to the water's edge and the crowd who stood around watching, as if the truck might suddenly resurface. Gradually they dispersed when it became clear there was no further entertainment to be had from the incident. By the time the police arrived, Nicole was sitting silently, watching the water alone. James had parked the car and joined them.

Nicole stumbled bewildered through the police interview. The officer asked several times if Nicole had any prior connection with the thieves. Much as he had been hoping to avoid it, James felt he had no choice but to explain exactly what Michael and Janine had been doing at his house. The story seemed particularly crazy, but it was backed up by the others. The officer could tell they had not been rehearsed. She relaxed and explained the grilling to Nicole.

'We get quite a few insurance jobs on trucks. The industry's pretty hard going. If you wanted out, these idiots have done you a favour. I'll need you to come to the station on Monday morning to sign the report. If I could just have the contact details of this Justin character, I think we'll have no trouble picking these guys up. I suggest you all go home and rest.'

'But my truck!' Nicole wailed.

'Nothing you can do about it now, and I don't think it's going anywhere. It'll have to be fished out.'

'Will I have to pay?'

'Don't worry about that now, Nicole,' Maureen interrupted. 'Thank you, officer, we'll make sure she comes in on Monday.'

The policewoman left. Everyone stood around

looking at each other, unsure how to react. It had all been very quick. One moment Nicole had a truck and the next she didn't.

'I don't know whether this is the best or the worst thing to happen,' said Nicole. 'Don't need to stress about not getting any truck work now, I suppose.'

'Might have guessed you'd come out OK.' Stephen thought he was being jovial. Nicole ignored him, taking a long last look at the water's surface.

'I need a drink,' Maureen announced, diverting attention. 'Let's find a bar.'

3.00 am

Given the time, finding a drink was not easy. The bars were closed. It seemed as if even this simple task would be beyond them until Tanya remembered the Taekwondo party was taking place at House, the huge dance club close to where the truck had taken a dive.

'That's OK for you, but they'll never let us in,' argued Irene. 'Look at us, exhausted people teetering on the brink of middle age in crumpled dinner clothes.'

'Leave it to me,' Nicole smiled. 'If there's one advantage to being a trannie in this town, it's getting into clubs.'

Discovering a post-trauma high, Nicole marched them over to the bouncers at the entrance. They stood silent and grim, their quota of PR pleasantry having been exhausted two hours earlier. It looked as if they would all sail in without the bouncers even acknowledging their existence until at the very last moment a hand went out and stopped them.

'You got a card or invite?'

'No,' Nicole challenged. 'Tell the manager Nicole's

here. I am a friend of Verushka's.' Nicole voice dropped an octave as she spoke. It was a voice none of them had ever heard before. It had never been that deep, even when she was Tom. The hand went up. They walked straight past the ticket office.

'I think,' announced Nicole, 'the dance floor may be a bit much for us. Let's find somewhere a bit quieter.' House was vast. On the mezzanine level, they got a sense of how vast. There were passages leading everywhere, levels below and above. People walked around as if in a shopping mall of dance. James headed to the bar as the others clustered on a balcony overlooking the crowded dance floor. It appeared to be a field, a crop of dancers waving in the breeze of lights that swept over them.

'I'm so old,' shouted Stephen in dismay.

'They're so thin and young!' Irene was equally dismayed.

Maureen held onto the balcony and swayed to the music as if the repetitive beats were familiar. She appeared to be lost in memories. Opening her eyes, she spoke. 'We won't be the oldest people here. In this light we all look beautiful. Stephen, you're more handsome than ever. Irene, you're radiant, and Tanya, you're positively childlike—if I worked here I'd be asking for ID. Nicole—alluring as ever.' They each smiled as Maureen delivered each compliment into their ear as if she were doling out pills. James returned with a tray full of shot glasses.

'No decent brandy, or glasses. The girl recommended shots of schnapps—said it would make everything "kick in" again.' He shrugged his shoulders in bemusement as everyone took a glass and held it up.

'To the next crisis,' he shouted and they downed their drinks.

'That's getting better.' Nicole felt the sweetness burn down her throat. The noise prevented post-mortems, which was just what she wanted. She felt as if a weight had been lifted. Without the worry of paying off the truck, she could get another job if she wanted. Unlike Louie, she was not trapped. There was still the afternoon's crash to face, but somehow she knew it would be resolved. She felt lucky, not something she experienced often. It might have been the euphoria of relief and the schnapps, but she felt powerful and whole, with a world of options in front of her. There was nothing she had to prove. She did not need to be the best friend, the perfect woman, the toughest trucker any more. She tried to imprint the feeling into her memory, in case it was not there in the morning.

Maureen drew her out of her musing with a gentle touch and inquiry as to how she was.

'I feel fantastic. This place is very distracting, that's good I suppose. What about you? You and James haven't spoken. That business in the hall, we couldn't help...'

The music, so isolating in one respect, created an intimate environment for conversation. There was no fear of being overheard by the person a metre away.

'I know,' Maureen replied. 'I'm terribly confused, and God knows what James is going through.'

'Sod James. This is about you.'

'Yes,' Maureen smiled. 'I shall be the model of selfishness.'

'I doubt it...We'll leave you two to talk. C'mon,' she said loudly, 'let's explore and see if we can find our lost youth anywhere. I'm sure mine's somewhere near that boy dancing with his shirt off.' She grabbed Irene and Tanya and set off. Stephen hesitated until Tanya turned and gave him a 'get the hint' look.

James and Maureen surveyed the dance floor. It seemed like the same record had been playing constantly, but a whoop went up from the crowd, indicating a new and much loved track. James had no words to say. He moved his hand onto Maureen's and squeezed it gently. The action sent a spasm of irritation through her. She pulled her hand away, recoiling.

'I'm fine,' she said.

'I'm not. How can you pretend everything is OK?'

'Isn't that what you want, what you all want?' she

answered. 'Want me to cope, make it easy, support you all.'

'Everyone cares deeply for you. I spoke to your friend, that Jasper. He told me what you did. I think I can understand.'

'Big of you...' she snapped and then relented. 'I'm sorry. I spent today trying to work out what I felt and I couldn't. Perhaps I don't feel anything at all. I'm just a computer program that simulates Maureen so well that the real Maureen's disappeared.'

'So you just pretend everything?'

'I don't know. When I think of you and the others, I feel, but I feel for you. I don't know if I can do it for me.'

James stared down into the crowd. The uniform field had broken up and been replaced with a floor of hell packed with tormented souls stretching their arms up in chaos, striving to climb out and pull him down at the same time.

'Do you want a separation?' he asked. Maureen turned to look at him. The understanding that had existed between them was cracking.

'Kick me while I'm down, why don't you?' She felt the anger and followed its prompt to leave. Storming off did not seem as spontaneous as she thought it was meant to be. It was melodramatic, but quite satisfying.

James looked at her back. Marching off was not Maureen behaviour. Even though he realised what he had said was a mistake, he had expected a reasoned argument as to why, not a rapidly disappearing wife. He had thought Maureen would be better off without him. He felt like a burden for her to carry, on top of her own problems. It had sounded like he wanted out. He chased after her, thinking he was following, but suddenly found himself standing half a metre above everyone else. The strip of carpet he had chosen to run down was a 'secret' catwalk. Designed for fashion shows and individuals that simply wanted to parade around seeking attention, it started at ground level and gradually rose up. James stopped. The young people standing around started cheering him. They could have been jeers, he couldn't tell.

'Strut it, then.'

'Where's the attitude?' called one young guy. James turned, angry at having lost sight of Maureen, embarrassed at standing out. He reached down, grabbed the boy by the top of his muscle shirt, and pulled him up to the catwalk.

'You do it for me, sonny, OK?' he growled in the youth's face.

He obliged, bending over and mooning as James

jumped off the end of the platform, knocking over two bottles of water.

•

'It's probably quieter on the top floor,' suggested Nicole. 'There's a cocktail bar where we can actually talk.'

'Like we haven't done enough of that tonight,' muttered Tanya. 'Perhaps that's where the Taekwondo party is,' she added, louder. 'Let's go.'

Nicole led them around to where she thought the stairs to the top floor were, but they had gone. Someone noticed their confusion and said they had to go down to the ground floor and up again at the other side of the bar.

Tanya and Irene pushed ahead, found the stairs and went up, eager to escape the crowd. There was a bouncer at the top blocking access. She allowed them in when Tanya presented her Taekwondo credentials. The others were not behind them.

'Oh,' said Tanya, not relishing a one-on-one with Irene.

'I dare say we can wait here a few minutes without causing a riot.'

Tanya shrugged her shoulders and they walked in.

'What a relief,' declared Irene as they passed through into the cocktail area. 'I swore when I was twenty I'd never say it, but I could barely hear myself think down there.'

'Yes.' Tanya was nervous.

'I'll get us drinks. What do you want?'

'A mineral water's fine.' Irene's raised eyebrow made Tanya realise that was not a satisfactory answer.

'Vodka soda,' she corrected.

At the bar, Irene regretted pointing out to the barman that the slim girl next to her should be served first when she ordered ten cocktails. It was some lime and kiwi fruit concoction, each drink having lime and individually scooped out kiwi fruit crushed by hand with a large candle-like pestle. It was frustratingly slow.

'They're worth the wait,' the woman who had placed the order offered, 'and all that fruit's good for you.'

'Just as well. It looks like you haven't eaten since you left school...primary school.'

Tanya walked to the balcony, a decking area that looked over the water. To the right she could see the garish flashing lights of the casino. The evening had not turned out as expected. She had thought it would be trying, but guns, car chases and breast cancer was over the top even for Stephen's friends. Everyone had surprised her. Maureen was suddenly not perfect. Irene had almost bonded with her when they both slapped Stephen. Stephen seemed as irritated with her as with Irene. She herself had almost murdered someone. The moment stayed with her—a flash of raw life and death in the sleep that was her existence. She remembered at school fantasising about killing Sister Judith with one swift kick to the head. Clean and sharp. It seemed like the ultimate in power. She had even thought about joining the army, but gave up when she realised that virtually no-one in the armed forces ever got to kill anyone directly. As she had grown older, the desire wore away and she stopped thinking about it. She had controlled it for so long, it did not feel like an effort, until tonight. Perhaps, she thought, Taekwondo was the wrong sport for her. There might be too much control. She could tour Asia and make her fortune on the illegal kick-boxing circuit.

'Tanya!' A voice brought her back from a caged arena in Hanoi. A large girl bounced up, her young competitor from earlier in the day. 'Where've you been? I've been looking for you.'

'You don't want to know. Shouldn't you be at home, it's late?'

'Mum's letting me stay up. She's here, sitting on that wall.'

The girl's mother raised her eyes and sucked on the straw in her cocktail saucily as she waved.

'Everyone's still talking about what you did.'

Tanya looked puzzled and then remembered what

had been her biggest issue of the day until the dinner party.

'That was a long time ago.' The focus and dedication that had filled her in competition and which had been frustrated by the legal challenge returned to her briefly. They seemed like excessive emotions now, as if she had been trying too hard to control things that should be set free.

'There are more important things in life,' she added.

'Like what? Taekwondo's everything, it's a way of life.' The girl had not been on the brink of murder in the intervening hours. Tanya smiled at her, like a serial killer eyeing her next victim.

'You'd better join your mum before she drowns in that cocktail.' She pointed to the mother, who was trying to drain the last dregs of alcohol direct from the glass and receiving a face full of ice.

'Sorry it took so long. Some idiot ordered a ridiculous quantity of a ludicrously slow-to-prepare drink from the ploddingly methodical barman. Cheers.' Irene pushed the vodka and soda into Tanya's hand.

'Cheers.' The conversation ended. They waited expectantly for Stephen and Nicole but both came to the realisation that some talking was required.

'So, tell me about…' Irene started.

'Don't say it. If you're all so interested in bloody Taekwondo, just do it, or talk to someone else. There's plenty of practitioners here. They're wearing black belts and big red spots on their chests.'

'A joke, marvellous. You're learning!'

'Don't start on me, Irene, not after everything tonight. I didn't know about the book. Stephen didn't mean to give it you. I didn't cause your break-up.'

'I realise that,' Irene hurled back and then changed her tone. 'I realise that. I bought the book myself this afternoon. I feel robbed and I can't blame anyone.'

'You must be upset about Maureen.'

'I don't know what's going on with her. I don't think any one of us really ever has, but we're only realising it today.'

There was another pause.

'Stephen was a bit of a prick.' Tanya was keen to keep the reconciliation going. Irene laughed.

'To which of the many points of prickdom are you referring?'

'He's not that bad. When we're alone he's great. It's just, well, you have an effect on him. He gets edgy and then says things. You're very clever. It can be scary.'

'Oh God, a scary woman. Is that what I am?' Irene grimaced.

'Sometimes. Look, I know Stephen's not the sharpest tool in the shed...'

Irene interrupted, 'He's a man! Sharp or blunt, they're all still tools.'

Tanya laughed. 'That's the nearest you're ever going to come to sticking up for him, isn't it?'

'Correct, and I'd swear blind I'd never have said it if it wasn't such a good line. Where the hell are they?'

'Stephen'll be in a panic about being left alone with Nicole. Poor man.'

'Poor Nicole. He's probably calling her Tom again.'

•

Stephen was staring at his breasts in the men's toilet. As the group had set off for the upstairs bar, a posse of dancers had rushed in front of him and Nicole. By the time they had passed by, Tanya and Irene had disappeared. He had decided to hide in the toilet for a few minutes. When Nicole had told him to enjoy himself, he thought it had been one of her jibes. Once in, he could see it was quite a spectacle. The urinal was a vast mirrored trough. Spaced at regular intervals were television screens, set in the mirror at chest height. It was a relief that there was something to watch. If you looked down it was impossible to not see every other penis in the mirror. Stephen watched his screen diligently. It was playing soft porn.

A girl with large breasts was sitting astride a man with telephone cables wrapped around him and Mickey Mouse ears on his head. Stephen had missed the intricate plot twists leading to this situation. The view switched to the woman's breasts: just the breasts jiggling around. Stephen stared. The screen image in the mirror appeared in the middle of the reflection of his own chest. They looked like his breasts. He watched them as they moved up and down in slow motion. Without thinking he started moving his own chest in time with the breasts, matching them swing for swing. He stopped, shamed by the realisation that he was not actually repulsed at the sight of breasts on his chest.

When he came out Nicole was standing on her own. For the first time in his life, he was pleased to see her.

'Someone come on to you in there?' she asked, smiling.

He explained what he saw.

'And I'm guessing it wasn't as revolting as you thought?'

Stephen looked embarrassed. 'I don't want a sex change. I love being a man.'

'I know, but?'

'But I don't know. Where are the others? We'd better join them.'

'But?' Nicole held him back. After years of snide comments he wasn't getting out of this. 'Tell me,' she challenged.

He looked at her hand gripping his arm. Her finger

nails were short and natural. He had always thought Nicole had long painted nails.

'Just for a moment I had a sense of what it was like to be a woman and it was, well, OK. I felt I could be weak.'

'Being a woman is being weak?' Nicole rolled her eyes.

'No.' Stephen was struggling. 'You know when you're a little boy...oh.'

'It's OK. I do, as a matter of fact.'

'Yes, well...you get bullied or something and you say you'll get your dad onto them and like he's this big guy that'll always protect you. That stops when you're about ten. Suddenly you have to be the big guy. You want to cry and you get told you have to be a man. And that's it for the rest of your life, forever. For that moment I saw the appeal of having some big strong person wrap you in their arms and take care of you. I don't think you'd want it all the time, but it would be nice just occasionally to not be "a man about it".'

'Is that why you always go for strong women?'

'Oh please!'

Stephen had barely time to finish expressing his contempt for armchair psychology when a solid parcel of muscle hurled itself at him. It was Merissa, the bodybuilder.

'Stephen, you came. Fantastic. The party's this way'.

She grabbed his hands and led him upstairs, Nicole followed. He looked back at Nicole and shrugged his shoulders.

'Just a friend,' he said.

'I'm saying nothing,' laughed Nicole.

•

James' spell on the catwalk gave Maureen time to escape. When he reached the spot where he had last seen her, there was no trace. With stairs going down, a corridor to the left, a passage that seemed to lead through a toilet and onto a long balcony down the side of the building, there were too many options. He walked along the balcony figuring that the broadest view in the venue gave him the best chance of seeing her. As he walked he thought he spotted her on the far side, back where they had been standing. When he arrived the woman he had seen, whether it was Maureen or not, had disappeared. He surveyed the dance floor, trying to make out individual faces and then realised it was ridiculous, Maureen was hardly likely to be there. He walked on, exploring every cranny of the club. Maureen should know he had searched high and low and had not given up until he found her. He wanted her to know he would not give up.

The venue unfolded continually, as if it was

expanding before him. Every area led to a corner which led to stairs which led to another room or another view onto the dance floor. He felt he had doubled back on himself several times, but each time he seemed to be in a new place that still skirted around the vast inner dance floor. At one point he even found himself in a shop. The club sold merchandising. Dancers could go home bearing a doormat with HOUSE emblazoned on it.

He contemplated asking people if they had seen her. His wallet contained her photo, so he could show it around. However, given the strange state most people seemed to be in, it was not worth it. He had been greeted with staring smiles, pats on the bum and offers of water. People had asked him for chewing gum, drugs and cigarettes. One girl even bounced up and kissed him.

'Sorry, I thought you were my uncle Trevor,' she had giggled. Madness surrounded him at every turn. Lights, music, people, the labyrinthine venue. It was all designed to strip him of his faculties and divorce him from the real world.

He was on the ground floor, level with the dance floor. He had to move higher. Looking down on it all he had a sense of control. Trying to retrace his steps, he found a stairway that looked familiar. He walked up it, passed through a corridor and emerged onto a

little balcony overlooking the dance floor. There was
a bench. He sat down. Through the perspex floor he
could look right down at the people dancing. This was
an erie where he could pause for moment and reconnect with sanity. His eyes searched the dance floor.
Time and again he glimpsed a face, the back of a head,
an arm that could have been Maureen, but it always
turned out not to be.

The music was all beat. Occasionally what melody
there was stopped altogether, and the beats got faster
and faster. The crowd loved it, screaming at the build-
up, tensing as if waiting to explode into relief. When
the melody erupted back, the crowd went wild. The
sea of heads was covered by a flotilla of hands. He
thought he saw Maureen's hands.

He was sure they were her hands. Metres away, in
poor and ever-changing light, but something told him
they were hers. He focussed determinedly on where
they were as the dance floor plunged into darkness.
The hands went down and faces were visible. He saw
her face, blissfully unaware of what was around her.
She was dancing with a group of people, looking like
one of them, like part of the madness. James had lost
her. She was too far gone for him to connect with.
Her face turned towards his erie and she saw him. He
could see no reaction, but their eyes locked. Her gaze

held him for a moment and then he dashed downstairs. He needed physical contact, direct proof in his hands that this was his Maureen.

She was still on the dance floor when he reached it. He charged through the crowd, which seemed to part instinctively, leading him straight to Maureen. She stood there, a captive empress in her dance-floor domain. A different smile played on her face. The crowd closed around the two of them.

'I think my drugs have kicked in again,' she said, continuing to dance slowly to herself. James thought he had misheard. She came close to him, pressed her finger to his ear to block out the music and spoke softly. The voice seemed to come from inside his head.

'I had an ecstasy tablet when I climbed the Harbour Bridge. It seems to be working again, or it's like my body can remember what the feeling was like. These people say the music can do that.'

'We have to talk,' he shouted at her. 'Please.' He took her arm and led her away. With her free arm she waved goodbye to her dance buddies. This time the crowd did not part. He had to push his way through, moving people aside, banging into others and tripping over empty water bottles.

'I have to get out of here. It's hell,' James said, once off the dance floor.

'OK,' Maureen replied. 'I suppose this has to be done.'

•

Merissa led them straight to Tanya and Irene. As Stephen attempted to facilitate conversation between Merissa and Tanya, Nicole spoke to Irene.

'I don't know who's more surprised. Tanya to see Stephen with this ball of feminine testosterone or Stephen to see you and Tanya chatting so pleasantly.'

'We've come as close to bonding as we ever will,' Irene answered. 'It's great. There could be nothing more terrifying for Stephen than Tanya and I in cahoots.'

'Don't be so sure.' Nicole was about to recount Stephen's toilet incident, but thought better of it. It was a confidence, her first chance to build any sort of a friendship with him.

'Where's your boyfriend?' Stephen asked Merissa, to let Tanya know she had one.

'Oh him,' Merissa replied, disappointed to be reminded. 'Gerard's off finding a protein bar. Doesn't wanna cannibalise his own muscles by getting hungry. He'll be ages. Come on, let's dance.'

She dragged Stephen off to an unofficial dance floor where several other of the physique competitors were dancing. The carpeted floor and turbo-charged shoulders did nothing for their dance technique.

The three women stood and watched.

'Should I be threatened?' Tanya asked, unsure what to make of this powerful interloper.

'She's very strong,' said Nicole, watching Merissa grab Stephen's hand and swing him around.

'Do you feel jealous? What does the Trinity tell you?' Irene asked.

'Dunno. I was worried we were going to have the talk about "where we are going", and he'd ask me to move in with him.'

'Don't you want to?' asked Nicole. She glanced at Irene, who nudged her quietly.

'Not really. I like my space. I get all uncomfortable actually living with someone.'

'Match made in heaven,' said Irene. Tanya looked wary, waiting for the second half of the jibe.

'Seriously, he's the same,' Irene said. 'I think that's been his problem all along.' Tanya smiled.

'Quick, someone get me a drink,' Irene added. 'I'm giving advice to my ex-husband's girlfriend. I can't think of anything more tacky.'

Tanya went to the bar, worried that Irene might launch into a tirade to compensate for having been nice.

Irene and Nicole watched as Merissa picked Stephen up and swung his legs to either side of her body in fine jive style. Then she sent him flying through her parted legs, turned and seemed to pick him up off the ground with a flick of her wrists.

'This makes up for his behaviour tonight,' Irene said. 'I wouldn't have missed it for the world.'

'I think that might be the boyfriend,' said Nicole. Bodies leapt out of the way. A vast man charged as fast as his pumped quadriceps would allow towards the rock 'n' rolling pair. It seemed like part of the dance action as Stephen rose up into the air out of Merissa's arms, and flew backwards, landing head first on the edge of table and rebounding off at Irene's feet. Gerard lumbered after him, shaking Merissa off like an annoying bug.

'What you doing?' he growled at the heap on the floor. The crowd drew back, apart from a few well-muscled men who presented a second row in the unlikely event that Gerard would fail in his assault.

Irene's hand went out to Nicole, as much to stop her doing anything foolish as for support. It was too late. Nicole had moved in front of Stephen and was facing up to Gerard.

'I've no fight with you, miss. Please step aside,' he muttered, his fake politeness expecting her to move immediately. She did not.

'Miss, I don't lay a finger on a lady, but this guy has it coming. I'm asking you to step aside.' The menacing politeness was backed up by veins popping all over his body. Nicole stood still, waiting for Gerard to make the first move. He did. Slowly he leaned forward and picked her up, pinning her arms to her body, and moved her to the side.

'Sorry, miss,' he said, staring all the while at Stephen on the floor. He had tried to pick himself up but was overcome with dizziness and had collapsed back down. He looked up at the vast shape of Gerard, so huge his head disappeared into the clouds of his blurred vision. He waited for the impact.

It didn't happen. Instead he felt a rush of wind above his head and saw Gerard stagger backwards. Tanya had let fly and landed a full point-scoring kick on his chest. She now stood between them, poised to strike again.

The music stopped and there was a flurry of movement. Irene dashed to stand by Nicole and saw that, out of nowhere, Tanya's Taekwondo colleagues had massed behind Stephen. The muscle men, outraged at the act of aggression, were ready to charge. Nobody moved, all waiting for the trigger for a battle of titans: muscle power versus martial arts.

Tanya was exhilarated. The frustration of pulling back from the brink at Maureen's house earlier would be repaid now. She was ready to let rip the full force of her fury. She wanted to take them all on alone. Move like a whirlwind and send carcasses flying out in all directions. She was stopped by a gentle voice behind her.

'Guk Chi.' She recognised the voice of Vernon, her competition trainer, reminding her of the tenet of self-control. She paused, silently thanked him and acknowledged the importance of what he said. If she had let rip wildly they would have torn her apart. This was no rule-bound competition performance in protective clothing. It was a brawl.

It could have gone either way. As if watching a coin spinning on the ground to see which way it fell, everyone was waiting to see if a fight would break out or if they would all back off.

On the ground Stephen groaned, he peered through his blurred vision at the scene. Shapes melted and new figures formed. He was in a court room. Irene and Nicole were in judge's robes, staring at him. James was fumbling with a stack of papers. They fell from his hands.

'You're defence, mate. Sorry. You're on your own. Just tell the truth.'

'Guilty,' shouted Irene, bashing her hammer down on a replica of Stephen's head and smashing it.

'He wants to be a woman: that's why he had sex with a bodybuilder,' Nicole said. Instead of a hammer she had a knife. 'Let's get rid of it. It's given everyone too much trouble.'

'Where's Tanya,' Stephen thought, and looked around the courtroom.

'Here,' she replied from the judge's bench where Nicole and Irene were placing judge's robes and a wig on her head.

'But we didn't do anything,' he shouted. 'We kissed and I wanted to, but we didn't.'

Stephen's delirious words, slurred as they were, rang out in the tense silent bar. Gerard lunged, Tanya parried and it was on. The bodybuilders trotted forward, determined to use bulk and raw power as quickly as they could. The martial artists swarmed like bees, darting in and out, stabbing here and there with arms and legs. The slower ones were met with punches. Vernon came up to Tanya's side, wanting to help against the might of Gerard, but was caught unawares by a punch to his face. He fell back.

Irene and Nicole stood still in the chaos around them.

'We've got to get Stephen out. Look at him,' Nicole said. Stephen had passed out. A pool of blood spread out from the back of his head.

'Come on.' Nicole dropped to her knees and started crawling along the floor. Irene followed her. When they reached him, Irene stopped Nicole.

'Perhaps we shouldn't move him.'

'If we move him out, we can get him to help.'

Memories of the afternoon flashed through her mind. It was her day for pulling injured men out.

Taking a shoulder each, they dragged him back towards the entrance.

'Urgh!' Irene cried, as a bodybuilder standing back to avoid a blow tripped over her. His hulking body fell over the three of them, trapping them on the floor.

'My nose,' he groaned and rolled around, oblivious to the bodies beneath him.

'Oh, disgusting!' Irene grimaced. Blood and mucus erupted from his nose onto her. Nicole tried to push him off while still holding onto Stephen, but failed. She had to let go of Stephen.

'You pull him out while I try to shift this brute.' Nicole wriggled out, kneeled and attempted to raise the man's shoulders. 'Pull, Irene!'

With a hand under each of Stephen's shoulders she heaved as hard as she could. He began to move and she pulled harder, finally liberating him from the body.

'Keep going. There's something I've got to do,' Nicole shouted and vanished. Irene got on her feet and pulled the groaning and increasingly heavy Stephen backwards. She reached the edge of the fray and looked around. Towards the entrance of the bar was a wall. She pulled Stephen there, sat down on the floor and rested with his head in her lap. She pressed her dress to the wound on the back of his head, trying to stop the bleeding. As her dress became more and more red she began to panic, realising his injury might be serious.

Looking around she could see no evidence of security staff, police or any means of ending the fight raging in front of her.

Nicole was approaching Gerard and Merissa, now united by the fight. Merissa had grabbed hold of Tanya, and Gerard was gearing up for a knockout blow, setting aside his no-ladies rule.

'Hang on,' Nicole shouted. Gerard turned towards her.

'One thing you should know,' she continued, 'I'm no lady.' She let fly with her foot at Gerard's groin and followed up with her classic right hook into his falling face.

'Works every time,' she said to Tanya, who was flipping Merissa over her shoulders and onto the floor in a reverse of her dance move with Stephen. The two women made their way to Irene. Progress was slow. Fighting couples, chairs and tables had to be pushed out of the way. Stephen lay on the ground with Irene bent over him, her lips pressed to his open mouth. The familiar sensation of his lips sent shivers through her. She looked up, blood smeared across her face.

'He's stopped breathing. Help. Please help.'

5.00 am

The water in the harbour was a black mass. Ripples appeared as flies touched the surface or something rose up from within. Most of the lights around the bay had been switched off, but some remained to bob on the water's surface. In the distance the casino lights continued to shoot up their mock tower and light their star. It was supposed to be exciting. James watched it as Maureen sat on a low metal bollard and stared into the water.

'The lights make interesting patterns on the water,' Maureen mused.

'Did you say your drugs had "kicked in" again?' James ignored the bobbing lights. Maureen nodded. James rubbed his forehead.

'I don't know where to start. Is that why you went to the brothel, because you'd had drugs?'

'It was the other way round. I got the ecstasy at Heracles and decided the bridge would be the best place to take it. I felt so perfect up there.' She glanced

343

over her shoulder in the direction of the Harbour Bridge, hidden by the city buildings.

James had never felt more irrelevant. The inability of his hands to compete creatively with his family was nothing compared to this. Back then he knew what he was supposed to do—he could try and fail. Now he could not even try. He thought of his mother in her pale blue nightgown and her scar.

'So, you want to leave me because I'm turning into your mother?' Maureen read his mind again. For a second he imagined life without her. For a fraction of that second it did not seem terrible. For the remainder it was his worst nightmare.

'No...I thought it might be easier for you if you didn't have me dragging you down.'

'Didn't it occur to you that you might support me, that I might actually need you?' Maureen turned and stared at him. The fury that had been in her eyes when James had caught her with Jasper in the hall had returned. It stung him.

'You seem to be managing pretty well without me, being fondled by another man in my hall.'

'I was just pleased someone could touch me. You didn't.'

'I didn't know!' he cried out.

'Liar. You've avoided it for weeks. We've been playing reverse cat and mouse in the bedroom, me pushing my breast to your fingers and you avoiding it. You used to grab the girls. You used to cram every square millimetre into your hands until I cried stop. When did you last do that?'

James could not argue. He remembered the last time he had grabbed the girls without a care in the world. He had felt it on the edge of his left hand, about two centimetres down from his little finger—a roughness that was different, some pressure pushing back into the side of his hand.

'You asked "what?" and then stopped.' Maureen narrated his memory. 'You were going to ask me what that was and you changed your mind. That was the last time you touched me properly.'

'I was scared. I was waiting for you to say something. It's your body.'

'You were scared! How the hell do you think I felt?' she shouted at him. Clubbers leaving House scurried passed. There was always a couple arguing outside a club. James waited until they had passed silently out of earshot.

'I didn't know how you felt. I never know. Nobody does until you tell us and even then, you say everything's fine. Everything's always fine. You always cope. Why should this be different?'

'This is serious, James. I can't do it alone.'

'Can't you? When have you ever really needed me?

You've been there for me, you've supported me and Irene and Nicole and the whole world but when have you ever needed anyone?'

'I have...When my mother died,' Maureen tried to offer an example. She wanted to be reasonable and logical, control the rage that was beginning to erupt inside.

'You went off on your own for a day, came back and were "fine", again. You grabbed my arm at her funeral and that's the only time I felt of any use to you. It lasted a few seconds and then you were organising everyone back to our house with grace and bravery. So Maureen.'

'What if I don't want to be Maureen any more. What if I want to be me?' she asked.

'And what's that? A drug-taking adulterer?'

Maureen screeched as loud as she could, hammering her fist on the bollard. Sheer frustration drove her hands harder and harder into the metal. She wanted to answer, she wanted to scream out who she really was, but could not. Noise and pounding were all she could manage.

'You'll hurt yourself.' James moved forward to grab her. She refused to let his hands grasp hers, shaking them free and hammering at James instead. Taking turns to pound her fists, scream into his face and pound her fists again. Her hair, always tidy and man-ageable, was wild. It flew around her head as she shook.

The hitting stopped. She took a step back from James, panting with exhaustion. With no control or decision, her mouth opened and she roared. The sound charged out from the depth of her stomach. Its power rattled her mouth. She could feel herself getting sore, yet her throat never felt so relaxed. People may have been watching as they walked past, buildings might have crumbled with its force and windows shattered, but she was oblivious to it all, releasing the massive noise through her mouth. James felt her breath on his face. The shock, the violence, all dropped away as Maureen's roar surrounded him. It was all around, a presence in the world.

She stopped, shocked but satisfied by what she had done. She felt solid, as if the noise, rather than emptying her body, had filled it.

They stared at each other. Her roar had drowned out other noises, which now returned. Sirens blared as police and ambulances pulled up outside House and a stream of people flooded out.

'Something's happened. The others...' James said, and started to head back.

'They can look after themselves,' Maureen said and he turned back. They looked at each other, surprised at who was going to help and who was leaving them.

James shrugged his shoulders. Maureen shrugged hers back.

'Let's walk.' James nodded towards the swing bridge at the other end of the bay. They walked in silence up the escalators and towards the middle, stopping to lean over the railing and look at the water.

'We came here for Australia Day fireworks,' Maureen said. They had stood on the swing bridge as the fireworks exploded around them.

'Your jacket got burned by a spark, we were so close,' James remembered. 'It was like there was just us and nothing else.'

'Irene and Stephen were arguing. They'd left Sophie with us so they could slug it out without upsetting her.'

'Your idea... of course. They were sniping at each other, not wanting to row in front of her. You knew they'd both explode if they tried to control themselves, so you asked to have Sophie to ourselves for a bit and we came along here.'

They both stared into the water remembering the magical feel of being right inside the light-bursts.

'What was that... back over there, that noise?' James brought them back to the present.

'I don't know. I feel full now, different. All day I tried so hard to find out what I feel and got nothing. There's something there now, but I don't know what.

Are emotions meant to be that difficult? Most people struggle to contain them, not struggle to feel them.'

'You're not most people.'

'When the doctor told me, I just felt sorry for her. I think that's why I ran off. When I'm with people it's hard not to think of them instead of me. I saw you all in the window of the house when I came home and it felt easier to step in and be supportive. Jasper threw me when I saw him in the hall. I suddenly wanted to be selfish again, I wanted to be focussed on me, but I was trapped into doing what I always do, and then...'

'...then everything happened.' James smiled.

'This isn't our life, is it? Guns, car chases...'

'...sex workers, drugs...riots.' James pointed over to the club were people were being marched out into police vans. Others were pushed into the ambulances on stretchers. They watched for a while.

'What *do* you feel?' James asked.

'I've spent so long thinking about others, I don't remember how to. I don't know when it started. Mother was strong on thinking of others. You know what she was like.'

'It was impossible to get her to express a preference for tea or coffee until someone else said what they wanted and she could have the same.'

'It was like that with everything, I suppose. What

everyone else wanted was always more important. Perhaps I never learned to know what I felt.'

'What do you feel?' James repeated the question.

'I feel angry towards you. Bitter that the one time I needed you, you've not been there.'

'Just tell me what you want and I'll do it.'

Maureen threw her hands half-heartedly in the air. 'I want to not have to tell you. I want you to know what to do.'

James felt tears in his eyes. He had finally been caught out after all these years. A pathetic boy pretending to be grown up. He wanted to say the right things and be supportive, he wanted to push aside his own revulsion, but could not.

'Maureen, I love you. You're the most wonderful person in existence. You took my dull life and made it into something extraordinary. I'll do anything for you. I'd jump into this water right now if that's what it takes, but I need help. I wish I didn't. I wish I could just do everything absolutely right. I want to help you but...but you have to let me.' He held out his hands to her.

Maureen turned to look at him. The love in his eyes was absolute. The desperate determination shone out. She could feel it and she knew she loved him. Despite the resentment, the anger and frustration, she loved him. She wanted to reach out to him. She could see the rude, tentative comfort he was holding out, but she could not move her hands to take it. Unable to stretch out, she still resented him for not giving her the comfort.

'What if neither of us knows how? she whispered. 'What if neither of us can do what we need to?'

'Don't say that,' James cried out. 'Please, there must be a way.'

The horror that love might not be enough struck them. The ambulances and police vans departed, sirens blaring. The quiet hum of the city receded into the background. They were alone in the busy world.

Maureen looked away and closed her eyes. Her hands gripped the railing in front of her.

'Can you hear the water?' she asked. 'It's rushing, pouring along. It's so loud, so fast. The bridge is giving way.' She could feel herself being carried off on a tide, swept away from the bridge and from James. In seconds she would be miles out to sea, left to sink alone on her tiny section of bridge.

'Help me, James, I'm falling.'

He jumped forward as her knees began to bend. Catching her from behind, he wrapped his arms around and kept her upright.

'I'm here, it's OK,' he whispered into her ear. Her body was tense, hands gripping the rail tight as if she alone could hold the entire bridge together. 'It's OK,' he continued, refusing to give in until her body slumped into his arms.

'James, I've got cancer,' she sobbed, feeling his arms around her. His hands held her up. They could support a mountain.

'I'm so scared,' she said, 'I'm *so* scared. What if I can't cope? What if they take it all off? I won't be me. You won't love me. You won't touch me. I might not want you to touch me.'

The fears poured out, more fear than James knew existed in the world. Like all the Eskimo words for snow, Maureen needed different words for fear. She dumped them on him and he held them. He could sense her drawing power from his hands. They were strong. She was relying on them.

'I can't get rid of the fears,' he said, 'but I can tell you you don't need to cope. I'll do that. Fall apart, if that's what you need.'

His hands squeezed her body even tighter.

6.00 am

Irene looked around at the other people sitting in the emergency ward at St Vincents Hospital. Bloodied victims of fights, drug overdoses, drunkards. It was the repository of the desperate who had not made it through a Saturday night in Sydney. No amount of private health insurance could bypass this emergency room. It was the great leveller, raising no-one above the lowest level. Her eyes passed over Nicole and Tanya. Dirtied, blood-stained and exhausted, they blended in.

She thought about her daughter, Sophie, and whether to call Stephen's parents. Perhaps they should be there. 'If there was a danger...' she thought, but went no further. She did not want Sophie to witness her parents mired in violence. She did not want this to be Sophie's parting image.

When they arrived the triage nurse had taken one look at Stephen's unconscious body and sent him straight through to stop the bleeding and perform a CT scan. It would not take long, she had informed them.

The ambulance ride had been crammed with attempted recriminations. Their relief at being out of the hell at the club meant they had started arguing again. Nicole had provoked Gerard. Tanya had let fly the first kick. Irene had done nothing. The argument had raged until the paramedic had shouted for silence. In the gap they looked at Stephen, breathing with the aid of respirator, but still unconscious. Tanya took his hand.

'If he hadn't been with that muscly little walnut, we wouldn't be here,' she said.

'Only Stephen could cause a riot and still have three women blaming each other for it,' Nicole observed with a wry smile.

'Your truck!' Tanya said to Nicole, as they sat in the emergency room. 'I'd forgotten. It'll still be there, in the harbour.'

'I suppose we've all left something behind.' Irene thought of the two copies of the *Chevalier*, one lying in her bath, the other somewhere in Maureen's house.

Nicole shifted uncomfortably. She would still have to go to the police station. They would have cross-checked her number plate and found out about the accident. She dreaded the return to suspicious looks and the same question over and over again.

'Maureen, James. Should we?' Irene said.

'Too much,' Tanya answered.

'She said they would know something quickly,' Tanya said after a two-minute gap.

They were not having a conversation, only punctuating the silence with words. Tanya jumped up from her chair. Exhausted as she was, sitting still was not possible. 'This must be a bad sign.'

'Not necessarily,' Irene tried to calm her. 'They are rushed off their feet.' Stephen had not been the only person rushed through. A heart-attack victim had flown out of an ambulance and straight through the plastic swing doors. Their's was not the only night from hell.

Tanya sat down again. They stared at the swing doors. Figures moved around, blurred by the scratched plastic. Every time someone seemed to walk towards it they hoped it was news, but the figure always veered off to the left at the last moment. Nicole smiled to herself.

'What?' asked Tanya, sitting up and looking at her. Nicole shook her head.

'What's so funny?' Irene asked.

'I was just thinking.' The other two gave up and sat back.

'So, Tanya,' continued Nicole, 'tell me about Taekwondo.'

Tanya's face turned to stone. Irene snorted and Nicole guffawed.

'If I ever hear that again, I swear I'll give a practical demonstration,' Tanya joked.

'You have. That flying kick you did, it was incredible.' Irene could not deny being impressed by her ability to fly.

'But what about her,' Tanya pointed to Nicole, '"I'm no lady." She's the one person who managed to bring that brute to his knees. We were all too busy aiming at imaginary red and blue circles on his chest. She had the right idea.'

'That girlfriend of his, Merissa. What was she like?' Irene asked.

'She was so bouncy, it was like kicking a tyre.' Tanya laughed.

'Can you imagine them in bed. They probably couldn't do anything because their thighs would keep them too far apart!' Nicole giggled.

'If any of you are interested...' the triage nurse brought their laughter to an end, 'Mr Lee has stabilised. We've stopped the external bleeding. The CTs revealed no internal bleeding. He's coming to, but we'll be keeping him in overnight. Two of you can see him.'

'You two go, I'll wait...' Nicole offered, but they had already set off through the plastic doors.

Nicole was not alone very long. As she sat looking at her feet stretched out in front of her, trying to picture her truck at the bottom of the harbour, a voice disturbed her.

'Nicole Barracks?'

Nicole looked up to see a policeman.

'I'm Detective Calvert. Do you mind if I ask you a few questions?'

'No.' Nicole looked about nervously, brought her legs in and sat on her hands as he took a seat beside her.

'I was down here collecting statements about the brawl at House when we got a call regarding your truck. Seems there was an accident earlier in the day. Anything you want to tell me?'

•

Stephen thought he was experiencing double vision as he peered up and saw two women looking down at him. He could not tell who either of them were yet.

'It's Tanya... and Irene.'

'I'm sorry. It's my fault,' he mumbled. He figured the one who had not spoken must have been Irene. He turned to her.

'The book, I really didn't mean...' Irene looked puzzled. He must be delirious.

'Oh, the *Chevalier*,' she realised. 'Ancient history. I wanted to blame you, but...'

'I'm sorry if I stopped you...' he winced. Consciousness brought pain with it.

'You're not dying, there's no need to put things to rights. We'll live to fight another day.'

'I don't want to fight.'

'Tough. I'll leave you two for a moment,' she said, and walked out of the cubicle.

'Is she serious?' Stephen asked Tanya. The unfamiliar experience of Irene joking with him was even more confusing in his haze.

'She kept you alive. Wouldn't give up on the mouth to mouth until help arrived.'

'Probably didn't like the idea of someone else killing me.'

'She's OK,' Tanya said.

'Oh God, this is a nightmare...The last thing I remember was you flying through the air, attacking that shaved gorilla.'

'*I* didn't want anyone else killing you, mate.'

'I've been thinking.'

'Bad for you, thinking.'

'Seriously. I do love you, mate. It's just...'

'Stephen, now's not the time. I love you too, but I'm not living with you. I like things as they are.'

Stephen smiled. 'You're not just saying that because I need good news to pull me through?'

Tanya sat down by the bed and held his hand. Even

in a semi-conscious state, he was obnoxiously charming. There was something about him that made her feel comfortable with herself. The confused girl from St Angela's could see the scared boy in him. She wanted to protect him in the playground.

'Did you kill anyone?' he asked.

'No.'

'Good.' He smiled and fell asleep clasping her hand like a teddy.

•

It took a lot of reassurance from Detective Calvert to persuade Nicole she was not in any trouble.

'The accident this afternoon, it wasn't my fault, honest. I just stopped.' She was sure no-one would believe her, despite the detective repeatedly saying he understood.

'I saw the crash and stopped to help. I've no idea who...'

'Why are you so convinced we think it was your fault?'

Nicole realised the police knew nothing about Louie. He was just checking that the two incidents weren't related. If she revealed what Louie had done, she might have been aiding and abetting. He would deny everything, mention their fight and then there would be more charges. In her mind a neverending charge sheet rolled out before her, ream after ream of accusations. She had to say something to deflect attention.

'I…I used to be a man,' she blurted out. The detective looked puzzled and Nicole felt she was back in her usual situation: tired, exhausted and having to justify her existence.

'You've lost me,' Calvert said. Nicole sighed.

'I've had a sex change. I'm a woman but I used to be a man.'

'I appreciate how difficult that must be to disclose, but I don't see the relevance to either incident. Changing gender's not illegal, you know.'

Nicole was stunned. He spoke without the slightest hesitation or awkward cough. She smiled.

'No, it's not. It's not relevant, it's just usually, it's best to…'

'Don't worry,' he smiled, 'some of my best friends.'

Nicole relaxed. The detective continued.

'We're not all complete bastards, you know. Some of us are quite nice really. I'm just talking to you to make sure there's nothing you haven't reported. Fights in clubs and wrecked vehicles—they can be hate crimes sometimes. Dimwits attacking people because they don't approve of their lives.'

'Don't I know it.'

'So everything's OK?' he smiled.

'Yes, fine,' she replied.

'I'm off duty now. I can give you a lift home if you like.'

Nicole went to check that Stephen was OK and that Irene and Tanya were happy for her to leave. She pushed her way through the plastic doors and sneaked into his cubicle. Stephen was asleep, Tanya and Irene were sitting in silence.

'Stephen came to, asked about you, and then fell asleep again,' said Tanya.

'Tell her the rest,' Irene interceded. 'He was probably being vile in his delirium, but you've a right to know. He also said "she doesn't need to try so hard, she should just be." Go figure that.'

Nicole understood what he meant.

'That's the sweetest thing he's ever said,' she replied, 'not that there's much competition from his other pronouncements.' Stephen was finally acknowledging she was a woman, she did not have to try.

'So, the nice detective is taking you home?' Irene's eyebrow shot up, sensing something happening.

'Don't be ridiculous,' Nicole giggled.

'We have to see him. We'll see you out.'

Tanya and Irene escorted Nicole back to Detective Calvert. They said their goodbyes, and watched them leave. They could just make out Nicole inquiring if there were any transsexuals in the police force and what the entry requirements were.

361

'I guess she's planning her post-trucking life then.' Irene smiled. They sat down, feeling dirty and smelly. With Stephen out of danger and light pouring through windows, exhaustion was setting in. They yawned in unison. Thoughts of life beyond the next five minutes came to them.

'We're not going to be bosom chums, you know,' Irene pointed out.

'We don't exactly have a lot in common, apart from...' Tanya nodded towards the plastic doors. 'What are you going to do about your book?'

'I don't know. I've been thinking of a quote.'

'There's a surprise,' Tanya let slip, and then looked alarmed at Irene. She ignored it.

'*Il faut cultiver son jardin*. You have to grow your own garden.' Tanya looked at her blankly. Irene explained.

'It sounds daft, but it's quite profound. It means more than grow, it's develop, cultivate. I haven't really been doing that. I've been too busy pointing out the weeds in Stephen's garden. Between his garden's and Sophie's, I've forgotten my own. Perhaps I should poke around, see what's there and see what I want to cultivate. It's a bit scary. I'm afraid I've killed everything off.'

Tanya looked at her and said, 'Baekjul Boolgool.'

'Indomitable spirit. I shall bear that in mind,' Irene

replied, and then added when she saw Tanya's stunned face, 'I have a smattering of Korean.'

'You are *so* scary,' Tanya replied, 'I like that. At school I was always the girl everyone was scared of.'

'I don't think that constitutes having something in common. I refuse to bond.'

Tanya ignored her. 'I'm going to lay off the Taekwondo for a while. I want something where I can let rip. There's too much control and precision. I need to be able to tear free...without killing anyone.'

'There's a relief. I was going to ask if you would teach Sophie some seif-defence. If you're going to be around, she'll need to establish some sort of relationship and, heaven knows, it's not something I can teach her. But if you're going to rip her throat out, perhaps it's not such a good idea.'

'I'd love to...teach her self-defence, that is.'

'Good—but if she kills anyone, I'll kill you.'

'I believe you.'

7.00 am

Maureen and James walked home. There was a lot to say and it was easier to talk while walking. It was agreed that James would ask Maureen every now and again how she was feeling and Maureen had to answer with anything except 'fine'.

As they walked along Elizabeth Street and passed the doctor's surgery, he asked. Maureen paused, looking up at the window and then at the convenience store next door.

'It seems ridiculous now, coming here on my own. I thought it would be more bother having you there, that I'd be too stressed about you. I didn't want to worry you if there was no need. I ended up worrying about the doctor. Anyone but me.'

'But how are you feeling?'

She cocked her ear as if listening intently.

'A bit silly, a bit guilty. I can still feel the drop in my stomach when she told me. I knew as soon as she moved her mouth to speak.'

'So how serious is it, really?'

'I was honest about that. It is a "relatively early" intervention. But I don't know how much will have to go. It might take several months, you know. It's not a quick fix.'

'I'm not going anywhere.'

They complimented each other on how good Maureen had been at expressing herself, and James had been at being supportive, and then continued walking.

As they walked up Liverpool Street, Maureen felt wistful, thinking of her time in the park. At Oxford Street, where young people staggered out of clubs, she felt wild and adventurous. She knew how they were feeling. As they passed a florist she remembered her anger at James and felt a flash of it again. As they passed a former women's hospital, now luxury apartments and a European-style shopping piazza, the fear came back and she gripped James' hand. It was always there, she said, like a sea, and every now and again a big wave of it swept up onto the shore.

At Queen Street, in their home suburb of Woollahra, she felt exhausted, trapped in a time warp that would never see them home. At the bottom of their street they stopped. The air had that crisp freshness once again as the morning breeze touched their tired faces. A mermaid walked down the street towards them carrying her suitcase, trudging home after a hard night on the rocks luring sailors to their deaths. She didn't stop, but raised an eyebrow as she passed. Behind her, seaweed, a chip packet and a plastic bottle caught in her tail.

'This isn't it, you know.' Maureen let go of James' hand. 'We're not sorted, the hardest is yet to come.'

'I know.'

'Do you? Really? I won't go back into that house into the old routine. A few days of office pressure, and you feeling too tired to do things differently. We're not just seeing me through this, we're changing everything. Breaking our habits, habits we've had for years, fourteen years.'

'Perhaps we should see a counsellor,' James suggested. Maureen looked shocked.

'To help us. I don't say we're in danger of breaking up, but let's get all the help we can. We won't be able just to slip into old patterns if we're seeing someone to keep us on track.'

Maureen smiled.

'That's a wonderful idea. That's ... ' she was lost for words. He had thought of something great. She knew how little he thought of psychology—neurotic housewives with nothing better to do. She knew how much the idea scared him.

'I feel ... looked after.' Maureen nodded her head,

savouring the new sensation. She took his hand, and bit her lip.

'Let's go home.'

In the house the living room had been tidied. The ship still stood, proud and motionless, but the table had been cleared and removed. Ulrika was curled up asleep in one of the deck chairs. The copy of *Le Chevalier* rested in her lap with Ulrika's ladle stuck through it as a bookmark. James woke her.

'There was no need for you to stay,' he said.

'I wanted to make sure you were all OK,' she replied and then remembered who she was. 'Besides, no-one storms out of my dinner without hearing from me. My food never takes second place.'

'It was wonderful, really,' said Maureen.

'Psh! I will be contacting the food section of the *Sydney Morning Herald* informing them of the fiasco. They will want a photograph of me here, so the ship must remain until Monday.'

'That would be good publicity,' said James. 'I'll tell them you're a complete tyrant and impossible to work with but the food is worth all the suffering.'

'Good. I'll be in touch.' Ulrika stormed out, slammed the door of the house, then of her car, and revved her engine as loudly as possible. As she reversed out of the drive, she leaned out of the window, crashed her ladle onto the side of her car and screamed, 'Ulrika does not work under such conditions. Never.'

The phone rang. It seemed like a long time since they had heard it ring. Normal life was encroaching. They looked at each other, wondering whether to answer it. The machine picked it up. It was Irene.

'We're at the hospital.'

Maureen looked to James, unsure what to do. He reassured her.

'It's OK to still care about people.'

Maureen dashed into the hall and picked the phone up. When she returned to the living room, James was aboard his ship.

'Everything OK?' he asked.

'I think so. We missed the final act. Stephen caused a huge fight between some bodybuilders and Tanya's Taekwondo people at the club and got concussed. He's OK but staying in hospital overnight. Tanya's with him and Irene's gone to collect Sophie. They're all getting on fine.'

'Stephen must be terrified. What about Nicole?'

'Last seen being escorted home by a rather handsome detective.'

'So they seem to be coping very well without you.'

'Yes,' said Maureen, listening inside again, 'I feel a bit left out. What if they don't need me anymore?'

James smiled, walking down the gangplank.

'The world will always need Maureen.'

'I suppose so,' she shrugged her shoulders.

'How about a little cruise before all the hard work starts. Would you like to come aboard?' He held out his hand and led her up the gangplank.

They nestled down on the deck, leaning against James' mini bridge.

'Where the hell did this come from?' Maureen asked.

'I made it...with some...with an awful lot of help. I just wanted to do something for you, something big and extravagant with my hands. I was so proud of remembering our little anniversary on my own and I really wanted to celebrate it. I know it's a sad day too. The anniversary of us finding each other is the day we lost so much else.'

'Not so little really...D'you think if the baby had...?'

'We can't know. It wasn't your fault, you know. It never occurred to me to tell you. I'm sorry.'

'Thank you.' She reached her lips up to his and kissed him. The affection grew into passion. He covered her face in kisses. She took his hands and pressed them to her cheeks, glorying in their feel. James unzipped her dress as Maureen moved to sit astride him.

He stopped and looked Maureen in the eyes, steeling himself for the moment to come. She reached her arms behind her and unclasped her bra. He watched as her breasts fell slightly with the loss of support and then closed his eyes. He put his hands out. She removed the bra and placed the girls in them. The weight felt blissful as her nipples pressed into his palms. He looked up at Maureen, tears in his eyes.

'Can I ever make it up to you?'

'I don't know,' she said, 'but I want you to try,' and he pressed his lips to her lump.

Acknowledgments

Thank you to: Chris Sims for constant support, especially through the inevitable authorial self-doubt; Lisa Highton for wisdom, fun and no ego-pandering (unless absolutely essential); Neal Drinnan, Mary Drum, Fiona Lincoln, Brett Woods and everyone at Hodder Headline Australia for their enthusiasm, commitment and creativity; Andy Palmer of Publicity Matters for being so good at his job; Heather Jamieson for such pain-free editing; Marie-Laure Bouchet for letting me write this; and Linda Hallam for information and 'tips'.

Bruno Bouchet was born in Spain of British and French parents and is now based in Sydney where he writes for a living and does the occasional performance. You can contact him via his website:

www.brunobouchet.com

REPS. 2000 CHOICE

the beauty of truth

bruno bouchet

a tale of ambition, revenge and domestic appliances

Truth, like **beauty**, is only **skin-deep**

What would happen if an average-looking whitegoods marketing manager suddenly became the most beautiful man in the world? Would female colleagues beg him to father their children? Would a loopy idea to put works of art on bench-top appliances become the greatest marketing success in history?

Mousy Mark Boyd recreates himself as a man of stunning, lust-raising good looks—and the results go far beyond his wildest dreams. But with success comes jealousy and hatred. Can Mark survive the raging emotions his beauty provokes? Will he learn where true beauty lies—and still turn a profit? *The Beauty of Truth* is a fearless send-up of the all-consuming power of marketing and the seductive allure of appearances. And it's what's been missing from modern literature: a celebration of domestic appliances.